The Stars Are Dying

An Anthology

Francesca Quarto

The Stars are Dying by Francesca Quarto

Printed in the United States of America

Believing in one's ability to tell a good story depends in part on the reaction of your most critical audience. My editor has always made it a painless process, bringing a keen eye to my work, and helping me to perfect my abilities and my tall tales!

Thank you, Elizabeth Hinds!

A Little Laughter Can't Hurt Much

Lying in the hospital bed was beginning to take a noticeable toll on his attitude. Unfortunately, I was his first visitor that morning after the nurse finished his bed bath and removed the bedpan. The pan was discreetly covered with a towel.

The patient was grousing under his breath about his privacy being trampled and trying unsuccessfully to cover his leg. This appendage jutted out like a white sail; metal pins and armor-like bands threatening any inquisitive hand. All this apparatus was suspended from a kind of pulley system that appeared to have all the comfort of a medieval torture devise.

I stepped around a tall, unattractive nurse, who was just exiting the room to announce myself with a warm smile, and a tin of his favorite biscuits. Neither did anything to deflect his growing discontent and malice toward all involved in his enforced confinement. But then, I really didn't expect much by way of gratitude for saving his sorry rump.

In retrospect, considering the circumstances that caused the injured femur, it could have been much worse. I mean, it's extremely rare for a Vampire to listen to the voice of reason. Though it sounds a bit arrogant, I must admit I have a rare gift when it comes to communicating with our blood-sucking adversaries. It has nothing to do with having a pointy stick and titanium bullets in my gun, and everything to do with being a rather attractive woman. I successfully used my feminine wiles to convince the Vamp we were no longer a threat, and after he gently kicked my partner's twisted leg, and studied his deadly pale face, he took off. Not appetizing I expect.

Seeing my male counterpart lying like a newly trussed turkey among the pillows and tubing made me breathe deeply of the germicidal hospital air. As cantankerous as Roderick is, he is still the only man I can tolerate within touching distance, that I don't have an urge to kill. His devilishly handsome looks are a plus, but it's his cunningly clever mind that has held my interest for fifteen years.

Good Mother! Fifteen years already as part of the elite Vampire Transition Task Force. Or, as the coppers from other departments have dubbed our team, Blood Sucker Exterminators. Being rather a fashionista, Roderick despises the image that expression conjures of us running around in filthy coveralls and wielding pitch forks! (Actually, I have been known to use that implement when visiting farmsteads in Braxston Shire. That whole farming community was being over-run with Vamps, and the toothy rascals seemed to like using the hay barns to drain their victims. So... use what's at hand, eh?)

Roderick and I have had a love-hate relationship from our first time fighting the Undead together. It's become ingrained in all we do together, from hunting and killing Vamps; to making love directly after, to help us bleed off our tensions. (Do excuse that choice of analogies.).

Our last case was literally thrown in our faces when our Team Commander was picked-up and hurled at us. We were in hot pursuit of the Vamp who kidnapped her a few days earlier.   He was hauling her under his arm like a sack of milled wheat when we spotted them. Our fellow team members knew our success record in these running battles, and suspected we would fall on our faces; we didn't disappoint! They took up the chase as we struggled under the dead-weight of the fleshy missile. Commander Maude Smithson is one heck of a cop, but she's also the size of a sturdy Angus steer, with a disposition to match. She is also Rodrick's greatest nemesis outside of the Vampires we hunt. They clash like siblings which, unfortunately, they are.

He's her twin brother and was sworn into the force the same day she was. Her upward trajectory was stellar, while his was, well, let's just say, a tad sluggish. Roderick spends lots of time improving his genius mind. He is fond of attending lectures on bizarre and arcane subjects. Two weeks ago, it was "How ancient pottery predicts the last cataclysmic event on earth," or something along those lines. He often can be found sitting naked in a near catatonic state on the floor of his cold garret. He'll be there for hours, practicing an obscure form of mediation, leading to out of body travel. He never seems completely present, so it must be working.

His fraternal twin, Maud, is tougher than the Harley she rides and fearless in the face of an attacking Zombie in full dining a la carte mode. Unfortunately, some of the spunk was taken out of her, along with a few liters of her blood, allowing the Vamp to use her like a tree trunk in a Scottish hurling contest. She had the misfortune to be snatched by the notorious Fang Man, himself an avid biker as we learned after her rescue, and he took off on a genteel BMW.

This latest mishap with my partner proved yet again that Roderick was a magnet, drawing the Fates to inflict severe bodily harm upon his person. In fact, his record of injuries is longer than the credits to the last episode of our TV show.

It's true. We star in our own telly series. It's based on the reality cop shows that were the rage in the long- gone days of high crimes and misdemeanors. For forty-five minutes between commercial bombardments, we're on live, hunting and bringing down the likes of the Zombie baker, or a Vampire gangster like Fang Man.

Our attempted rescue of Maude from the suave gang boss, gave an unexpected boost to our viewership and our ratings shot up like Maude in her inaugural flight. I'll try to keep Roderick from learning one critic wrote our performance was, "The perfect comedic relief for these tumultuous times..."It seems our viewers were actually rooting for Fang Man after his launch of the much-depleted Maude. They especially enjoyed the segment where Roderick and I were buried like two well-dressed manikins under an avalanche of black leather. Maude's knee found my ribs and the bruising was nearly worse than the one to my ego!

The Producer is already planning a sequel. Stay tuned as they say. As soon as he's released...wait a minute.... that big nurse is back to draw blood. I hope Roderick will cooperate. That's an awfully big syringe. She certainly has a familiar look.

I need a break from this medical environment, and the view from his room is so boring. Only the parking facility below and... hmm... is that a BMW bike?

Roderick's scream is somewhat muffled under the large hand pressed over his mouth and nose, but it's immediately clear to me, 'Nasty Nurse' isn't fluffing his pillows. In my best Bruce Lee move, I spin around, planting two spiked heels into her broad back. Unfortunately, the hulking woman merely twitches her shoulders and I lose a four hundred credit pair of shoes.

Roderick is insensible with lack of air, and his eyes are unpleasantly rolled back in his head. The nurse pulls the large needle she jammed into his carotid artery, where it dangled like a bloated leech. My partner must have objected to her nursing practices and that caused her to smother his cries for help. Standing barefoot, I'm yelling at her to back away from Roderick, when I notice there's no blood on her uniform where my stilettos are deeply imbedded in her muscular body. Huh...

I reach under my long skirt and between my legs and the Vampire's eyes show their true red color. Did she really just lick her lips? Gross! Pulling my titanium packed gun from the holster between my legs is the easy part. The big nurse is tugging at the corners of her face and chin. With one quick rip she's peeled off the unattractive nurse face, only to be replaced with the even less attractive face of Fang Man! I am looking into Fang's red eyes and they are glittering like a hungry rat's about to feed. Damn!

Roderick keeps trying to say something, but his voice is a strangled croak. Another injury in the line of duty. This will make eight medals for him to my zero. No wonder the other agents question my courage when only my partner ever gets hurt. I back away from Fang keeping my gun behind the folds of my skirt. While I'm thinking of how to stop him from killing Roderick, or worse still, turning him because of that weird twin-thing he talks about occasionally. I've always wondered if they were even related…let alone twins! But Fang has plenty of Maud's blood fueling him right now and may have acquired a taste for the brand.

Fang is moving backward toward the bed and the now groaning patient. I see the needle appear in her hands and he grins at me as he releases the contents in a red stream down his throat. Before I can say 'ugh,' he has driven the hypodermic into Roderick's artery for another fill-up. I've had enough. If he thinks I'll stand by while he drains my partner, he's only partially right.

I pull the gun from behind my leg and put two neat holes in Fang Man's forehead. When he slumps to the floor and begins to shrivel, I move to Roderick's bedside. I think he's trying to thank me when I put my third bullet between his cloudy blue eyes. The first sign of change. Fang must have thought I wouldn't notice the small punctures in Roderick's throat as he lay among all the pillows. He was dining on my recently deceased partner since he was admitted to the hospital no doubt. He had a real taste for twin blood it seems.

Well, I can't take a risk on Roderick turning into a Vamp in the middle of a show, can I? The viewers would flip out if I shot my costar during a Vamp take-down. Anyway, I like the idea of going solo on the show. Think I'll retrieve my shoes. Fang's pretty much withered like last fall's apples. Guess it's time to check in on Maud. She's in the room down the hall. Good thing I packed extra bullets.

And Now, A Plague

"It won't just drop into your lap, you know? You have to put some effort and energy into it! And since you are the laziest man I have ever known, you'll never write more than one book and grocery lists!"

The flimsy door banged shut, leaving behind the echo of her anger. It didn't really trouble Azad; she'd slammed lots of doors in his face, even as his adoring eyes begged for her forgiveness. It was true of course, and he knew it. He scarcely made any attempt to work on his manuscript, many times, pretending to ponder over a page when she walked by his hunched figure, likely to spy on him. His first novel, *The Tiger's Child* had become an instant success, flying off the shelves everywhere, especially during the hard times they'd been experiencing. Its tender love story captured the power of hope, the sturdy raft, on the rough seas of life.

But that was nearly ten years ago. The modestly lucrative royalty checks, had long since dried up like the fields surrounding his village, before the monsoon's brought relief and destruction. On days like this, he felt as if he'd melted into a brown puddle like the ones outside their front door. He felt bland and useless.

Azad had insisted they remain in the modest, rough built house, even after his book supplied enough money over time to improve on his lower, middle-class status. He was hesitant to leave the home and community he'd been born into, for the frenzied life in a city like Calcutta. His young wife chafed under the yoke of his final word on the subject and was becoming more outspoken as the months and years slipped through the God's hourglass. He didn't regret much of his sixty-three years, but he did wish he had not rushed to marry the beauty he met at a bookstore in that cursed city of Calcutta.

Aalia was almost twenty-three years his junior, but his growing fame made him something of a local celebrity. This glitzy status surely blinded her to his thatch of white hair, and dark, sunbaked face, marked like the many roads he'd already traveled. She came to his book-signing table just after a plump girl with a forgettable face, making her own great beauty that more obvious and intoxicating. She wore a light blue sari, shot through with silver thread, smoothly moving over her slim figure. He thought he beheld a goddess! The long black braid of her hair swept over the tabletop when she leaned in to hand him a copy of *Tiger's Child*, and he thrilled at her feather touch as her fingers brushed his hand, taking back her signed book. Seven months of passionate courting, and her upper middle-class family rejoiced beside the new, poorer relations, after the announcement of their engagement, and then again, at their lavish wedding. A few other royalty checks paid for most of the festivities.

Still delirious with love, he never noticed the fading ardor in his bride's luminous dark eyes, as weeks and months passed without any envelopes coming from the publisher; in fact, they seemed to have forgotten him all together. Aalia watched him from under her thick black lashes whenever she brought tea to his tiny workspace. He was always sitting at his cluttered desk in deep thought or so it appeared. She had no idea her older husband had reached the bottom of his well of inspiration. While he scraped around for new stories buried in the muck of his thoughts, the Muse he sought so desperately, fell further into the darkness. There was no inspiration. There were no other tales to tell. Now, there was only the drifting light of twilight as it began to cloud his mind.

His ardor for the still lovely, though slightly plumper Aalia, never faltered, nor did it die back into a dusty corner of his mind.

He still found himself deeply in love with her, or perhaps, the thought of her. For her part, the restless Aalia found many opportunities to scurry off to the city, taking a rickety bus into the heart of Calcutta. That was her only mode of transport, and it galled her to have to share space with unwashed children, or women holding caged chickens on their laps. She learned not to lean against the window side, discovering they might be smeared with any manner of filth. While these trips turned her delicate stomach, she trained herself to focus on the person awaiting her arrival at the Calcutta bus station.

Azad decided to take advantage of his wife's latest excursion to see her Auntie, to pick up his second book manuscript and begin a long-overdue revision. He brewed himself a pot of Chi tea and tossing some biscuits onto a plate, began. Reading through words so distant from his memory it seemed a stranger had written them. He began to relax and fall into the story as if it was a feather comforter to roll around and wrap himself inside.

The story was untitled but took the reader to medieval days when the Black Death descended upon the semi-conscious world of men and science. He'd studied this period of history extensively and was becoming something of an expert on the subject when he was at University. His parents were fortunate that Azad had a brilliant mind, and he was accepted there, in spite of his lower breeding.

"I'll call it *"And Now, A Plague"* he said into the dancing dust motes coming off the road through the open study window. It felt perfect since the hero had overcome so much to finally reach his pinnacle of power, only to be cut down by the black boils under his arm pits.

Azad could relate to this man; smacked down, time after time, by circumstances he could never control. In the story, his stalwart hero rushes off to the never-ending wars between kings and queens, loses an arm in battle, only to overcome this to become a left-armed swordsman of deadly capabilities on the field. The hero returns to his own lands after meeting great perils, to find them plundered by marauding bandits taking advantage of his absence. Once again, he finds the determination to defeat his enemies, before falling victim to the Plague silently stalking the many lands of the known world. He is abandoned by his terrified wife to his coming fate. In the final chapter, the hero sets fire to his manse, releasing the flames to consume his death ridden body.

"Yes. This is a good story! I'll send it to the Publisher immediately!" Azad slipped the thick bundle of papers into a sturdy yellow envelope, writing the name of the publishing house in London on the front, in his concise hand. *My love will know I am no sloth...merely a methodical writer,* he thought as he added the address.

Late into the night Azad waited by the small window in the front of his house, watching for his wife's familiar figure to appear out of the shadows. He was found there by the mail carrier, who thought he was asleep, and seeing the thick envelope snatched it up to be mailed. He knew Azad would reimburse him the postage needed.

That evening, the front door rattled open, and the heavy perfume his wife favored followed her into the small front room. Her heart nearly stopped in her chest when the lamp she lit revealed the ashen face of her husband, sitting stiffly in his chair. His eyes were focused on the small window, and like the yellowed glass, they were dingy and lifeless.

Aalia was free at last. She ran to their bedroom, snatching up the old suitcase she shoved under their bed on her wedding day. She frantically began to throw her best saris and belongings into it, the snapping of the latches sounded like rapid gun shots in the deep quiet of the small house. She knew she'd have to walk for at least an hour before the bus began its route and she could take it into Calcutta, but her body was filled with a new energy. She didn't bother to look upon the body of the elderly husband before she closed the door behind her empty life and fled the dusty village.

A month after his burial the Postman carried a letter to Azad's house. It was now occupied by a distant niece who inherited his things under the terms of an old will discovered in his desk. He meant to revise it after his marriage, but never seemed to find the time as he pondered over birthing his next novel.

When she opened the letter, his niece was stunned to find it was a letter of acceptance on his latest book, *And Now, A Plague*. They intended to release it immediately and had great hopes it would become as popular and lucrative as *The Tiger's Child*.

And so, it was. The niece had all rights to his works, using the royalties to move into a flat in Calcutta where she could follow her uncle's footsteps, and study to become a writer. The circle of life was completed as it should be and always will be. Karma is everything.

The Stars Are Dying

**Captain's Log: HMS Star Chaser; Twenty-ninth Cycle
Year of Apocalypse, Galileo Sea**

There is little time to do more than mark our identity here, and the date of The Ultimate Cataclysmic Event. No time to list the names of my crew, who, having served His Majesty with valor, have all preceded me in death. Alas, my only companion is my ghostly reflection in the glass of my cabin window. It is clearly visible against the pitch-black void surrounding the ship. A never-ending, unbroken night batters my senses and smothers all hope. Only the stars, like a scattering of shiny pebbles, provide interruption in this vast expanse of darkness.

We have been drifting upon this black sea for three cycles now, without benefit of crypto-sounding devices, or cosmic scanners. All went blind and deaf just as we entered these dreadful waters and the night subtly blended into a darker element. My First Mate was among the valiant men to leave the relative safety of the ship, to investigate what appeared to be an impenetrable wall of nothingness. He took a small party, including the Chief Engineer, in hopes of identifying the mass of indigo-black we'd sailed into. The rest of the crew and I soon heard sounds of distress a distance from their Starboard departure point. Bursts of laser beams suddenly streaked through the night, as the cries of my men rose-up from below our bow, smashing like screaming gulls upon our sides. The twelve never returned from the landscape of the void. I dared not send others in their wake, and there were no volunteers stepping up either.

We searched the waters, the light spilling from our ship in all directions, onto the black firmament below us. Not a single trace of the twelve, or any wreckage from the small, doomed Racer, was spotted. My remaining crew became more agitated as we drifted further and further from the area of the unexplained disappearances of their shipmates. According to my Second Mate, there was whispered talk among the crew, of a creature, not unlike the mythical Kraken of the Norse sagas, rising from the deep to wrap long tentacles around the Racer, crushing it and all the souls on board, and dragging the lot beneath the inky waters.

Star Chaser was unresponsive to the prodding of the Engineer's Mate. He worked relentlessly to move us out of the murky channel that held us fast to an uncharted passage. It was clear to my remaining crew we sailed on evil waters, and no longer plotted our own course.

My tenure of service was known to all my men. I'd like to believe it gave them some comfort in the perpetual night, as we were pulled like a child's toy ship over the flat face of this brooding sea. But nothing had prepared me for this phenomenon. Nothing short of a Perseus Soothsayer could have given me the insights needed to prevail. None, but a prognosticator, could have provided my crew with answers and quell their primal fears in the face of what happened to their friends.

When we began this expedition, our planet had already endured prolonged distress. World-wide food shortages, ravaging plagues, and relentless environmental degradation, reduced all of civilization to mayhem and backward thinking. The Star Chaser was launched secretly by order of His Majesty, to explore this possible refuge for the remnant of life found upon our return home. It would be a mission of indefinite length, but infinite importance to our kind.

With the loss of all navigational equipment, we turned to the stars, the silent witnesses to our distress. They have guided seafarers on any world, for as long as they stood at a helm. These heavenly bodies were poor beacons to us, however, while we floated in this dark soup. They were mere pricks of light, seen through the dense curtain draped over us. The ancient Star Charts were brought from my cabin, and stretched out on the illuminated wall where I could clearly see their unique patterns. Even though we were held fast in the course plotted by this cursed sea, I wished to determine our current location. This chart might somehow point to a final destination.

I put my Second Mate in charge of assigning crew to study the smooth dome of our constant night sky. They were to note our position in relation to the known placement of stars as shown on the ancient Star-maps. The first cycle passed uneventfully, until the last man took his place at the watch atop the Skyscraper Bubble.

He'd only begun marking the placements of the bleak dots on the Virtual Sky Chart he carried, when he shouted a garbled warning over his transmitter. When I arrived with some of the curious crew, my Second Mate ordered the man to report. He rode the small cage down to the deck, where I asked for an explanation for his alarm. His response chilled the hearts of all who listened to his findings.

"I saw a star explode sir, and before I could take my next breath, two more exploded into fiery ribbons. Another did the same as the cage descended, sir."

"Was there any indication that these stars were in some sort of cosmic distress, when you began your scan?" the Second Mate asked.

Deep concern transformed the young sailor's face into a grim mask. We all had a sickly pallor from the lack of natural light for so long, but the sailor standing just outside the cage looked drained of blood.

"I detected no other cosmic activity sir, prior to the explosions. There was one thing though, sir. A kind of humming sound. It was faint, like it had traveled over a long distance, but I definitely heard something up there."

Much of the crew had joined us on deck by the time the man made a fuller verbal report. With little to do on board, there was no concern about deserting their stations. When they heard the humming sound, the air around me filled with speculation, until a stern word from the Second Mate quelled the excitement. We all knew something was out there. Something that was capable of destroying the very fabric of this world. Something was killing the stars. I have, in truth, never felt so vulnerable. Even now, alone on this vessel, I bear all calm, because I understand my fate is already written.

The men were sent back to their stations as the Second Mate and I discussed the implications of this horrendous occurrence. If the stars were truly dying, what about our own puny lives? We had no defenses against an invisible, destructive force, and were already prisoners on a seemingly endless journey.

It is now two cycles since the last crew member vanished beneath the ebony waters, released by me to find a peace I know doesn't exist. I've accepted I shall never set foot upon my home world. In fact, according to the Star Charts of the Ancients, I believe little is left in this part of the Galaxy. Sailing below the eternal dome, I have watched as stars, and planets alike, are scrubbed from the vastness of space.

After so much time elapsed, the spirits of all on board were at their lowest. One by one, with all hope crushed from their spirits, my crew willingly drank the poisoned waters from the sea that holds us in its grip. They fell like quiet obelisks, under the great winds sweeping Mars. As their Captain, it was my duty to put off my own, ultimate escape, until the last was gone.

I returned to the observation post in the Bubble, bringing this Logbook to complete. I sit inside the useless barrier of the cage, listening to the increasing humming sound, as it pierces the thin atmosphere of this world. There is nowhere to hide, so I offer myself as a final tribute to all life forms in the Universe. Better, have gone before me, but I wonder what will follow?

Star Chaser -Captain Jes..................

Me, Wicked, and the Dark Angel

My story starts out with me, Wicked, and the Dark Angel. But before I launch into that tale, let me put to rest any speculating here and now. Wicked is my mischievous baby sister. I've been watching over her now...well...since I started robbing banks and shooting folks at fifteen, to feed her and me. Our folks were burned up, working the fields in the Panhandle bottoms and passed a week apart. I figure they couldn't tolerate the separation.

That was long before the Vamps turned me and Wicked, New Year's Eve in nineteen-double- ought at the stroke of midnight. The *Dawn of a New Century!* The papers named it. Lots of celebrating and fireworks shooting off and such, for just another day as I saw it. All that hoopla must have brought the blood suckers rising out of their holes like night crawlers after a good rain.

Well, we had it pretty rough back then, Wicked and me. No Teleportation, no Mind-Hookups, and definitely, no living past your prime. 'Course back then, a good ol' age lingered around forty-seven years. Our daddy had already been treading water in life's swamps for fifty years, when he finally took a nosedive into a patch of sorghum. I'm not that sharp at numbers, but I figure I've already added on considerably to my own life above the ground since the Vamps made me and little sister a better offer than a noose.

I was clearing twenty and Wicked was fourteen at that particular moment. Appears I'd caught the attention of the notorious Bounty Hunter, Miguel Sanchez, and if you'll bear with me, I'll explain how life was changed forever after.

I'd heard stories about Sanchez around the dusty border towns, when I visited for a day, or so, before making my 'withdrawal' from the local banking establishment, or Dry Goods Store if we were low on some staples. He was described as The Dark Angel because he always preferred the 'Dead' part of 'Dead or Alive' as his method of bringing in his prisoners. At several of the bars I visited, gathering information on Banking Hours, potential guards, and such, the locals would turn jittery and pale if I brought up the name, Dark Angel. In one bar, I struck up a conversation with the town's Undertaker. Like many of his profession, he was a friendly drinker. He said the bodies he'd seen after the bounty hunter brought them in for his reward, looked like they'd been dipped in candle wax, and left to dry in the noonday sun. His hand shook upon the recollection and a few drops of the fiery liquor spattered the bar. I must admit, I felt a tad spooked, but considered it my companion's influence, and ordered him a new drink.

At home that very same night, as the clock ticked away like a beating heart toward the new year, I had the pleasure of meeting the Dark Angel, Miguel Sanchez, for myself. I was in the back stable, rubbing down my mare after a quick departure from a bank several towns away. I heard a horse, clippity-clopping over the hard dirt that long ago gave up growing anything green in front of our shack and sauntered over to check things out. I knew it couldn't be a law man that quick, so I relaxed a bit and smiled as Miguel got off a gleaming black horse. That beast must have stood at least seventeen-hands, and when it moved its huge head to give me a look over, I saw its eyes were a fiery red!

Miguel, on the other hand, had a broad grin creasing his round face as he looked me square in the eye. Standing a good six-foot, he was built like two men were stuffed inside his black shirt and road-weary black denim pants. Right off, I noticed the black leather boots he wore. They'd been expertly hand-tooled, with a pattern of lightning bolts flashing in yellow around the ankles and circling the boots above the calves. His skin was a deep, burnt-cinnamon brown. I guessed he'd come out of the wild country, somewhere in the mountains of Mexico. All in all, he was a remarkable looking man, and his friendly smile put me off my guard some.

Wicked, as I recall, wasn't so easily taken in with his smile. She hung back, just inside the open front door. I saw her reach in and grab her rifle she kept ready for just such unexpected visitors. She didn't show it but stood close to the door frame to conceal her little surprise until she needed it. Wicked is some kind of warrior that girl is!

"Afternoon, mister," I said as I watched Wicked ready the gun from the corner of my eye.

"Don't get many strangers out this way. Care to state your business?" I said friendly like.

Guess my neighborly smile didn't fool him, because he said, "No need for alarm, Senior. I mean no harm to you, or your young sister. I am here to offer you a better way to get rich than robbing these poor farmers of their money."

"What the hell you talkin' bout mister?"

Just then I picked up Wicked's move as she pushed away from the door.

"I suggest you get back on your monster of a horse hombre and ride out of here in the saddle...rather than over it!" Wicked backed my comment, with the distinct sound of cocking the rifle.

"Senior, I don't give a pile of steaming cow turds about your little enterprise. I am only interested in offering you and your sister...Wicked, I believe she is called... I want you both to join me in an everlasting adventure! You will have riches beyond your wildest dreaming, and the lifetime of an Angel to live those dreams! No more midnight raids thinning your neighbor's herds of stinking cattle to sell across the border to Mexican ranchers. No more bank robberies to fend off long hungry winters. And most importantly, no more suffering the pains of growing old and shriveling up like your parents did."

Wicked stepped off the porch, her lever-action rifle pointed at his middle.

"Go on Senorita! Pull that trigger and test my promise of eternity." He lunged toward her and Wicked sent a blast square into his broad chest. He was blown backwards and fell to the ground, landing on his back, still as a black crow hit with sling shot. We both came close to standing over him.

Sudden as a rattler, that big man sprang back onto his boots, wearing that same cocky grin. The front of his shirt was shredded, the pieces of fabric flapping in the dry wind. There was a hole the size of a squirrel's head in his chest, but it was closing up so fast we hardly saw it before it vanished. Now we knew what the stranger meant by having the lifetime of Angels!

"I believe you already know who I am. I've been...shadowing you, you might say. I want to recruit both of you now, before the Sheriff in the town you just left, finds your trail. He's part Apache and a very excellent tracker. You'll both be hung for murder, cattle rustling, bank robbery, and likely for killing off some of his posse when they get here. You'll be dragged out of here to the nearest tree and fitted with a hangman's loop. Trust me, Senior, these men won't care if one of you is a young woman. Her feet will dangle over the dirt just like yours. I'm here to offer you eternal life, and you've both seen with your own eyes, I have that power."

It was pretty awful the way he was going about our future demise, and thinking about my little sister suffering a hang-man's rope gave me pause.

"What do we have to do for you mister, to get all that life and all?"

I was surprised to hear Wicked's voice since she never speaks up like that, and never to a stranger.

"Do, Senorita? Why, just invite me into your home, and we'll have a little bite to discuss your future. All will be revealed shortly after. Oh, and I did bring an associate along, so you could both meet her before we conclude our business."

A woman stepped out from behind Wicked. I never saw her sneaking up on us, but all of a sudden, she was there! I swallowed hard to get my heart out of my throat. Wicked's eyes were wide as she backed away from her, angling in my direction. The woman stared into Wicked's panicked face. Reaching out she gently took the rifle out of her hands as easy as taking a rattle from a baby. I blinked twice to be sure of what I was seeing. The gal was about Wicked's size, small and thin. She took a clump of my sister's hair and pushed it away from her neck. The next thing I saw was Wicked standing as passive as a cow at milking time, as the woman sucked on her neck for a minute. When she pulled away, her mouth was covered in blood and Wicked dropped heavily to the ground.

I wanted to help her to stop the attack, but I couldn't move. The Dark Angel had somehow moved unnoticed to my side. He laid a hand on my shoulder and pushed me down to my knees. I tried to shout out, when he leaned over me. I saw his grin was wider, he'd unhinged his jaw like a prairie rattler. Two long teeth hung out of his mouth.

Like a ship in heavy fog, uncountable time has passed since that New Year's Eve. Wicked and I have seen hundreds of celebrations so far, and figure we'll be seeing hundreds more. The Dark Angle and his woman dropped out of our little gang after the first twenty-years or so, because they got tired of what they called, the thin blood of the hardscrabble farmers and ranchers.

With all the money we could want, Wicked and I wonder how to spend our endless time. We are limited you see, because she's still fourteen, and will be forever. And me, I'm still a tad over twenty. I've dodged two wars that I know of, hiding in this swamp. We moved here to New Orleans in kind of a rush. Our last dinner guest at our fancy mansion, was the town Mayor. Unfortunately, he let the City Council know exactly where he was spending dinner that night. We only eat when I can find a gator hunter, but it's getting pretty rare these days.

Lately, I've noticed Wicked giving me some strange, side-long looks. I caught her whittling on a long piece of wood the other day, and said it was to relieve the stress of living. I decided to write down this story so there's a record of our lives for whoever stumbles across our cabin. Life must go on…and on…

"George! Over here!" The air boats skimmed the greenish-brown water, its growling motor causing a disturbance among the population of the swamp.

"Looks like a hut, or cabin over there."

The two crafts made for the small dock jutting out from the muddy bank. Within twenty minutes George and his buddy found a headless corpse with a stake sticking from its chest and wormy wood boxes filled with rotted cash and gold coins. They were in the process of loading their booty onto the bobbing decks when a young woman's voice called out.

"Stay for super fellas?"

Killing the Last Hero: A Prologue

How I came to be the unofficial biographer for the life and times of Patrice Amundi is another story entirely. For now, I am simply concerned with telling you about the last hero of our hard-won revolution.

Though our country is barely a speck on your maps, and even less in your memory, it is a place of great beauty and magic to us Farlanders. It would be best if I used this Prologue to share a very brief history of our island.

It was named Farland by the rather unimaginative man who discovered our Paradise, sweltering under the sun and fanned by cool ocean breezes. His name was also Patrice Amundi, but he was the first of that name. He was from a very distant time and place, and after his arrival here, he planted a flag of his own design, along with seed of his own loins. One, in the rich black earth, the other, in the barmaid Matilda, who fled with him from an unknown scrub-town along the Ivory Coast, after, it seems, an altercation involving coin and murder.

Folklore tells of Matilda giving Patrice five sons and six daughters, before dying of sheer exhaustion from the demands made on her body. It seems Patrice was determined to populate his island with as many offspring as possible. Fortunately, none of the siblings found any among their numbers attractive enough to couple with, so no morons were produced, though his two youngest sons were questionable.

After Matilda was set adrift on the outgoing tide, a clean way of disposing of mates today, Patrice set sale for other islands, roughly noted during his first voyage. He then proceeded to lure, or kidnap, many young men and girls off these outliers of floating jungles and bring them back to his own island with the help of those five strapping sons, and two rather sturdy daughters. The sons provided needed muscle, if the girls charms failed to convince resisters.

Once home on Farland (again, a truly bland name for our fair isle) Amundi set himself the task of matching mates with the new arrivals, relying, it is said, on no more than who got caught first by an excited mate-to-be. There are alarming stories of recalcitrant participants among the non-Amundi group, but never mind that. I'm not writing this to stir your prurient interests. In the end, all were matched, wedded and so on and so forth! Babies began popping up all over Farland, strapped to the backs of all five wives and the six Amundi daughters. In due course as these things went on, these children grew, and found suitable mates, and the cycle continued until the island of Farland was bursting at the seams with progeny!

Over subsequent generations there was always a Patrice Amundi to be found and hailed as undisputed leader. And, amazingly, like the first of this name, they all carried the spirit of adventure, or as some might say, they were scoundrels. It is the last of these Patrice Amundi that I serve as Recording Historian of his life.

My work is stuffed like a Cornish hen on Farland Patriots Day, with tasty morsels and tidbits of astonishing avarice, immorality, rampant egoism, with a dash of mysterious deaths or exiling of any perceived enemies. Meticulous investigating on my part, turned over several mossy rocks, revealing wormy schemes for expunging rivals. Stephen Agape was one such rival, and I shall start and finish this Prologue with him.

Stephen Agape

Just as his family name implies, Stephen was filled with love. Love for his kinfolk, love for the wild remedies he culled from the natural world around him, love for his homeland. His role as Healer for Farland's population, helped carve-out a powerful place for him, and his own progeny, on the political stage of the island. Though never elevated to the status of high command, for generations the people of Farland looked to the living Agape clan Elder as their anointed *Guardian of the People*. This was rooted in Farland tradition from the first dawning of Amundi leadership and was manifest into every generation of Amundi leadership to follow. The Amundi dynasty never went unchallenged, or totally unchecked as long as there was a living Agape Elder to speak for the people. This vigorous defense of the voiceless among the populace, was met with arrogant disregard from the first Patrice Amundi, to this current one, but Stephen Agape's voice of dissent had the ring of iron behind it.

Men and women armed themselves with every kind of conceivable weapon and at the word of Stephen Agape, stormed the mud-daubed walls of the Amundi Compound. The bodies of Amundi's elite Homeland Guard, were strewn like wheat chaff across the ground. The whole of the Amundi clan was snuffed out until only Patrice was left. Battered, and stripped naked, he was taken prisoner for public execution.

And so, dear reader, you may assume Patrice met a gruesome demise at the end of a pitchfork, or several, but that was not to be. He was placed in the village square on a pile of faggots and cow dung. The leader of this coupe, Stephen Agape, addressed the crowd with stirring words of forgiveness and the solemnity of life. He told them enough blood had been shed, and freedom from tyranny was planted in the hearts of all, now, and forever. His words brought tears to the eyes of some among the blood-spattered mob. Stephen placed his arm in a forgiving gesture around Patrice Amundi's hunched shoulders. He hugged the sobbing despot to his chest, smiling up to the heavens. That simple act was an uncanny trigger to one onlooker.

The excited village simpleton broke from the ranks of armed folk. He ran forward, laughing heartily as he jammed a burning brand over and over among the branches and dung. The pile quickly burst into a conflagration before Stephen Agape could react. The crowd stared silently, watching the confused look of betrayal melt from Stephen's face into the orange flames.

So ended the life of the powerful Patrice Amundi, on a pile of cow turds and sticks. Of course, it also ended the life of the Healer, Stephen Agape, at the hands of the simpleton.

Thus concludes this Prologue. To this chronicler's eyes, this proves yet again, some idiot can always undo the careful judgement of the wise among us.

Bernardo, Farland Keeper of Memories

The Last Ride Home

"There's really no reason to follow me home," Miranda said firmly to her friend.

Betsy's pickup truck sat idling in front of the vehicle in question on the side of the road. Both women were just off-duty from their night shift as nurses at Good Samaritan hospital in the nearby town.

"Honestly, Betsy. I'll be fine. My car is just temperamental in this kind of weather. Some oil must have splashed onto the hot engine over these bumpy roads. Get out of this rain for heaven's sake and go home! You've got a longer drive than me, and I'll call you when I get to my sister's place."

Miranda was shouting to be heard over the pelting rain and constant booming thunder. She saw her friend's barely concealed relief in the next lightning strike. It was miserable out, and they were already soaked through. Miranda's little Volkswagen Beetle began billowing smoke a few miles back. Betsy, who'd been driving behind her, said it was like following a crippled fighter jet!

She had pulled off to the shoulder of the empty country road, black in the moonless deluge. The Beetle sat stuttering as her hands slipped a few times trying to pop the hood. The smoke dissipated in the heavy downpour while she attempted to check for loose hoses. That was the extent of her knowledge of a car's engine. Miranda noticed it made labored coughing sounds when she pressed the gas pedal, and she was afraid to turn it off. She was certain it was good enough to get her back to her sister's ranch, about three miles away. Miranda gave her anxious friend a reassuring smile as she pulled her head out from under the dripping hood, telling her again, to get going.

"I'll be home before you!"

After a split-second of considering her options, Betsy gave her a quick, wet hug, and ran back to her idling truck. She pulled out onto the road, glancing back at the squat, dome-shape, silhouetted against a frenzied night. The wind had picked up considerably, and the black sky looked as if it was being cracked open by spikes of lightening. She made a quick check in the rear-view, relieved to see Miranda behind the wheel before the overhead light went out. Rather than driving right off, Betsy slowly drifted down the road, looking back to see how Miranda was doing. After several long minutes, the headlights on the VW flashed three times to signal all was well. Betsy gave her car some gas. Before long Miranda's car was just a pair of distant yellow halos melting on her rear window.

Miranda felt every bump and ridge of the rough, gravel road. At one point, she considered getting out and walking the rest of the way to the Lonesome J Ranch. She was already wet right down to her undies. Crawling along under ten miles an hour, afraid to put too much strain on the sputtering engine, she was beginning to regret flashing her lights to give Betsy the all-clear. The rain was coming straight down in opaque sheets, as the wipers struggled to clear the heavy downpour. She had the eerie feeling of driving under a waterfall. The floorboards of the old car vibrated when the thunder growled over-head and a bolt of lightning found its mark.

Squirming around in her seat, Miranda tried to ignore the chill creeping into her body from her wet clothes. She reached down to turn on the heat. When she looked back through the streaming windshield, a tall figure was standing in the road directly in front of her moving car. Miranda pushed hard on the brakes, immediately putting the car into a slide. The Beetle swerved sharply on the shifting gravel. She felt the small car pick up speed, as the world turned upside down once, then again, and again.

Stopping with a jolting thump, Miranda's body shot forward and her head smacked against the windshield. It took a minute to gather her wits. Her headlights were still on, but barely lit the scene since the front bumper was buried up to the pale globes in the muddy wall of a deep gully. The car's engine made a sickening sound like a patient taking a last breath. Miranda sat stunned, trying to understand what had happened. Suddenly, the form of the dark figure flashed into her mind.

Had she hit him? Is he lying on the road dying? She pushed against her door. It was stuck because the car was tilted on the driver's side. She had to crawl over the stick-shift and climb out the passenger's side. The deep trench the car was mired in was beginning to fill with water. The rain hadn't slowed, the winds were still strong, whipping her long hair around where it stuck to her wet face and neck.

Miranda felt like she'd stepped into a river as she desperately struggled to climb out of the fast-filling ditch. She was nearly blinded by the stinging rain as it pelted against her upturned face. When she reached the edge, there was an outstretched hand waiting to help haul her up. Without hesitating, she grabbed hold and her rescuer wrapped a hand around her elbow and pulled.

She was covered in mud and dead grass. Her nurses' uniform was badly ripped. Miranda took the edges of her light sweater and pulled them tightly across her chest, hoping to save some body heat. It finally dawned on her, she was standing on the side of the road and someone else was with her. Blinking rapidly to clear her vision, she found herself staring into the pale eyes of the man she almost hit.

"Thank God you're alright!" she blurted out when she finally found her voice.

He stared back at her, a slight smile tugging at the corners of his mouth. Miranda was too distraught to notice, going on about narrowly missing him.

"You came out of nowhere!" she added, still trying to explain the near mishap.

"I surely come out of somewhere, Miss Miranda, and I'm definitely fixin' on going back! It would be most agreeable fer me to hitch a ride in yer auto-mobile to hasten my journey."

Miranda began to wonder if she smacked her head harder than she thought. Reaching under the weight of her plastered hair, she felt several deep lacerations on her forehead and scalp. Distracted by her serious injuries, it took a minute to process what the stranger said, as it filtered through the beginning of panicked thoughts.

"I don't know if you've noticed, but my car isn't running well at the moment," she said.

She tried to keep her growing annoyance at this man out of her voice, when it dawned on her, he'd called her by name.

"How do you know my name? Were you one of my patients?"

This time he smiled broadly, showing a mouthful of broken teeth, and holes where many were missing.

"No Miss. My maw learned me to decipher some, and I read thet there bitty sign yer wearing."

Miranda was taken aback by his odd comment and stilted language. She looked down at her name tag, hanging askew from her sweater. She began to study the man more closely.

He could have stepped out of the late eighteen-hundreds. Even his long coat and rough looking shirt and pants all had an antique, home-spun look to them. Looking at him up and down, she noticed he wore a pair of high, well-worn, leather boots, and his coat was actually some kind of canvas rain slicker. She took a step backwards before she pointed down the gully to the silent hulk of her Beetle.

"My car is not going anywhere. It would be best if we just started to walk to Lonesome J, my sister's ranch. It's about three miles from here. We can call for a tow truck for my car, and my sister can get a ranch hand to drive you home."

She noticed how pale the man looked under a stubble of beard. He nearly glowed in the dark! Even his sunken eyes had a dead look about them. She was surprised at his reaction to her suggestion, shaking his head from side-to-side, laughing softly.

"Oh Lordy! Can you believe it? The Lonesome J! Of all things! Why that's jest the place I'm headin' fer. Need to find my ol' restin' place. Truth be told, the whole cemetery were dug up...oh, back in '08, the best I ken figure it. Any hows, lots of us boys were badly disturbed as a result. Most, jest wandered off inta the mountains round Santa Fe town, but I weren't none too happy at the prospect of being so distant from my roots ya' see."

Miranda studied this odd man more closely, wondering if she was safe in his company. He was talking gibberish about being buried at the ranch, or maybe, that's what he wanted. But she knew for a fact, there was no cemetery anywhere near the house, or in any of the pasture-land surrounding it.

"I guess we'd better start walking," she said to the man, trying to focus him on the urgency of their need to move.

He grinned and said, "I got an even better notion Missy. How's bout I whistle fer ol' Clopper?"

"Who's ol' Clopper?" she asked taking another step away from the stranger.

"Why, he's only the best cow pony this side of the Rio Grande! Don't you fret none, Missy. He ken carry both of us, seein' as yer just a fly speck of a gal!"

Miranda felt the weight of her rain-soaked clothes weighing her down. It was as if her body was encased in plaster that was shrinking tighter and tighter. She began to feel light-headed, like she wasn't getting enough oxygen. Her heart raced inside her constricting chest.

"I think I may have a concussion," she mumbled. The man gave her a wider grin, showing all his rotted and broken teeth.

"It won't be long now Missy. I hear ol' Clopper coming to get us right quick now!"

Miranda was rooted in place, or she would have run when she heard the sound of horse hooves coming toward them. She blinked slowly, letting the rain cascade down her face like a bride's veil. A strong arm was slipping around her waist and she was suddenly being lifted off her feet. She found herself sitting in front of the stranger, on the broad back of a sway-back horse every bit as tall as a Clydesdale. She could feel the ridge of his rib cage against the back of her legs.

"Time for us to go Miss Miranda. This being our last ride home, you jest lay yer head back and close yer eyes. This is gonna be a smooth trip, seein' as ol' Clopper here has done made it more times than cat's got whiskers."

Miranda felt her body relax against the boney chest of the stranger. His long fingers looked skeletal with the reins wrapped around them. Miranda felt the horse move after the man made a clicking sound. It was like floating and she closed her eyes against the battering rain.

The Trench

"I don't see how you can save me from the gallows, Penbrook. My story has been recounted in every yellow rag... even turned into one of those cheap Penny Dreadful serials, I'm told," he barked out a crazed laugh, and added, "The publisher is just waiting for the last chapter to be written, when the trap door opens beneath my feet."

He'd been pacing his cell like a caged tiger, but stopped to take a deep breath, as if feeling the hangman's noose slip around his neck.

"My beastly crimes have cost me everything including my freedom, and soon, my life! No. There isn't any sense in rehashing this sordid nightmare."

Charles Burgoyne dropped exhausted onto the narrow bed, causing a threadbare gray blanket to slip onto the filthy cell floor unnoticed. A chill winter light from a portal window set high in the stone wall, barely penetrated the heavy gloom. A narrow cold beam settled on his broad shoulders, and the thick blond curls at the nape of his neck. He bent over, leaning his elbows on his knees and cradled his head in his hands, silently shaking it as if denying the existence of his mean surroundings and ultimate fate.

The Solicitor, hired by his parents in a desperate act to save him, stepped closer to the filthy mattress, careful not to brush against it with his dark wool coat. When the blanket fell to the floor, he noticed the rough stuffing poking through the ripped seams of the naked mattress. The cell reeked of unclean bodies, and the foul human and vermin droppings left in an overflowing bucket and its dark corners. There were two other prisoners being held in this cesspit, and his client, the once dashing

Charles Burgoyne, looked as out of place among the rascals, as an exotic songbird would in a chicken coop.

"Charles, I have been your family's Solicitor for many years. Your father has tasked me with freeing you from this unjust incarceration, and I intend to do so. Your living conditions here are utterly deplorable!"

The young man looked up. It was nineteen-sixteen, and two years of fighting in a seemingly endless 'War of the World,' had hallowed out his once handsome face. He smiled weakly at the older man.

"There is truly nothing here worse than what I have already seen and experienced. The other men in here were found guilty of desertion, and they are to be shot. For me, it's the Gallows, where I'm to swing like a church bell. I have the dubious honor of being the only Officer in His Majesty's Service, to ever have been found guilty of mass murder of my comrades. I'm told I am to serve as an example of how criminals of any rank will be treated if they commit such heinous crimes.

Shall I review the facts for you Penbrook? Did you know all but two men from my squad were slaughtered because of my deranged behavior? Even shooting at me had no effect or slowed down my rampage. The two survivors testified they were only able to escape because I was systematically butchering their friends in a frenzy of blood lust. They crawled through the trenches until they reached the next command position. The Officer in charge immediately reported my insane behavior, ordering that I be brought back alive to face justice. Though I'd hardly call my current state being *alive*."

The prisoner chuckled to himself, then took a long breath of the foul air before adding, "There. Now you have the whole story, sir."

Penbrook left after a few more minutes spent trying to convince the young man that his plight could be avoided.

"You need only divulge the full truth about the incident," he insisted yet again.

The Solicitor's spicy cologne lingered for a brief time, until it too, was overcome by the heavy stink of despair. Charles lay back on the hard bed, his arm flung over his eyes. Wrapped inside the closeness of the cell, he soon drifted into another fitful sleep. He saw himself in the same nightmare as it played out yet again behind his locked eyelids.

He was on his belly, covered in mud as torrential rains turned the trenches into stinking bogs. He was half-crawling through the gouged earth, trying to reach each of his men to relay his orders and give a personal word of encouragement. They had fought together as a squad for several months now. Their numbers dwindled over time by another kind of rain; the withering torrent of bullets that awaited any man who stuck his head up too far over the lip of the trench.

He could never quite remember how many months they had fought, side by side, covering each other's backs. The war was as blurred as his vision in the downpour he slithered through. The men were squatting along the wall of dirt. All of them had stunned, far-off looks in their dull eyes, and expressions of horror etched into their faces. They dug this trench days before, advancing yard by yard, toward enemy lines. They had to keep reinforcing it as it continuously slid down with the frequent downpours, and the constant fusillade from across the River Somme.

They were in the north of France and had been engaged with the enemy for almost one-hundred days already. So many thousands had already died or been wounded. Charles found it difficult to swallow after considering his next order. As a Captain in the British Army, it was up to him to show a rigid backbone to his men, no matter how wretched the circumstances.

He finished speaking with the last man, retreating for a few minutes of rest under the make-shift shelter that was his command post. Out of sight of his men, he removed his helmet, running filthy fingers through his thick blond hair, and rubbing his eyelids with gritty palms. He sank to the ground, propping his head against the lose end of the tarp ceiling. It seemed as if his burning eyes had just drifted shut, when he distinctly heard a woman's voice call his name. His eyes flew open.

There, with the strobe effect of field artillery painting her naked body in garish hues, stood the most beautiful woman Charles had ever seen. He froze as if suffering shellshock, staring at this voluptuous apparition. He gasped when he spotted the stubby wings, covered in shiny scales, protruding from her slender shoulders. His mouth hung open, but no words were spoken. He blinked in rapid succession until he knew what he saw was real, and not a vision likely to fade. He managed to ask, "Who...How did you...?"

"I'm only with you for a few minutes Charles, but I've a gift for you. It will save you from this mindless slaughter and bring you the peace you've longed for."

Charles watched as she floated to where he lay sprawled, legs akimbo with a deadening fatigue. She leaned over him; her full lips parted in a seductive smile. This close to her open mouth, her breath smelled of a mixture of floral scents and the coppery smell of fresh blood. His body was rigid with an all-consuming desire this strange winged-woman inflamed in him. He tried speaking, but she laid a slender, cold finger on his lips, hushing him with a small shake of her head. The movement of her long black hair sent shivers through him, as he watched it brush across her full bosom. With the same chilled finger, she pulled his filthy collar away from his neck. He was looking straight ahead, but his peripheral vision picked up the long incisors hanging from her mouth just before they sank into him.

Time stood still for Charles while he listened to the strange sucking sound close to his ear. He couldn't move a muscle. When the woman pulled away, it sounded like someone pulling a boot out of the mud. He watched blood dripping from the corner of her lush mouth and down her delicate chin.

"You will be very hungry when you awaken, Charles. More ravenous than ever before. But out there, lies a feast for you. I'll feed again later, after you've had your fill. Ah, let the blood flow!"

She vanished into the muddy shadows under the tarp. Charles stared at the spot she stood a second before, seeing only the hard pellets of rain beat into the exposed earth. He shook his head hard then stood.

"I am famished!" he declared to the darkness around him. He felt his mouth shifting oddly as if he was sprouting new baby teeth. He touched the sides of his mouth where the sharp incisors had dropped neatly into place.

Charles attacked each man while they slept in war-induced stupors. None had the chance to scream out after he ripped into their throats and drank deeply of their life's blood. This went on into an endless night. Before dawn, Charles saw the last two men rouse themselves. Seeing the torn bodies, they scurried like squealing rats through the black trench, covered now with the free-flowing blood of their comrades.

As always in his macabre dream, Charles returned to the small lean-to and finding his knapsack, dug out another yellowish pod. He knew he was addicted to pure opium, but it was the only way he could survive the horrors of this war. He'd do another quick bowl before he had to rouse the men for a charge out of the trench, toward the withering fire awaiting them from the enemy line.

As he fingered the annoying insect bites on his neck, he took a deep drag on the pipe and smiled at the preposterous notion of death. Nothing could be worse than the trench.

The other prisoners in the cell watched as his body jerked and tossed in his fitful dreaming, waiting for the screams they knew would follow. They whispered to one another that his death would surely be the only relief he'd ever find in this world. The older of the two condemned men wore a field jacket that still had the traces of his Sargent stripes left after they were torn from the uniform he disgraced. He was more than familiar with the demons possessing the disgraced Captain.

"In the damn trench, a bloke's got to forget everything except his name, and even that don't matter when you hear the order ta charge! I seen other officers lose their nerve, this one's no different. Only instead of running away from the bullets and bayonets and slaughter, he used the yellow poison from the Chinaman, and became the butcher like they say.

The trench can twist a man's mind until he sees angels one minute and devils the next. There are more ways to escape than the one we took kid. He'll likely hang still screaming about a woman… Hey…did the captain just say he's hungry? Damn, not again! Get the rat sticker kid! Guard! Guard!"

The Servant's Tale

There was no doubt in his mind. He had found the entrance to the treasure cave used by the infamous Lord of the Realm-turned Pirate, Sir Creighton March. He'd been obsessed with locating the storied site of fabulous jewels and uncounted coin for over twenty years, following every lead no matter how scant, and leaning heavily on written accounts from the last man who stood in his place years before.

The driving force of his life, his quest ruined every relationship he ever entered, drove friends to decry him as mad, and reduced him to pauperism as it swallowed his last farthing. But now, he stood on the brink of total vindication as he closed his eyes momentarily, to bask in the shallow light at the cave entrance.

"I have found my Nirvana at last," he murmured reverently.

Only the long shadow he cast upon the cave wall bore witness to this glorious moment. He'd been deserted by the handful of ignorant sailors, along with the Expedition Scout, after the poison darts of the ghost-like savages took three of them down. The Scout left him huddled under a flat palm fern in the middle of a moonless night, deserting him after their third day under siege. He, and the mutinous crew, took their beached dinghy and returned to their small ship. The next morning, the boat's masts and square form no longer filled his brass scope. The savages were also gone, believing all the white devils were driven off no doubt. Tales of this island, calling it a sacred site protected by blood thirsty savages, had proven as true as they were once thought totally preposterous to his enlightened mind. He guessed the deserters were sailing back to their last port of call, at least fifty nautical miles off.

"The fools will never survive in these uncharted waters. Not with the undetectable reefs surrounding it," he said defiantly into the morning haze. His sole companion nodded agreement encouragingly as he pushed the palm ferns away from his own eyes.

Petry, his nearly invisible Manservant, had loyally stayed with him throughout his long years of decline, unable to break his oath of service. However, his master hardly counted him as a witness to this auspicious moment.

Now, standing slightly behind his Master, Petry was set to become the second man alive to clap eyes on the fabled March Treasure, lost to history nearly seventy years before. Petry leaned against a wall, feeling the chilled moisture seeping through the feet of dirt and rock that formed the entrance to the cave, while his mind wandered. His velvet-blue uniform was reduced to colorless tatters, yet he insisted on wearing it, seemingly oblivious to its deteriorated state. His body was as thin as the material of his breeches. Any exposed skin sagged and had turned a strange shade of yellow. This went unnoticed by his red, rheumy eyes, or indeed, by his once fastidious master.

His master's voice snagged Petry's meandering attention. He sounded as if he addressed the Society of Unthinkable Exploration, the elite group he founded as a young University student with three others of like interests. Their mission was to search-out answers to the inscrutable mysteries that peck away at logic like birds at scattered seed. The Treasure of Lord March was one such mystery.

"Now, Petry...we must proceed with extreme caution from this point forward," his master said, adjusting the flame in his lantern as he spoke.

"The Society garnered written testimony from a few fellow hunters, stating the Pirate, Lord March, turned to the Dark Occult in an effort to conceal his fabulous treasure. These riches are supposedly safeguarded with ingenious traps of illusion and Magic. It was reported that anyone getting too near, suffers a mercurial grasp on reality, leading them deeper into the cave's interior. Several Society members who made it this far, turned back after being lost for days in these catacombs. Two were lost forever and this place became their tomb. Of the six members of the Society who ventured here over the past fifteen years, only one, my dear friend Claude Beauchamp returned, giving a first-hand report to me, and the few Society members still faithful to our mission."

Lighting Petry's lantern next, his master began to move like a dancer on tip-toe, into the heavy gloom. He proceeded to recount some of the treasure's history to his Man Servant, in a barely audible whisper. To Petry's ears and vivid imaginings, the crinkle of the parchment his master clutched like the Holy Grail in his grubby hand, sounded like the laughter of tiny elves. His master continued his tutorial.

"The Society listened to Claude's rambling report, dictated from his death bed, poor man, recounting the disappearances of fellow members who searched these caves with him. The members all agreed, searching further for the March Treasure, was far too dangerous a mystery to pursue. Claude's untimely death shortly thereafter, cemented their resolution to drop any further attempts to locate the treasure trove."

"But my dear Petry," he added, turning back to catch his servant's rheumy eye, "the other Society fellows were unaware that I pried this map from Claude's stiffening hand before they could learn of its existence. It shows every twist and turn in this damnable maze, until it eventually opens into a large cavern with a vaulted ceiling. This... is where Lord March stowed his treasures!" he concluded breathlessly.

Petry knew the significance of finding such wealth to his impoverished master. Yet, inside the shadowy passageways of the cave, he began to have a clearer view of how this would impact his own life. Though nearing fifty, Petry looked decidedly older. The rigors of this journey, and countless others over years of serving his master's myopic quest, had taken a supreme toll on him. He had enjoyed neither family, nor hearth, in an endless stream of wandering through strange ports, sleeping on boards of endless boats and ships, carrying him half-way around the world, and back again. All their meandering finally brought them to this swampy island. Infested by every kind of crawling and flying insect life, and a band of wild men, with an odd resemblance to himself under their sun-blackened skin.

Petry believed this could be the conclusion of his own life's journey. A bitterness began to take root in his thin chest, beating stronger with the thumping of his lonely heart. He watched the emaciated back of his Master, once broad with muscle and flesh, and followed in a near stupor through the ever-narrowing passageways.   Rows of somnolent bats were roused on occasion from their upside-down perch, as the glow of the two lanterns passed under their foxlike heads, the yellow fingers of light penetrating their hooded eyes. Petry felt a coolness settle around his near-naked limbs, reaching thin arms around himself to retain a little heat.

"Petry! The treasure room is just ahead. I can feel the vastness of the cavern, just as Claude described it. Come! Hold your lantern up man, so I can better see!"

His voice held a worrisome edge of recklessness and near hysteria. Petry hastened his own pace to keep the hunter in view. He could hear the echo of his master's boots as the sound bounced back at them from the lofty cathedral ceiling. The servant knew his master would throw all caution to the wind as he rushed forward into the unknown chamber.

The meager glow from the lanterns could barely stave off a heavy darkness he felt was about to swallow the two of them. Petry gave voice to his rising panic, yelling out.

"We can't just rush ahead my Lord! There may be unseen pitfalls. And what of the Magic used to seal the treasures from looters? Surely you must avoid triggering the magical mechanisms before we ..."

Petry's words were cut short when his over-wrought master grabbed his arm, jerking the lantern out of his grasp. In the same aggressive movement, Petry was launched head-first into the yawning mouth of the cavern. His screams were captured like stones from a sling, shooting around the open area, bouncing off granite walls and floor. His master's voice called out to him.

"Petry! I'm sorry. But I needed to test for any wards, or magical spells that Lord March might have contrived. Answer if you are able man! Can I proceed?"

Petry was no more than a cluster of shadows as he moaned, unable to move his limbs. He answered automatically, not thinking of the implications of his master's actions.

"I am unable to move more than my head, my Lord. I fear my back was injured when I hit something within."

The servant watched as a single lantern bobbed its light like a giant firefly off the hard surfaces of the cavern. Believing his master was coming to his aid, Petry called out, "Sir, I'm over here. Please, hurry..." Petry gave a resigned sigh when he realized the other man was focused on one thing only.

He was several feet away, mumbling to himself as he ran his hands through piles of coins and mounds of jewels. The booty winked back at the servant like a mischievous imp, where he lay watching his master's obsession take hold completely. Petry raised his head slightly to take in a limited view.

Treasure was scattered around the floor of the cave, some in overflowing wooden chest with rotted leather strapping, others, lose and twinkling under the small flame of his master's lamp. Petry bit-off a groan and listened as his Master panted like a man caught-up in the tempest of an orgy. He opened his eyes wider when something moved above his head.

"Master..." he tried to push air through his words to be heard. "There is...something..."

His master was lost in his moment of possessing wealth beyond all dreams. He didn't hear the beseeching voice of his loyal servant, until Petry screamed. Jerking his attention away from the caskets of treasures, he finally took note of Petry lying in front of a casket the size of a small cottage. Tearing himself away from the mountain of gold and glittering gems, the greed sodden man gave his servant a hard shove with his foot, rolling him aside to better access the huge trunk. He threw back the heavy lid and leaned over to peer into its murky interior. He was about to right himself, seeing only unbroken blackness, when suddenly the figure Petry had seen stirring overhead swung down, roughly pushing his master into the vast chest. Petry heard the lid slam shut, sealing off his master's scream. The sound of bolts being shot home, quickly followed, with the finality of death itself. If he weren't already paralyzed, Petry would have been too frightened to twitch a hair.

"Your master is no more," a shrill voice rang out in the nearly black cavern.

"He was already lost in his own greediness and obsession. My own master, Lord March, awaits him as he did the other seekers. You, servant, will not leave this place a broken man."

The single lantern cast the shadow of the old hag scuttling like a beetle toward his broken body. He lay unable to resist even if he'd had a mind to. He felt her lay a bony finger on his forehead while chanting a few garbled sounds. His transformation was complete, and he joined the other bats hanging listlessly over the darkened riches. Before she returned to her own place above the giant chest, the Witch looked up.

"Your loyalty has been rewarded in kind. Let us wait for the next fools blinded by unquestioning allegiance or driven by greed. It's all the same to me."

Good As A Blind Man's Candle

"Ah, yes. There's a story to be told tonight, but are you all certain you have the steel in you to hear it?"

The men regarded Thomas with sly looks, trying to judge the Englishman's sincerity in the matter of a promised Halloween Tale. The six rough looking ranch hands lounged around a large campfire on a brisk October thirty-first. Some still scraped their tin plates clean of beans with hunks of gritty corn bread, while others sipped coffee strong enough to wrestle a steer to the ground.

Thomas was a camp cook, on his third cattle drive with these wranglers. Rolling behind the ranch boys, he bounced on the hard seat of the covered wagon for hours, listening to the rattle of cooking gear while he ate and breathed the dust of their wake. They were moving twelve-hundred head, from the Double Barrel Ranch, heading to the railhead outside Santa Fe, where the cowpokes would then prod the cattle into the freight cars.

The ranch hands had been eating Thomas's grub for the better part of three years, and they still didn't know much about the stringy old coot. He had a strange way of talking that somehow stopped them cursing or spitting in his presence. Even though he trundled along in a cloud of their dusty grit most days, he somehow managed to stay clean and tidy looking when they rode back to the orderly campsite he prepared, for their evening meal.

One night, the youngest among the saddle-sore cowboys, asked Thomas if he was "...some kinda doc, with that fancy talk ya'll got?"

In his usual quiet, unhurried manner, Thomas answered that among other things, he had been a thespian in London's finest stages.

"A what?" the youngster blurted.

"An actor, young man."

After the crew learned of his past profession, a few shyly began asking him to entertain them with stories of what they clearly saw as his exotic former life, while they sat around the fire eating their mean victuals.

This night was no exception. It was the youngster, on his third plate of ham and beans, hoping to secure a minuscule piece of salted pork, who spoke up as he settled on a log close to the fire.

Thomas seemed reluctant at first, telling them, "Stories of Hallow's Eve are best told on any other night! Recounting tales of spirits and ghouls, encourages visitations from ghosts who roam freely this night."

The six men, reeking of leather and cows even in the sweet mountain breeze, would not be dissuaded, the youngest insisting they were not fearful of "nothin' without a gun!". And so, Thomas settled in, sitting erect as a preacher on the log the others always left vacant for his expected story-telling each night. And so, he began.

"There was a gentleman of great wealth, his mansion tucked into a corner of a small Shire, twenty-odd-miles distant from London. He was a powerful man in this county, made-up mostly of poor farmers, and cottagers struggling to make a living at one of the many businesses he owned throughout the area. In his own village, that business was the Candle Emporium Factory.

Understand, this was an innovative concept for the times. Fine beeswax candles were created by many hands, in many different sizes, shapes and even colors. These were then sold throughout England to Churches, civil servants, and for any private residence that could afford them, rather than the rough-made tallow candle of the poorer classes. The wealthy man designed the special molds and refined the dipping process himself, but all of that, was before his accident."

"What kinda accident?" the young cowpoke sputtered, corn breadcrumbs scattering into the campfire.

"He was gravely injured, when one of his candle molds literally exploded from excess use and heat, splashing liquid wax onto his face and into his eyes. His eyes were sealed shut for several minutes before the wax cooled enough to remove. Hiis eyes were scalded to the point they no longer had any color but looked as white as the underbelly of a dead fish."

The youngster drew in his breath at this description, the others smiling to themselves at his queasy nature. Thomas continued.

"The wealthy owner was whisked out of his busy factory by the floor manager; a towel thrown over his head, hiding the severe damage done to his face by the molten wax. The workers later spoke of the smell of burnt flesh lingering in the air for hours after, like the unwholesome fog that floats over the marshes.

The injured man returned to his sprawling mansion for the long convalescence his physician recommended. The doctor secretly held little hope for much healing and couldn't bring himself to completely remove the bandaging.   Several weeks went by, with the doctor checking daily on his patient's progress. He reported on the workings of the rich man's candle making business but gave scant information to him on his slow recovery from his burns, merely keeping watch for any sign of infection showing on the bandages.

After a month spent resting and sitting quietly in his gardens, the man grabbed for the doctor's hand as he began to re-wrap the top gauze covering his face.

"Undo the bandages, Dr. Phips! *All* of them this time! I have had enough of this languishing about. It is time to move on with life!"

While he sounded optimistic, the man guessed he'd been blinded, and more likely, greatly disfigured. The doctor worried about his positive attitude, toward what would surely prove a disastrous outcome. Phips stood behind his patient in the rich surroundings of his bedroom. He slowly began to unwind the long gauze wrap.

"Well, come on then...what'd' the doc find, Cookie?"

It was the impatient young cowpoke again, squirming on the log to hear the answer to a man's fate.

"He found the rich man's eyes were sunken into his skull! Two black holes looked back at him from a face covered in ridges of angry red scars, cut into his flesh by the rivulets of hot wax. The doctor couldn't repress a gasp of utter shock at the hideous visage he gazed upon. He didn't know how to respond when the man asked him why he hadn't removed the last covering from his eyes. He stood mutely, until the frustrated patient lifted his hands to his face.

"There are no bandages here, Phips! So, I am truly blind." he ran his hands over the deeply carved creases and mounds of scars on his once handsome face.

"You may leave me now Doctor. I know what I needed to learn."

"What in God's green acre does *that* mean?" hollered the young cowboy.

His rather unimaginative query bounced off the hills around them, and the others heard a few of the cattle lowing into the darkness with their answers. Thomas smiled thinly at the impetuous young cowboy, which subdued him considerably, then quickly slipped back into his tale.

"The rich businessman knew his chances of ever seeing again were as remote as the Orient to him. In desperation, he decided to turn to something more powerful than the doctor's puny medications. A secret hidden deep in his family's past...the use of the Dark Arts."

Thomas let the low hum of growing agitation from among his rapt audience quiet down, before he resumed.

"The rich man ruminated night and day over the possible use of the mystic arts but was too afraid to do more than contemplate such an extreme plan at first. He'd been a foundling babe, you see, and was told all of his life by his adoptive family, that his true parents were drowned in a calamitous river boat accident. Years later, after he amassed his great fortune, he used it unsparingly, hiring private detectives to put to rest any questions about his lineage.

Accessing county records, and musty old Church documents, they discovered his father had been named as the notorious leader of a cult that practiced the forbidden teachings of the ancient Druids. His mother was among his first disciples. Together, they forged a band of thirteen men and women, called a coven…who pledged their lives to the mystic life, and used ancient magic to serve their dark purposes.

The rich man sat, day after day in the isolation of his eternal night, undecided about turning to this arcane Magic to return his sight and unscared good looks. Alas, in a moment of feeble character, he decided to reach out to the only living member of those Druid worshippers. Her identity became known to him, when he discovered his parent's Satanic past."

His listeners shifted on the rough seats, each looking as if he was ready to spring into flight at some unheard signal. Thomas lowered his head for a second, smiling to himself.

"Soon thereafter, Doctor Phips called on him to deliver ointment for his scared face. It wasn't lost upon his patient, that after squinting at his destroyed face, Phips couldn't leave the great house, and its deformed owner, quickly enough. The wealthy man, could almost smell the good doctor's repulsion, and knew it was time to implement his plan.

He rang for his manservant, Bushard. He ordered him to go into the heavy woodlands on the outskirts of the village. There, he needed to locate the cottage of the Druid Witch, Lydia, reported to live there by his private detectives.

Bushard could barely look at his master's face, with its blackened orbs. He tucked a fine woolen blanket around his master's legs against the Autumn chill, stirred the embers in the hearth, added new logs, and left the house on this desperate errand. Coincidentally, it was Hallow's Eve...as it is this very night!"

Thomas looked at his listeners, noting how they were giving one another side-long looks. He smiled as if gratified at their unease and resumed his tale.

"Bushard heard the shrill voices of some village children, as they went about their Hallow's Eve mischief in the square, and around the scattered cottages. He soon stepped into the deep, green silence of the woods, breathing in the sharp scent of pine mixed with the loamy odor of decaying forest debris. A full moon rode high on its black stead of night. It created thin pools where it penetrated the dense branches, appearing like curdled cream upon the dark lumpy earth.

He'd heard village gossip of a witch living alone in a hovel, near a small running brook. Bushard stopped for a moment, listening for the sound of burbling water, under the sound of the crunching leaves he trampled. He was about to take another step, when he felt a soft brushing of air near his ear and smelled a sour odor.

"Do yer young master send ye fer me then?"

The manservant almost watered the ground in his terror at the old woman's sudden appearance."

The young cowpoke snickered, as the truly immature will tend to do, but caught the flash in the cook's eyes, and thought better of interrupting him.

"The old hag agreed to accompany Bushard back to the grand manor house, after he read to her the message sent by his master. It divulged who his parents were and stated her services were urgently needed. The servant brought her to his master's study, moving into the shadows that had settled in the room, outside of the low fire's glow.

The injured man told the crone, he would have his sight restored, nearly shouting in his anxious request, "I know you were part of my father's coven of thirteen Druids! You have the power to do as I ask! I want to see as well as my mother and be as handsome as my father."

She responded in a croaky voice, "I ken do fer ye, m' Lord. I needs only a single candle from yer precious shop."

He didn't question her, but sent Bush, whom he sensed hovering nearby, to his factory to fulfill the odd request."

At this point in the story, one of the cowboys got up from his seat to put several logs on their dying fire. They were all so immersed in the story the cook was narrating, no one noticed how the years seemed to fall away from his animated face while he spoke. He resumed as soon as the man retook his seat. The flames jumped up as if excited at the prospect of finishing the tale.

"The old woman left, but as the hour approached midnight, came a heavy knocking upon her cottage door.

"The Master has asked that you come immediately, woman!" Bushard nearly screamed in her wizened face.

The toothless crone merely cackled at the man's pretense of courage.

"Ye return by yer own path, boy," she told him, leaning heavily on a stout, tree limb, and moving a few feet off. Bushard head her begin to chant in a strange language. He was greatly relieved to be getting away from the filthy hag, turning for a second to look back at her hunched figure. In that instant, the Druid Witch shot up above the trees. He watched amazed as her black silhouette crossed the face of the bulbous moon, sitting astride the limb, her ragged dress, streaming behind like a following dark cloud. The sight inspired the poor man to run as if the Devil could smell his fear. He returned to the mansion, taking the marble steps two at a time. He rushed into the master's study, where he'd left him in front of the fireplace a mere hour past, to seek out the witch.

The woolen blanket lay in a heap on the floor. The chair was empty except for a wax figure, twelve inches tall. Bushard edged closer to the strange object, seeing it pulsating with a yellow-white light from within as it sat on the rich brocade of the chair. He reached out his hand, picking it up carefully. He leaned in closer to make-out its features.

The long screams erupting from Busard's mouth, bounced off every wall of the empty house. He tried to throw the wax doll away from himself, but it clung tenaciously to his hand. He banged it against the arm of the chair, but it wouldn't dislodge. He ran around the room, and then the house, trying different methods of prying it lose, cutting it off, even trying to melt it, but merely succeeding in burning the sleave of his uniform.

Finally, exhausted from his long night of terrors and exertions, the servant found himself back in the master's study. He threw himself into the chair, closing his eyes for a moment to gather his wits. When he opened them, he saw the room had gone completely dark. The glow from the fireplace was gone, and not a shred of moonlight penetrated the heavy velvet drapes. Bushard felt like he'd fallen into a bottomless well. He struggled to breath, realizing he no longer felt the weight of the wax doll hanging from his hand.

In a flash of insight and stark terror, he raised his hands. The ragged ridges of deep scaring covered his entire face. His fingers tingled as they moved upwards, finding the empty orbs where his eyes should have been. Now he understood why it was his own face he saw carved on the evil wax doll. He was meant to take his master's place in this eternal black pit that was to be his life."

One of the cowboys had nodded off somewhere in his story, but the others were as silent as the gray clouds scudding across the face of the October moon. Until the youngster spoke up.

"That there's a crazy story, Cookie! I figured it out some, when ya said that Bushard fella saw the wax doll. That's where the candle went, right?"

Cookie stared into the young cowpoke's eyes. "Why you clever boy! But one thing you need to know. Every Halloween the candle must be replaced to keep the rich man alive, and in his current state of wellbeing."

"Well, we sure don't need no candles out here!" the young man responded, laughing at his own slim wit.

Thomas's hand slid into his pocket where it poked about until his fingers wrapped around a single, stout candle with the face of the youngster meticulously carved there, He smiled at the innocence of youth and bid them all happy Halloween.

He slipped into the covered wagon and dropped the flap, waiting for the slow acting herb he put into the bean pot to take effect. Their sleep would be relaxed and untroubled, but the morning would see the English cook vanished and the young cowhand, strangely subdued. But then, the wild west country has a way of tempering a man's disposition some.

The Trunk

The Steamer trunk sat among the detritus of cast-off life, for well-over a century. The house where Charlotte and Bernice found it in the attic, appeared to have been swallowed whole by nature, thick vines covering walls and moss clinging like a hood over roof and porches. The girls had been making adventurous forays into the woods and fields around the small town since they were five. At fifteen, they searched out mysteries just as avidly, when Bernice visited her grandparents over summer vacation, and renewed her friendship with Charlotte.

They couldn't puzzle out how they'd never discovered the large, two-story house years ago. From its size alone, it appeared to have been the home of a fairly well-to-do family. Any paint stubbornly clinging to the house faded to a dull blue-gray, or if non-existent, insect infested wood showed through. Every window gaped out into the thick woods surrounding it, pane-less and inviting to any wild creature. From evidence of a battered tin plate and cup, it might have been visited over time by a deserting Confederate soldier, or a runaway slave. This was Charlotte's vivid explanation, after spotting the items on the warped floorboards near a flagstone fireplace.

"After all," she said knowingly, "this *is* the South, and that sort of thing happened here all the time I expect!" Her conclusion went unchallenged as always.

While the two girls searched the first floor, Charlotte spoke about a possible treasure trove of items they might uncover. Bernice's voice dropped to barely above a whisper, as the floors creaked, and felt to her as if they shifted underfoot.

"It's like being on board an abandoned ship in the middle of the ocean!" she tried to laugh, but her friend was too engrossed in turning over scattered items to notice the fear creeping into her comments anyway.

They cautiously maneuvered around the front room, avoiding piles of dried excrement, gone white with age, and rotted furnishings, so broken they had no discernible identity. Twenty minutes of poking about in the kitchen, uncovered the remains of a feral animal close to the black, pot-bellied stove, and heaps of grayish dirt and dust in the doorless cupboards. Charlotte became bored with their findings, and decided they'd search the second floor.

"There might be some lost jewelry, or silver combs and brushes in the bedrooms," in her effort to convince her hesitant friend to use the rotted staircase.

Charlotte led, taking hold of the banister. It felt spongy under her hand. She jerked it off, seeing the greenish patina of fungus, dented where she'd gripped. She shuddered, giggling nervously as she turned back to Bernice.

"Don't worry, it's only a little mossy from the damp."

The stairs moaned like dying cows as they stepped carefully on each tread. When they reached the top, Charlotte moved into the first of two bedrooms, telling Bernice to check what appeared to be a small sitting room. They were both coughing with the dust they stirred and gagging with the smell of a rotting raccoon carcass. The creature had made the unwise choice of entering the house via the fireplace chimney in the master bedroom. It became impaled upon the poker, somehow stuffed into the grate point up, and now its desiccated body hung over the long-dead ashes.

"Let's get out of here, Char. There's nothing here, and it stinks to high heaven! I'll never get that smell out of my nose!" Bernice whined.

"Let's look in the attic first," Charlotte said, adding they needed to be thorough.

They located the pull rope for the attic ladder at the end of the hallway. It was surprisingly sturdy looking.

"Looks like the stairs are pretty good," Charlotte said, bringing the short ladder down. They stepped into the murky confines of the large storage room, with its canted roof, a few minutes later.

Charlotte was always well prepared for these adventurous excursions and pulled her father's flashlight from her jacket pocket. Bernice stepped closer. Charlotte began moving the light in a slow circle, exposing the remnants of lives long gone. Cobwebs streamed down from the pitched, unfinished beams, waving gently in the dead air stirred by the girl's warm breath. Decrepit, cast-off chairs and legless tables were piled into one corner; a small mountain of decay to give witness to lives lived and spent decades ago. They uncovered an old dresser under a canvas tarp.

"This could have once been used as a tent by a visiting rebel soldier," Charlotte said dreamily.

Something reflected back at the girls when Charlotte's light swept across it.

"It's a trunk!" Bernice blurted excitedly."

They moved around the cluttered floor, shoving boxes out of their way, making a path to the rear of the attic. A narrow light from a large hole in the side wall, helped illuminate the features of a massive steamer trunk sitting beneath it. Both girls stared down at the hulking travel case as if they'd discovered Leprechaun's bucket of gold!

"Char! It's huge! It must be crammed with silk dresses and maybe even jewelry, moved up here to hide from the Union boys. Remember what Miss Parsons said in third grade, about the blue coats riffling through all the houses in search of money and valuables?"

Their history teacher, an avid Civil War buff, inflamed the imagination of the girls with her tales of pillage and rapine, all of which occurred solely in her own hyper-active mind.

"Here! Hold this so I can open it," Charlotte ordered, thrusting the flashlight into her friend's hand.

"Shine the light on the front. Darn! Someone's forced the lock," she reported, preparing them for another disappointment.

The paddle lock dangled ineffectually off the top iron loop. Charlotte told Bernice to help lift the heavy top of the trunk. Bernice laid the flashlight on a nearby parlor table, its light directed at the front of the trunk. Kneeling beside her, they each grabbed a side and pulled upward, grunting with the strain.

"It's like someone is holding it down on the other side," Bernice said through gritted teeth as she increased her effort.

"Keep pulling up, we almost have it," Charlotte answered.

The sound of their labored breathing, was accompanied by the loud creaking from the joints of the steamer lid, as it was pried wider and wider. Suddenly, it hit the back wall with a resounding thud that seemed to shake the whole house. The vibration caused the flashlight to roll off the table, onto the floor behind them. The weak light from the hole in the wall was blotted out for a moment as something huge emerged from the steamer trunk.

The girls screamed as they shuffled backwards like crabs, trying to get away from the shadowy figure. They got to their feet, trying desperately to navigate through the maze of clutter, strewn across the attic floor, knocking over things, tripping and falling, sobbing in their fear.

Charlotte made it to the wooden ladder, when she heard her friend call out to her, "Char, wait!"

Charlotte had one foot on the first rung, looking back into the murky shadows. Bernice sounded strange.

"Bernie, get out of there!" Bernice's voice held absolutely no fear when she answered.

"Charlotte, it's...wonderful!"

The next sound in the dead silence was a wet sucking noise, as if someone was using a plunger in a clogged sink. Charlotte moved onto the next step, trusting her instinct to flee from whatever they freed in the old steamer.

"Bernice, please! Come on!" she yelled back into the recesses of the attic.

The sucking sound became more frantic, when it stopped, she heard a loud thud. Charlotte knew the trunk lid was again closed, but this time her friend was inside. Her flight down the ladder and through the gloomy rooms, took her less than two minutes.

She sobbed as she pushed through the Cyprus trees and knots of vegetation cloistering the house, her eyes blurring from the stream of tears. Leaving her friend to a gruesome fate, she was overcome with shame.

When she finally stopped long enough to look back at the rotting house, she knew she'd have to return one day soon with another friend. The Master had an unending appetite.

Little White Lies

"August 10, 1951. Interview with Mr. Charlie Poke, of Knuckle Lake, Arkansas, for the Jasperville News. Peggy Parsons, interviewing. You may begin, your story, sir."

"Ahem. I'm ninety-four now, and my memories are kinda blurred, like looking for fish through frozen pond water. Mostly, they begin as a five-year-old, scruffy boy, left to my bachelor uncle, Jackson, along with my daddy's farm. Mama was just a rough tinplate of a girl, no older than fifteen, sitting over the fireplace, to watch over me while I ate. Always wished I'd known her some. But that wasn't to be. When my daddy was laid next to her in his own patch of earth, I felt like I'd been thrown onto strange shores by mighty waves, I can tell you!

As a kid, I never told any real whoppers. I leaned heavily on little white lies from time to time. I found those crumbs of fibs, much easier for people to swallow, than a whole, messy meal of facts. Being a cute, tow-headed tike, didn't always carry the day for me, and I was partial to covering over little mishaps instigated by me, rather than take a whupping from my Uncle Jack, as I came to call him."

"Mr. Poke, please try to confine your reminiscence to times relating directly to your uncle's murder. That's what the readers are interested in hearing about."

"Well now, Miss, your newspaper boss did say he wanted something he called "colorful background." To my mind, my growin'-up years should count for something in my story."

"Of course, but we're under a deadline. Can you jump ahead to when your uncle married perhaps?"

"That's quite a leap, but I guess I can stretch a bit!" he chuckled good-naturedly.

The old man adjusted his boney rear on the hard chair, took a swallow of black coffee from the chipped mug, and centering it in front of himself on the rough table, he continued.

"Uncle Jack, had a reputation as a loner among the other farmers, scattered for miles on all sides of our small patch of farmland. He never asked for help, and he never gave any. One year, when we got hit with a drought that lasted near ten-months, the crops withered-up like old apples left layin' in the sun. Jack lost a whole field of corn, and near lost all the hardier soybeans. We had only a little money left to make it through the winter months. Our supplies were low, and we were pretty-much down to eating beans and tough biscuits, since Jack didn't want to slaughter any of our few livestock. I was secretly glad, because I looked upon most of them as my pets and suspected Jack was fond of them too, since they'd been around quite a while, uneaten.

Neighbors knew Uncle Jack had bottomed out bad that year, and that he had a young boy to feed besides himself. But Jack was pigheaded and proud, a bad combination, and refused any offers of food from those good folks. Many had traveled miles, through drifts of snow and ice, to get to us with provisions to help us through. I can tell you, those kind people had little enough for their own when they brought that food to my mule-headed uncle!

Well, that Christmas, I'd given up on dreaming of meat and potatoes, and was just fiddlin' with an old harmonica Jack gave me, said it had been my daddy's, when we heard a loud knocking on the front door. Jack tried to open a crack, but the wind took it and flung it wide open. And there stood this angel, except for missing wings! She was a vision I can tell you! Even from this distance in time, with the snow whirling around her like she was a princess inside one of them snow globe knickknacks. We never saw who dropped her off at our place, but there she stood, smiling from ear to ear and bustled herself inside. And that's how Uncle Jack met his wife, Alice Ann.

Alice Ann won his heart on the spot, and the roast and fixings she carried in a crock wrapped in a blanket, won mine! Uncle Jack and her got married in March of the new year, and I thought life couldn't get much better."

"Mr. Poke, were there any signs that his new wife was really a crazed killer?"

"Hmm. Well, she purely loved chopping the heads off them chickens for Sunday suppers. But it all came out of her, you might say, with the pig.   She had a terrible row with him when Uncle Jack refused to kill our only pig. He said he planned on buying a mate for her and raising up some litters like my daddy did years before.

In the end, Alice Ann took it upon herself to round up that lonesome sow, commencing to whack her over the head, and chop her up like cord wood. Uncle Jack wept for days as I recall, hiding his grief in the empty pigsty.

That kinda set Alice Ann off. I called her 'Miss Alice' by the way, on account of her age. She was no more than sixteen when she blew into our lives, and still had that fire in her eyes that young people have, before experience tamps it down some. Guess I was too young myself, to recognize that fire was some kind of crazy demon, eating away at her brains like a leach.

Nothing was said about the slaughtered sow all week, and Uncle Jack kept to himself most of the day until he wandered in after dark. He barely ate the supper Miss Alice put out and went directly to bed.

The calamity befell our lives when Miss Alice served up a boiled shank of that pig the following Sunday. I can almost smell it today; the farmhouse filling with the salty-sweet smell of fresh ham. Uncle Jack went stone-still when she brought the platter to the table and set it down with a small smile.

We only had the one pig, so it wasn't a reach to guess the sow he'd been grieving was being served up. Uncle Jack slammed his fists down on this very table, making the forks and knives jump like they were alive. He shot up to his feet, grabbing Miss Alice by her apron front, and dragging her close to his face. He looked downright possessed by some kind of spirit; maybe the spirit of that dern sow! Uncle Jack's eyes were burning hot, while his face went as red as the blood that stained the barn floor, from the pig's butchering.

I don't know how he missed it, but Miss Alice was holding the carving fork in one hand when he took a fistful of her apron. She swung up her arm and stuck it into his stomach like he was a roast. Guess he was, 'cause she next took up the carving knife and shoved *it* into his chest.

Uncle Jack didn't move, nor did he say one word of protest. Just stood there with a surprised look. The redness and fury on his face drained away, and he was as white as the winter snows. Miss Alice took her hand and gave his chest a little shove. Uncle Jack fell onto his back, and after he stopped twitching, Miss Alice turned to me.

I know I hadn't closed my mouth, and my eyes were fixed wide as a barn door. I can still hear her words exactly, like she said them that afternoon as she took Uncle Jack's chair and sat herself down.

"Let's say our grace, Charlie, before this all gets too cold."

I think I heard a kinda sigh, from down below the table. Guess Uncle Jack was joining in the praying. I made up my mind on the spot, as I helped myself to a big slab of ham. When they ask me what happened to my Uncle Jack, I'd just tell a little white lie and say he dropped dead at Sunday supper. Probably one of my best ones if I do say so."

The Sharing Circle

Her eyes darted away from the group, up to the high windows. They had the same heavy security meshing found throughout the Center for Cognitive Health. It made her feel claustrophobic. Sitting straighter on the cold metal chair, she shifted, trying to find a comfortable position on its unyielding surface. The others squirmed on their own gray seats. They knew from her first time in the Sharing Circle, the old lady had been a Professor of Anthropology at some Ivy League University, snickering behind their hands when she said her extreme fatigue was misdiagnosed as a mental upheaval. Of course, they knew the letter opener sticking in her secretary's back might have had an impact on her case.

"I've been wrongfully committed here by my family," she protested over a few out-right laughs.

In past sessions of the Circle, the woman used her time as opportunities to lecture them as if they were students. This looked like another boring monologue about Neanderthals foreshadowing the brutality of males in society. Her voice was soft, sounding small in the large, mostly empty room.

"Good evening," she said, primly crossing her ankles. "There's nothing about Angels that hasn't already been shared over millennia. Probably since it dawned on mankind it was a good idea to have some help from a higher power.

We've long believed these beings walked among us, taking various forms to play their part in safeguarding us, within their own limits. Unlike much in the human experience, there's no gender bias in selecting who gets this special protection. I, for one, have experienced the influence of Angels on many occasions. My first notable encounter came many years ago, while caring for my two small children. Their father was away on business at the time. I had just learned a few weeks earlier that I was expecting my third little miracle. Little did I suspect the miracle would be my own survival."

The listeners became more attentive. Perhaps this would be more interesting than her discussion on morality and pornography.

"I was alone in our house, with my three and one year old; all of us sleeping soundly. Suddenly, I awoke to a knife plunging deep into my gut! My eyes flew open! After searching the shadowy room, I understood this was no intruder, but my body was surely under attack! Staggering in pain to the adjoining bathroom, I made it as far as the tub before everything blinked out like a bad light bulb. I passed out twice more, and finally, half-crawled back to my bed. My only hope was a friend, married to a doctor. I pressed the numbers on the bedside-phone, not really conscious of what I was doing. How did I remember that number in the state I was in? you might ask.

"Jeff is on his way! Unlock your door for him!" my friend instructed me.

Now, I faced an even scarier situation than getting to the bathroom. My bedroom was across from the children's. That meant I needed to get downstairs to the first floor! By now, every time I tried to stand, I passed out. I crawled out of my room into the hallway and to the head of the stairs. Looking down on them, the twelve steps might just as well have been the rock face of the Grand Tetons! Desperate, I called my three-year old. After several attempts to rouse him, he finally stood, rubbing his eyes, and looking down on me where I lay on the floor. He did what any toddler would do at that point. He was thrown into a panic! Mommies aren't supposed to wake you up in the dark and lay outside your door whimpering! I felt guilty to have woken him to such a stressful situation, but I was overwhelmed with desperation. I had to unlock that door, or my only hope would be snuffed out like a candle.

Propped against the wall, I sent my frightened son back to bed, telling him mommy would be going downstairs. He bobbed his head, and I watched as he climbed under his covers. I had no time to lose now. I felt like a bomb was ticking out the seconds of my life. My friend lived less than a five-minute walk away. I figured with dressing and getting to my house, he'd arrive any minute.

Using the wall to push myself back to my feet, I gripped the banister and began my unsteady descent. The pain now enveloped my entire lower abdomen and seemed to be rising into my upper torso. It felt as if another living being had taken possession of me, growing stronger with every breath. I made it to the third step when I felt a hammer slam into my body, and I began to crumple on the stairs.

When I awoke, Jeff was kneeling over me. When he knew I was conscious he said, "I've already called an ambulance. They'll be here soon. Thank God you got the door unlocked before you passed out. I wouldn't have seen you lying here at the bottom of the staircase."

I knew I'd passed out and fallen down the flight of stairs. There was no way I unlocked the door and its dead bolt. I confirmed my story, when my son told his father he'd gotten back out of bed when he heard his mommy groan and he'd seen 'mommy roll down the stairs and fall asleep at the bottom.'

The mystery of how that door was unlocked took over my every waking moment of my eleven days recovering in the hospital. There was only one feasible explanation, and since I believe in unseen powers, it became obvious to me; I had been saved by an Angel! Not just any Angel mind you, but my Guardian Angel. Assigned to me for the duration of my time on this earth."

The listeners shot sideways glances at one another. This wasn't the answer to her mystery they'd expected. She didn't welcome their doubting looks and wouldn't answer their questions. Instead, holding up a hand, she went on to what she knew was the conclusion of the story.

"My Angel is a nameless, supernatural spirit, who has likely been circling around my life since I swam in the waters of conception. He is with me even now, as I share this life-changing experience with all of you."

The others sitting in the circle sat mutely as she made her final remarks. She interpreted the shocked and unsure looks on their faces, to show the awe they felt at her revelation. They were simply overwhelmed in the presence of one who'd been touched by an Angel in such a definitive way.

The speaker's smile never faltered as she looked from face to face, weighing the impact of her story on each listener, until she reached the dark eyes of the thickly bearded Dr. Carville. Their eyes locked in a long breath and her smile slowly faded. The doctor's words were crisp and final, leaving no options.

"Our session is finished ladies and gentlemen. You are excused to your rooms or the rec. room." Turning to the Anthropologist he added, "Not you my dear."

When the room was empty of the last echo of shoes passing out the door, Dr. Carville gave his patient an exasperated look.

"Why do you insist on sharing our little secret with others? Can't you see how difficult it makes my job when you go blathering on about your past with these befuddled folks? I wasn't supposed to open that door for you, you know, but I just couldn't allow you to die. I've gotten used to our inter-twined life together. In any case, I didn't want to be reassigned."

As the woman stood silently under his disapproving gaze, an Orderly walked past the open door. He looked inside and stopped. After a few seconds he stepped inside, going right up to Dr. Carville.

"If you're having trouble controlling her, let me take her for a few minutes and she'll be a new woman."

The dark eyes of her Guardian Angel, flashed like obsidian orbs. He reached out his right arm and drew her closer to his side.

"That won't be necessary."

The woman jerked loose of his grasp, screaming something about imposter, and flung herself at the orderly. The startled man had a hard time controlling the flailing, screaming woman. Two other orderlies rushed in to help restrain her. Dr. Carville had a bite on the back of his hand. He told them they needed to sedate her and put her in isolation.

Leaving the struggling woman to her screams and the orderlies, he returned to his office. He shut and locked the door. The blind was closed against the prying eye of the sun, as he stripped off his lab coat and dark suit jacket with its false shirt front and proceeded to unfasten the bindings on his wings.

"Phew! what a relief. His forked tongue darted out and pressed against the bite.

"I hate it when they recognize me. It never ends well for them," he muttered.

The red wings with their thick black veins, stretched to their full span, blocking the muted light from the window and casting a shadow of the demon over the floor. Looking down at his shadowy figure made him acutely aware of his state of complete isolation. He sat behind his desk, closing his eyes and letting his thoughts roam like a herd of wild horses.

I had to intervene in that dark predawn, even knowing her days of sin and repentance and more of the same, lay ahead in her long life. She was just human after all. And now, after all this time, we are reunited in pain once more. In this hospital for the criminally insane, I feel nothing but contempt for its inmates. Except for the woman I saved in my last act as a blessed spirit, and before my own spectacular fall from grace.

He stood slowly, weary with his pseudo life and dressed once more as the doctor in charge. His patients would never be free to leave, and just like him their sins weighed them down like heavy stones around the waist of a drowning man.

He walked back to the isolation area, where prisoners were placed until they were deemed safe enough to rejoin the others. He was still thinking about the morning he opened the door and saved the woman's life.

The woman's story proves the human heart is more than a pumping station. It holds a mysterious power to call upon angels. I answered when her life mattered to me, before my holy light was snuffed out for all eternity.

Ah, well. Time to bring her story to its conclusion and see if she'll enjoy my companionship once more. Not as her Guardian Angel, but as the bringer of closure to her story. The last chapter until eternity begins.

A Crime of Fashion

"The body was laid-out like a store mannequin, perfectly posed to simulate a natural nonchalance. Only, there was nothing natural or carefree about this blond beauty. The only thing she wore was a look of surprise, but then, she probably wasn't expecting to have her throat opened up like a can of tuna.

She was stretched out on a cream-colored sofa in a sumptuous fitting room, big enough to hold a party. Her arms, were carefully arranged over the pillows and back of the sofa, to support the lounging effect. Her left leg was draped casually over her right, covering her like a fig leaf. The victim was good looking, if you ignored the glassy blue eyes and the bloody gore covering what was once a well-endowed figure.

In her mid-teens, a seriously dangerous age for women around Trinity Parrish, Louisiana, at the time. She fit the profile of the other ten females that turned up dead in our tourist-driven, Cajun Town. Filled with raucous xylophone music, cheap Po Boy Sandwiches, and the best Gumbo this side of heaven. *The Cage*, as the locals lovingly call it, doubles its population with every college Spring Break and holidays.

The young victims had two things in common, besides being dead; they were discovered at trendy fashion boutiques that dotted the Cage, and their throats had been ripped out.

I was shadowing the lead Detective because that's what I do when she calls me in. I'm a specialist. Only one of a kind actually. The Trinity Police Department lists me as their Paranormal Activities Consultant. The guys on the job just call me, Father PAC Man, or Father PAC for short. The Bishop disapproves of my work, but can't deny, the End Days are at hand when a Vampire roams the Bayous once more. This was a plague we thought eradicated back in the early nineteen hundred, for the love of Mary! The Church has been vigilant for this kind of resurgence. The world is growing darker with every trip around the sun, and that's the perfect environment for evil to move among us.

"This guy likes the rich donuts, but only eats the fillings," the ME quipped to the Detective hovering nearby.

Mary Louise Bloom hovered a lot. I noticed she didn't smile at his sick attempt at a joke. The body hadn't been drained of all her blood. Mary Louise hadn't said a word to any of the Crime Scene techs since arriving at The Bellamy House of High Couture.

Standing next to her, I heard her mumble, "High Couture, my ass! The name is the only fashionable thing about this place! Looks more like designer clothes for Drag Queens and hookers."

Lt. Bloom, was known to carry on conversations with herself around the Station, so I didn't bother to comment. From experience, they all knew to expect long silences while she made mental notes at the fresh scene. That was just Bloom's MO. Squireling away what she saw for future reference during an investigation. Bloom had an uncanny memory. Some said it was better than the camera team at recording things before they got shuffled and moved around. With all her talents, Bloom still called me in after the sixth girl was found. Three months later, here I am again.

"Mary Louise, we agree it's a Vamp that escaped The Great Purge, but I still think it's a female. The naked corpse is to throw us off, using sexual innuendo."

We were entering her office. The Detective clearly didn't want her own theory challenged. She developed it over the past weeks, and her conclusion was set like Bayou mud on a boot. I persisted anyway.

"You think it's an Ancient One, male, who has enormous powers, and has shifted to avoid our hunters. But I believe that a particular kind of Beast would be less fastidious in how he left his victims. A female, on the other hand, would have some compassion left in her, especially if she was turned when she was younger. This Vamp always sets the scene, like an artist posing as a model. According to the mother of our last victim, Lori Flynn, Lori was visiting the Bellamy Boutique to meet an artist for a potential modeling job. According to her, Lori got the lead from a girl she'd met at a party in The Cage. Her mom said Lori was excited about being a model for a real artist."

"So, Father PAC. You think Lori's new BFF is the murdering Vampire operating in Trinity these past months? Even though every case had significant sexual connotations."

"But only in the way the victim is presented, like a painting in blood...Wait! That's it!" I jumped out of my chair.

"We're looking for a turned fashion designer, with a grudge and an appetite!"

We decided to return to the Bellamy, entering the shadowy boutique after six. The evening had grown dark, with the threat of more rain. The store was filled with displays of every outrageous design that could pass for clothing. All they lacked was a mannequin wearing meat like that fabled icon from ages ago. I suggested we separate to cover the large building more thoroughly. I took the first floor; Mary Louise went up to two, using the elevator. Twenty minutes into searching potential hiding places for a Vampire needing to lay low, a tortured scream shattered the dead air, raising the hair on my neck and arms.

Running up the steps of the frozen escalator, I picked up the sound of a garbled voice. *Mary Louise,* I thought, pulling racks of clothes aside as I tried to locate her. I spotted a sign reading *Futuristic Fashions* and ran back to its Fitting Rooms. The first two rooms were empty. The third room, the same one we discovered Lori Flynn's body, was closed behind yellow police tape.

Mary Louise's voice came from behind the closed door. She was yelling, "No more," over and over. I called out to her.

"Don't come in here, PAC! Run! It's a man..."

The door was locked to prevent anyone messing with it and I threw my shoulder into it. I was getting ready to slam into it again, when everything around me went black. The Trinity cops found me stretched out on the floor in front of the door. They'd been alerted by a passerby, hearing horrible screams coming from the Bellamy and seeing our flashlights bobbing around the place.

I was covered in her blood, even my mouth and teeth were coated. Mary Louise was ripped open like a pinata, and like the other women, naked. In her case, her gun was still in her shoulder holster and she didn't have a casual look. Her face was a mask of sheer terror. They cuffed me, and as we passed through the shadowy store, I swear, I saw one of the sexy mannequins blow a kiss goodbye to me. "

My new cell mate chuckled to himself saying, "Nice story old man. Using extinct Vampires to murder the cop lady!"

But I did figure out Mary Louise's last words. They weren't "It's a man..." I wonder as I look over at the smirking cellmate, if that *mannequin* is still showing off her fashionable deaths.

I should be getting out of this prison for the criminally insane as soon as they realize I'm sane or when the murders start happening again...whichever comes first.

I didn't mention to my cell mate that Mary Louise was dug up after her burial and when they discovered her open casket, they saw someone had plunged a stake into her heart and left her severed head resting on her chest. Guess the Bishop believed me anyway!

The New Year's Eve Monster Club

"This is not the way I wanted to spend my New Year's celebration, Monty! It's quite hideous of you to drag me down here on the pretext of our enjoying your Club's secret New Year's rituals. You made it all sound so alluring, and glamorous and it's anything BUT!"

Gladys had been going on in this manner for a good twenty minutes now. She sat huddled in her furs on a solitary stone bench in the dank crypt. The only light was shed by four torches set into corner wall sconces, but all they truly produced, were deeper shadows around the square stone interior. A large stone sarcophagus stood menacingly in the middle of the room; its lid laid across two sides. Gladys, peering in earlier, and in a moment of unaccustomed imagination, announced the inky interior looked much like what the gaping maw to Hades might appear. Now, sitting across from it, she shrank deeper into her silver fox wrap, glaring at the rough stone coffin, as if it was the symbol of every discomfort she ever had to endure.

Coming here to the cemetery, was to be the high-point of her revelries that night. And making it all perfect, she would enjoy the intimate company of one of London's most pursued bachelors, the wealthy and rakishly handsome Montesquieu Rathburn.

Monty's reputation as a debauched scoundrel, appealed to the bored and self-indulged Gladys Mortenson. Her father, deceased since her fifteenth birthday, left her too young, and too rich, to control her appetites and actions. Long ago, it was determined her mother was simple minded. Coincidently, this occurred after Mortenson Esquire had been exposed in yet another of his many illicit affairs. She was promptly committed to a lovely sanitorium, twenty miles from the Mortenson estate. This left her four-year-old daughter, Gladys, for the indifferent parenting attentions of her father. He encouraged her sexual promiscuity and spent-thrift ways by simply ignoring her completely.

The young woman looking peeved and uncomfortable, was enticed into coming to this odd and remote place in the country by the charming Monty. There were hints of a sexual orgy that his secretive men's club indulged in every New Year's Eve, along with some kind of sacrifice to a Dark God.

"It's exciting beyond description," he had rhapsodized to the wide-eyed beauty, Gladys. And so... he didn't. He knew the beautiful heiress would be bored with details in any case, thus his conscience would have been clear... if he had one.

Gladys had detected an odd aroma upon entering the crypt, and mentioning it to the ever-attentive Monty, was assured it was incense used to purify the stale air.

"We haven't held our ceremony here since last New Year's Eve my dear, so naturally, we needed to refresh the place. And more so because you are to be joining us," he added as smoothly as the silk pulled tightly over the rise and fall of her ample bosom.

At half past the hour of eleven, the heavy wood and iron door to the mausoleum creaked open. Gladys' heartbeat faster as the soft moonlight revealed the face of one handsome man after another stepping through the doorway. When the last entered the crypt, there was the sharp thud as the bolt was thrown into place. She thought it odd to have a bolt on the inside of the mausoleum, but like most of her more astute observations, this too was fleeting and lost to her easily distracted nature.

Monty sidetracked any further questioning that her brain might have endured, by taking her hand and bringing her from her seat, into the center of the quickly forming circle of devilishly handsome young men.

"These men are all here to satisfy deeply hidden cravings, and you my dear, shall be their feast!"

Monty's hand looked pale to her as he reached over and unclasped the fur at her throat, letting it slide down her body, onto the dark slate floor of the chamber. Gladys shivered, exposed as she was to the chilled air. Her long silk gown would offer little warmth in such a cold place. The five men all moved in almost choreographed step, closer, tightening the ring around the blond beauty. Without realizing it, she began to turn in her own tight circle, looking into the faces of each man closely. Each was more handsome than the one beside him; each had a look of hunger in his eyes, as if she would be their first and last.

Gladys enjoyed the heat of desire directed at her alone. She smiled her most alluring smile at each man in turn. When she faced him again, Monty reached out to brush the long, silky tresses from her shoulder and throat, wrapping his arm around her slim waist. She threw her head back and closed her eyes leaning against him in anticipation.

His mouth was wet, his kisses leaving moist trails on her luminous skin as he worked his way around her slender neck. At one point, a low moan escaped Gladys' partially open mouth, and her eyes flew open when something sharp scraped along the exposed top of her quickly rising and falling breasts. Monty had been replaced ever so subtly by one of the others, and it was he who smiled back at her surprised look.

"Nothing is sweeter than rotten fruit, I always say!" the handsome stranger murmured.

This was the trigger for the others to join in the feasting. Monty helped them lift the now screaming Gladys up and into the spacious stone cradle where she would be rocked to the core, and reborn as one of theirs.

"Happy New Year, all," she heard Monty call out as he stretched out his arm and the heavy cover to the stone casket flew up, slamming down and plunging them both into an eternal darkness.

Love's Trap

Thom Love was an unusually clever twenty-eight-year-old. Even as a young boy on the fast and furious streets of Brooklyn in 1911, he was considered a sharp kid. He had a reputation for always besting the local gang of bullies. After years playing the avenging angel for his baby brother, Albert, he had plenty of time to perfect his tactics.

The fates were unkind to little Albert. He came into this seething cauldron of poverty and ignorance, generally known as The Devil's Parlor, blanched as white as a rich man's sheets. Seeing the tears leaking from Albert's pink eyes always moved Thom to greater schemes, protecting him from the brutes that targeted him endlessly for his waxy, unhuman appearance.

Albert enjoyed little in his pale life. Bunty Park, a patch of scraggly trees fighting for light under the shadows of the tenements, was his favorite place. Women, hanging laundry on endless rope lines, set like fluttering islands between the buildings, saw everything. They often spotted Thom, his hand wrapped protectively around Albert's, making the painfully slow journey over four city-blocks, to this green Mecca. Watching the sturdy ten-year old and his spindly, freakishly- white little brother, brought some of these life-hardened wives to tears. To others, it made them raise a thumb and forefinger in their ignorance, to ward off the devil.

Thom found ingenious ways to foil attempts to harm or tease his albino sibling. He became astute at reading the signs of planned ambush along their walk to the park. Some of the gang members shadowing them would grow bored with their pursuit or frustrated with Thom's ingenuity in avoiding their traps. With little else to occupy immature, cretin minds, the others persisted in their efforts to fool young Thom, in hopes of tormenting the ghostly looking brother.

Thom prevailed in these bouts between brains and brawn. After years of protecting the milky-white Albert from harm, he became something of a folk hero, using his unique talents to protect other social misfits up and down the streetcar line that was the demarcation of his neighborhood turf. His calling in life seemed life seemed predestined. Thom became a copper.

Called 'Lovey' on the street since he wore short pants, as a man wearing a police uniform, his incredible sleuthing talents soon transcended his nickname. He rose quickly in the ranks to become a highly decorated Detective, earning a new name on the streets; 'The Ghost.' His area of expertise was organized crime. To Thom, that still meant gangs.

He'd already scared, maimed and terrified several of the notorious criminals roaming the gritty New York streets like war-lords. Many were well-known to him as thugs from his childhood days. The Ghost didn't leave a clue when he stealthily took revenge on any guilty of tormenting Albert and casting long shadows over his short, tortured life.

After five years on the force, Thom managed to ferret out every man from the old neighborhood, who had been part of Albert's years of misery as their freakish target. The ring-leader of those local urchins, passed from street bully, into politics. A seamless transition in Thom's mind. Thom watched as this man now wielded his thuggish powers over his neighbors, from behind the Police Commissioner's desk.

Thom was obsessed with bringing his revenge to the man who orchestrated the slow killing of Albert's spirits, eventually making him so desperate, he took his own life in the fast-moving waters under the Brooklyn Bridge. The Ghost would complete his revenge by luring the Commissioner into his own trap; an ambush he'd never survive.

A letter found its way onto the Commissioner's desk, listing the political cover-ups and crimes he was engaged in for his own profit. The letter was clearly an attempt at blackmailing the man, demanding ten-thousand-dollars in small bills and directing him to arrive at two o'clock the next morning, at the entrance to the Brooklyn Bridge.

Thom, dressed completely in black, concealed himself just below the street-level approach to the bridge. The Commissioner's sleek, black Packard, slid out of a haze of streetlights and onto the darkened entrance to the bridge, rolling to a stop. The engine was switched off. He wasn't alone, just as Thom had predicted. The burly figure that exited the driver's side, was quick to melt into the shadows. All went according to Thom's guess about the Commissioner's own plans.

The portly figure of the Commissioner exited the back seat. His steps echoed in the heavy silence. He walked slowly to the side of the bridge where the money was to be left on the high railing. One hand carried the paper sack with the money, the other, kept close to his side, held a small revolver. The Commissioner was prepared to kill his blackmailer; an easy prediction for Thom to make.

Thom waited until he saw the bag placed on the ledge. Knowing the bodyguard was watching him to make a move toward it, he put the next phase of his trap into play. Holding two flashlights as far apart as possible, he pierced the gloom where the thug hid. He surprised both the bodyguard and his boss, who reacted by lumbering toward the safety of his car.

Foreseeing the whole scenario, Thom had arrived earlier that night, disabling the few lights leading onto the bridge, and causing the area to fill like a well, with deep shadows. He switched off his flashlights, throwing them onto the bridge in opposite directions. The sounds hung ominously in the night air. Thom was moving like a cat, up the side of the ramp, toward the large vehicle. The Commissioner opened the driver's door, sliding his large girth behind the wheel. He started the engine, ready to abandon his thug to his own fate. As he drove forward, the tires of the heavy Packard were ripped to shreds on a long plank of nine-inch nails, laid by Thom, anticipating the coward would make a run for it.

The Commissioner threw open the car door, scrambling to get out, and screaming for the lurking bodyguard to help him. Thom heard the big man panting as he ran like a dog to his master. Thom grabbed the huge bucket he had strategically placed across from where the nail trap was laid. He came up behind the Commissioner as his thug threw the spike strip aside and began looking at the ripped tires.

Thom poured the thick, white paint, weather proved to be used on the bridgework, over the sputtering Commissioner's head, leaning close to his quickly clogging ear.

"Remember the albino? You made his life a living hell until he ended it here. Care to join him?'

Without another sound, the Ghost shoved the blinded, starkly white figure toward the edge of the bridge and ordered him to walk forward. The thug stopped his futile efforts to salvage the tires, when he saw the ghostly apparition approaching, moans and gurgling words coming from it. The shots from his gun filled the night. The apparition tumbled backward over the lower railing and into the waters below.

Love's trap was sprung. The Ghost faded back into the night smiling at the sound of a heavy splash.

The Boarder

Three of the four men currently rooming at the Darby Boarding House, were of the same opinion regarding their landlady. It was a cold November night, foreshadowing heavy snows to come. Their patronage of the Boar's Tusks had become a ritual after dinner at the boarding house each evening, helping to relieve the tension of the day's work and the loneliness suffered by young men in their circumstances. After a few pints loosened their tongues and fogged-over good sense, they boisterously began sharing their thoughts around the table.

"Georgianna Darby is as warm as a cow turd! " Henry blurted out, enjoying the reactions on the faces of the others. A tenacious line of beer foam, rimmed the droopy mustache he'd been cultivating of late, over his mouth. It nicely highlighted the sneer on his florid face.

"Well, maybe a recently dropped turd!" he added to the guffaws of his listeners.

Henry used the back of his hairy knuckles to mop at his whiskers until the laughing died down around their table, and the tables nearby of accidental listeners. He went on describing the named woman in even courser terms.

"I have yet to see a glimmer of a smile on that pasty-white face. Always scowling like an old witch over her brew," he added with a flourish of his hand, tipping some of his brew, onto the lapel of his shabby suit. Ignoring one more stain, he went on with more rapid-fire snide remarks.

"She's as tight with her good humors, as the braids she wears like a black crown on her head."

His unguarded comments opened the way for the others to speak their minds, befuddled as they were becoming with the arrival of a third pint for each of them.

"I've taken note of how she only joins us at our dinner, never breakfast. Even then, she barely speaks," put in Tomas, the youngest man staying at the Darby House.

"It's mostly just 'yes' or 'no', to civil attempts at conversation."

Tomas was a newly minted accountant and always spoke with the precision of that profession.

"And she never eats, only sips at her wine. I swear, her bones already poke through those black dresses she wears, without a glimmer of color on her person!"

"How long has she *been* in mourning, anyway?" Ralph asked, looking around the table. As an insurance agent, Ralph was always concerned with health matters.

The three turned a bleary eye to Carter, the only one who hadn't offered insights regarding the cold, dour, and emaciated Mrs. Darby. In fact, he rarely spoke more than a few words on any topic. However, Carter's surreptitious glances at the landlady during her stony visits at supper, spoke volumes to the other boarders. They all noted how he pulled out her chair like an attentive suitor. They observed how the lady of the house, leaned in, directing whispered remarks for his ears exclusively. For some opaque reason, Carter was interested in this eccentric, scarecrow of a widow. Oddly, Georgianna Darby became almost attractive in those moments, with Carter looking up from his meal to stare momentarily into her dark eyes.

"Come on Carter, being a Copper, you probably know something of Mrs. Darby's background," Henry said, giving the taciturn Peace Officer a hard elbow on his arm.

"I've only been at the Boarding house for three weeks. I can't say I know any more than you lot," Carter answered in his usual soft-spoken manner.

"But you have to agree," barked Ralph, "she has some peculiar ways about her. And then, there's those noises we've all heard late at night. It's like the old bird is having a party somewhere in the house!" he said looking around at three nodding heads.

Tomas joined in saying, "The noise seems to be coming from the cellar. Though upon questioning the cook, she'd only say the lady of the house was putting away wines, and food stuff in their bins down there."

Mention of the cook, brought other oddities about the household to light and comment. All the men, with the exception of Carter, had strong opinions on this hugely over-weight woman, though all agreed they ate well. Only the finest cuts of meat graced their table each evening, and the cook was never stingy in their portions. At the conclusion of graphic descriptions of the bloody-red roast they enjoyed just that evening, Carter stood up, swaying ever so slightly on his feet.

His current assignment, impersonating a lowly Patrol Officer on the streets of the Fourth Precinct, New York City, placed him in the boarding house nearly a month ago. In reality, Carter was a highly successful Investigative Officer for a burgeoning constabulary. He' d been assigned to look into five Missing Persons Reports filed on boarders who resided at the Darby House just prior to disappearing off the face of the earth. So far, Carter discovered each of the disappeared men had been given the same room he now occupied, and that all, like him, were unattached. In fact, it was their employers who filed reports when they failed to show for work after several days. And of course, there was the blurry past of Mrs. Darby.

After careful questioning, Carter learned from the current boarders, all five of the missing fellows had become strangely smitten, with the wraith-like figure, and sickly pale looks of their landlady. To his chagrin, Carter found he too, felt she exerted some sort of influence over him. He felt more and more drawn to the darkly crowned woman, even experiencing some strangely vivid dreams, with her lying intimately close to him in his bed, speaking in a hypnotic, soothing voice. He always woke when the dreams became overly intense, and he'd been suffering extreme fatigue and lost focus over the past few days.

Returning to the boarding house took several halting minutes while he struggled to regain his sobriety. *I only need a good night's rest;* he thought as he opened the door and entered the dimly lit foyer. The gloom was heavy with the scent of wood polish and the cloying smell of Mrs. Darby's fragrance. He noticed it the second he walked into the boarding house weeks ago. It permeated the air, the drapes, the carpeting and every stick of upholstered furnisher. For some reason, it was extremely strong when he laid on his bed.

Smelling it so strongly now, he shivered, knowing the woman of the house might be nearby. He only wanted peace and rest and didn't want to hold any conversations with the landlady at this late hour.

"Mr. Carter," came her silky voice out of the inky recesses of the foyer.

"I see the pub has gotten the best of you," she gurgled like a gently flowing brook.

"Let me help you to your room, these stairs are very steep, and I couldn't live... (she cleared her throat) ... if you suffered an accident."

"What d'ya mean, 'suffered', Carter slurred.

"If you suffered a mishap, of course. Now, shall we get you to your bed?"

She'd already managed to slip her bony arm through his, using his elbow like a rudder to guide him up the long, polished wood staircase, to the second floor. His bed looked so inviting to him, he put up no fuss when Mrs. Darby laid her hand on his chest, and gently pushed him down onto the fluffy comforter. He began to doze off immediately as she busied herself, humming softly while divesting Carter of all his clothing until he lay as innocently naked as a babe. There was a stirring, more like a rumble coming from the narrow bedroom closet when its door was thrown wide. He watched through half-opened eyes as the cook pushed her great weight through.

She peered long and hard at his lean body. Carter struggled to move, but his body was frozen, and felt as if he was in a block of ice.

He heard her the cook's gruff voice, "This one will drain quickly, Mistress, but we won't get much meat off of him I fear."

"No worries, my dear. Just be certain to fill the wine bottles well, and don't spill any. You know how I detest waste. The others will be back soon. Let's put that uncouth one with the droopy mustache in this room next. We'll tell him it is the best room in the house, as it surely is…for me!"

Her laugh sounded like scratches on a chalkboard. "We can tell them Mr. Carter was called away suddenly due to a death in the family. Burn his belongings in the furnace and don't forget the shoes this time! It was difficult for me to convince the police they belonged to my late husband.

Carter began to succumb to a deadening feeling in his limbs, feeling his heart slow in its beating. As he felt himself fall into a dark hole, he heard the rotund cook remark irritably, "I hate when you refer to me as your 'late husband' my love."

This inspired the expert Investigator to mentally force his eyes wider. His last view in life would not be of the stary night or setting sun, but of the cook removing the gray wig covering his bald head before he began to collect Carter's belongings.

A Garden to Die For: A Eulogy for Spring

"It's absolutely breathtaking, Meg!" gushed one of the Mornay twins. Meg couldn't tell them apart, so she merely smiled, bowing her head demurely. Meg Randall was hosting the 'Mississippi Bountiful Gardens Society' at her country estate. This was their first gathering since reforming, a process that occurred on a yearly basis as members always seemed to drop off after the first meeting. The current group had high hopes of avoiding that outcome.

Meg noticed a few of the young matrons wrinkling their noses earlier, as they passed through the musty hallway on the way to the dining room, and the entry to her gardens through a set of grit-covered French doors. They clearly expected little from this visit to meet their high horticultural standards. In the current mood of the privileged class in 1921, those standards had evolved to include the proper accouterments of wealth and style. Meg's shabby estate, landed well-short of that bar.

When Meg threw open the doors leading out to the patio, there was a unanimous intake of breath, as the eight women stepped through. The gardens spread out before them, shimmering like a piece of art by one of the Old Masters. Vibrant, and alive with color, this was truly an Eden of exotic plants and flowers, swaying like the graceful Salome, wrapped in soft breezes. The carefully blended design of trees and shrubbery, lent an artful backdrop, keeping the mystical blooms from dancing out of sight. Some of the ladies spontaneously lifted their long skirts to take the inviting flagstone path, leading deeper into a glorious banquet of fragrance. One woman was moved to exclaim, "It's as if we're surrounded by rainbows!"

Their newly installed President, the starchy Mrs. Grumwalt, curbed their enthusiasm, reminding them that tea was ready to be served. They reluctantly moved back to the wide skirt of the flagstone patio where a maid finished the preparations. One of the Mornay twins whispered behind her hand that the corpulent President, would never miss an opportunity to sit down to a meal. Meg's sharp hearing caught the remark, and she indeed saw the plump woman licking her lips in anticipation. No one noticed her own tongue dart out in a similar fashion.

Meg seemed indifferent to her role as hostess. She sat stiffly in her chair, relying on the rather elderly maid to pour tea, and offer the freshly baked scones and delicate cakes around to the women. She spoke to no one. No one spoke to her. She made herself inconspicuous by her stillness.

Her guests unanimously held the opinion that Meg Randall had a strangeness about her. Where did she come from? How long had she occupied Randall Hall? They just reformed their group, when Mrs. Grumwalt received a musty smelling book titled, *The History of the Mississippi Bountiful Gardens Society*, supposedly sent by a past Secretary. It stated Meg Randall had hosted every annual meeting since its formation. The Society was founded many years ago, according to the dates, yet Meg Randall looked timeless. They argued among themselves, over the veracity of the claim, and none of the previous members were around to be questioned. However, as recorded, routine visits never changed. The Society seemed compelled to come to Randall Hall yearly, like the lemmings to the sea cliffs.

Outside of a few pleasantries extolling the delightful scene before them, they took little notice of her stoic figure, and no notice at all of how she ignored the sweets they all hummed over like bees gathering nectar. None seemed aware that she studied each of them in turn, from under her long, dark lashes, while appearing to fuss with her uneaten strawberry petit four.

Privately among these women, Randall Hall was referred to snidely as The Randall Mausoleum. The sprawling mansion was more cathedral than home. With its tall, lifeless windows, and guarding gargoyles at each corner of the tiled roof, heavy stonework covered with tenacious vines, Randall Hall was as warm as the inside of catacombs and nearly as sprawling as those discovered under Roman streets.

The women had arranged themselves around a perfectly laid table. It gleamed invitingly, as the mellow spring sun swept over its glazed glass top. The cups of the delicate porcelain tea set, were almost too fragile to hold. Its floral pattern was an exquisite reflection of the many varieties of flowers and plants surrounding them. There were constant outbursts from the younger Mornay twins, as particularly lovely plantings were spotted further down the path leading into the heart of the garden. As they nibbled cakes and sipped at their cups, every color of the prism tantalized and bedazzled them. In one corner, bright yellow tulips, shot through with royal purple, or deep red slashes, like the sleeves of medieval ladies at the English Court, captivated their hungry eyes.

A restless enthusiasm settled over the group. Some were too agitated to have more than two scones with tea. Meg never lost the thin smile that carved her full crimson lips, as she watched her chattering guests from under sweeping black lashes of half-open eyes. She was quite blatantly ignored, as her guests dove into the creamy yellow butter, slathering it on their warm scones.

The women all appeared to be in their late twenties or early thirties. To Meg's mind, the perfect age of reason and life. They fell upon the treats with the appetites of the young, and quickly began to relax under her penetrating hooded gaze. Their hostess held her fragile cup carefully, raising it to her deeply red lips. Meg shunned rouges and powders; her pale skin was flawless. She appeared to be as delicate as her tea service.

Undeniably beautiful, the young women still found her clothes as dated as her furnishings. But she did have a presence, an unsettling vibration coming off of her, not dissimilar to the chill most felt staring up at the snarling gargoyles, as if they'd fly down on them at any moment from their perches at the corners of the rambling manor house.

Meg rose to her feet like Venus rising from the sea, smoothing the front of her dark skirt to its perfect folds around her slim figure. Taking this as their cue, the women quickly gathered themselves behind her as she wordlessly stepped off the patio, onto the inviting path.

"Time to visit my precious children, ladies. Follow me please and do keep to the path. My garden is fragile, and somewhat unpredictable if it feels…threatened."

A few eyebrows shot up at this odd comment, but not a word was uttered as the small entourage trailed the ethereal figure of Meg Randall. None of the young matrons took note when the broad yellow and black heads of towering sunflowers turned to watch them as they passed. Just as they never noticed the glistening beads of red that sweated from their thick stems.

The spicy tea had a wonderfully calming effect on them, certainly making gathering them like a living bouquet so much easier. Meg knew the old maid followed close behind. *The young are so self-absorbed* she thought, stopping only after following the stone path deeper into the gardens.

Enclosing the exotic plants here, was an impenetrable wall of strange bulbous shrubs, giant ferns, and moss-hung trees linked tightly together with the tentacles of gnarly vines. Beds of blood-red roses carpeted the ground beneath the green wall. Meg's soft voice floated back to the women as she invited them to breath-in the intoxicating fragrance as it wafted around the heavy humid air of the gardens. None demurred, bending deeply at the waist, each inhaled the smell of decay and death, yet none gasped in revulsion.

The maid stepped in behind them as silent as a shadow. She moved from one to the next, efficiently dispatching the women while they hung like a row of broken marionettes over the soft petals using the freshly sharpened ax in swift arcs. Watching each head fall, she watched as it trailed gore under the broad leaves of the Caladiums that formed the natural wall of trees. The wide, pale red leaves were veined in a deeper red and shook with anticipation when the heads rolled among them.

"My garden will be well fed this season, mother."

"And so shall we be my dear," the old maid answered. "Now, open the trap door beneath the poppy garden, daughter. This lot will remain fresh as a bouquet of roses in the cold ground while we drain them at our leisure over the next months. By the time our larder empties, the Mississippi Bountiful Gardens Society would have reformed under our friend's leadership and the cycle shall begin again."

The old woman was chortling softly to herself while she watched Mrs. Grumwalt walking toward the bloody grounds. With the mesmerizing effect of the garden's exotic bounty, and the carefully tainted tea, the club women never noticed their president's absence among them, while they drifted over the flagstone path like lambs to the slaughter.

"Shall we store our harvest ladies?' the dowdy Grumwalt asked the others.

With the strength of three ancient Vampires, the bodies were quickly stored among the bones of dozens of others of past Society members. The careful art of creating beautiful gardens had proved a dangerous hobby for them.

Passing a blood-red eye over the vibrant flowers surrounding her, Meg sighed with contentment, knowing her gardens would never wilt or sicken and like she and her mother and aunt, they would thrive. She began down the path toward the patio leaving the other women to restore the grounds around the carnage while she collected the tea service and disposed of any trace of tea. Just thinking of the feasting to come made her long incisors drop down, distorting her lovely face. Along the way to the open French doors, she leaned down, snapped the stem of a purple daisy-like flower and tucked it behind an ear. The brushing of her long skirts over the stones filled the cloying air and the flowers all swayed.

Love Me for What I Am:
A Fairytale Without End

A sadness settled around her like a heavy woolen shawl. She covered herself in the weight of her sorrow, hoping to crush any feelings that might stir as she looked down on the body. The motionless, broken man was once her love. The only person in her universe she called *My Heart*. Oh, yes.! He once brought life to her; her pulse raced with his every touch, his caressing looks, his murmured endearments. She was like a constant flame, burning with the sun's intensity. As if the fat of her body had become the tallow holding the heat as he stoked her inner fires. But, in the end, all was consumed in this sacred conflagration.

Her love, her mind, his life; all lost to the Mirror of Truth, and the curse upon her kind. Confirming the truth about her new love, became irresistible to her. She was driven to find validation of this pledged union of hearts.

The Mirror of Truth hung within the Witch's stone cottage, huddled at the edge of the woods tightly surrounding the village. The old hag had covered the mirror's ancient, veined face in a silky black cloth years before. Now, this hung in tatters and spiders wove their own threads among the torn.

She was warned by the Witch's foretelling glass, that this man was full of deceit, and fed his base appetites with the flesh of other women. The Mirror shimmered and rippled through the shreds of black, like something stirring within a fog. It spoke of how this beautiful man made his fortune seducing women of great wealth, choosing only those women who were spurned by other men because of their singular unattractive or repulsive looks.

Her body was so ball-shaped with her prodigious weight, that she'd lost sight of her tiny feet and these appeared incapable of carrying her to her next meal. Heavy breasts beneath the lose fit of her expensive gowns, hung pendulous, swinging like counterweights when she walked, which she seldom found the need to do. Her face was round and bloated with flesh; a mouth and nose though present, were more discernible upon the face of the moon. Her button eyes, under thick folds of eyelids, were as pretty as a snowman's bits of coal, black and dull. There were at least two chins visible above her short, creased neck; each quivering like a rooster's wattle. To find her arms inviting in an embrace, would be like submitting to a bear's hug.

She eagerly bent her head of pale-yellow hair, to the man she so adored. She was like a fat bumble bee gathering the sweet nectar of his compliments. At his insistence, they wed in secret.

On the night he became Lord of the castle, and its vast estates, she came to his bed unbidden. She dressed in gauzy linen, the color of fresh churned butter to match her hair, hanging down her back. Her flesh, unencumbered by stiff corset or muslin, or any other restraint, shifted like wave upon wave upon the face of an undulating sea as she lumbered toward the bed.

Her eyes, newly alight with an aroused passion, she flung herself upon him while he lay dozing face down in a haze of wine and greedy dreams. The sound of his back cracking, was not unlike the ice being pushed aside by the prow of a ship. She lay upon his inert body, feeling the warmth slowly leaving him, just as the Mirror of Truth had foreshadowed.

"My love!" she cried over his chilling flesh.

"The Mirror warned of your betrayals and showed your end as surely as I see it before me now. You have proven the foreshadowing by breaking like a twig under foot."

The mountain of flesh lifted off the still form, lying akimbo amid the silken sheets. She would see the Mirror of Truth many times she was certain, before a true heart was revealed.

Sighing deeply, she knew the curse was still intact, as it was a hundred years or more. She Returned to the Witch's cottage, squat and ugly under a finger of moonlight.

Once You're Dead: A Political Fantasy

"I don't know how much more I can take of these endless questions! I've already told everything to the Cerebral Monitors, the Modified News Collectors, and gods help me...the chosen relatives of the poor thing they pulped.

It isn't my fault she decided to go rogue on me. It's well known the altered human species doesn't lose its stubborn inquisitive nature even after your alterations of genes and whatnot! She had to form her own opinions about things; things she had no right to question. I only acted as her host Nutritionist, for the love of Janus!   She fed off me until she could mature enough to be detached as scheduled.

I was created as a comforting feeding station with a rational mind, and that isn't easy you know, but how would you...you're just like her! My only pleasure in life, not that you'd care, is that I get to talk, while you have to listen. Can't talk with your mouth full, right?

Speaking of mouths, she had one on her, that one! Almost as soon as they removed her succors from my body, she started spouting crazy things about "freedom of speech" and "freedom of beliefs"...really radical stuff right out of the history holograms! Naturally, they accused me of watching that crap and influencing her mental pictures. She did talk about some seriously warped stuff though. Dangerous as anything shouted by those freaky females, the "O Plus Freedom Fighters", or even the Planet Crusaders, for that matter, whenever the Company catches that lot. She actually yelled that the whole gestation process was a way for the Species Oligarchy to control the humans they were breeding.

What a pile of yellow offal! I was born in the flesh labs too. My sole purpose is to feed you Class-One brats! I was made to be your personal nurse maid, your sentient smorgasbord. My only pleasure while you feed is having these conversations. Bet it frustrates you Class beauties, to have to listen while your host gabs as freely as those flying birds creatures from before Cataclysm Day.

Oh, did I tell you...hey, not so hard with that sucker on my back...anyway, did I tell you, that crazy Class One tried to detach her nursing-mate from his host? She botched that job I can tell you! He shriveled up like an empty brown bladder. Guess she didn't know only the Monitors can detach a Class-One.

They keep asking me how I missed signs of her discontent with the program. She was a nice symbiont as they go, actually. Never too rough on me and always left a little for later, so I didn't have that empty, lights out feeling. Speaking of that, you should slow down or you'll be sucking air...

Anyway, the Monitors keep asking me why I never noticed she was not growing the reality blinders like she should have been. She had a clear view of everything without them, that altered her mental patterns and thoughts they said. Hey, I'm not in charge! I only work here and follow directives from somebody higher up the food chain. In fact, when you're done slurping away on me, I guess the Monitors are sending me to the Heap. And you and I both know, once you're dead, there's no re-do.

Speaking of blinders, yours are slipping a tad...don't want a repeat of my last symbiont. I'll just keep feeding you and you keep those on. Not much going on anyhow!"

Time Enough to Die

His lawyer, Gracie McFarland, stepped away from the bench with a graceful pivot. Her client heaved a deep sigh, knowing she had been successful in getting a key piece of evidence thrown out. The state's attorney, a woman with impeccable grooming and style, and as much personality as a store manikin, returned to the Prosecution's table, averting her eyes from his.

The trial had lingered on for over a month. The jury was beginning to show the wear and tear, squirming and shifting in the tightly packed rows confining them. He studied each one from behind his dark wrap-around glasses. The Prosecutor loudly objected to these at the beginning of the trial; saying they would be used to intimidate the jury. She quickly relented when he removed them, showing her a mutilated eye socket where his left eye should have been. That was a much more disturbing sight she figured, than a pair of sunglasses. Also, she didn't want him to get sympathy. She wanted him to get the needle.

"Getting you off from a murder charge, won't be the slam dunk you're used to Carter!" Gracie McFarland was in her scolding mode.

"Your money won't impress the jury one bit. Getting the Court to throw out the necktie only raised more speculation among the jurors about your relationship to Pati. And I'm not satisfied with your answer regarding that either, I might add."

Carter Koble was one of the country's magnate-playboys. He inherited a small fortune, growing it into mega billions through his Interstellar Investment Corporation. IIC employed thousands throughout the colonized Galaxy. They had huge holdings in mining and resource reclamation, on a dozen or so planets, and held rights to explore on a dozen more. Carter liked to brag that he ruled the universe, but that was before Pati.

He was in his Terra Verde offices when her antiquated spacecraft seemed to fly out of the old holograms, landing at the archeological site once known as Canaveral, a launch station for space crafts like hers. The world went wild with excitement as the story unfolded.

"Female astronaut steps out of history, lands at space port after centuries in cryogenic state!" screamed the digital papers.

The news feeds were blazing hot with descriptions of her and her condition. The fact that Interstellar owned the old space station, meant the visitor had become part of Carter's space interests. He jetted down the coast the next day to meet his newest acquisition.

Pati was lying in a sea-green hospital room in IIC's Medical Arts and Enhancements building, on what was one of the old Keys in Florida. After the oceans rose, the Keys were inundated, eventually replaced with what amounted to floating cities. The huge complex of pontoon-like structures was old technology by the time of Pati's arrival, but like everything else around her, this was a new world.

When he walked into the Passive Environment suite she occupied, Carter was struck by the unique opportunity he had to speak with a space traveler from the distant past. She would be very impressed no doubt, in fact, *awed*, by the progress in space flight. Her back was to him when he stepped into the hushed environment of the softly lit room. The figure on the special, non-intrusive restraint bed, was slight, almost child-like.

He was greeted by a six-person team of doctors and nurses, sitting in a long row of consoles, monitoring the patient's every breath and change in pulse rate. The lead doctor shot to his feet when he saw the visitor was none other than "Mr. Universe" as he was jokingly called by his staff.

"Sir! Welcome, sir. We had no idea you would be here so soon. Allow me to brief you on the astronaut's medical condition."

Carter listened intently to the information thus gleaned by the team of specialists in Space Medicine. Summed up, Pati (her name was carefully stamped on the coveralls she had been wearing), had been stabilized, and she would be ready to be interrogated any minute. She was rotated in a smooth movement until she was on her back.

When her eyes fluttered open, Carter was fully expecting her to be disoriented and very frightened in the strange surroundings. Instead, he saw her slowly turn her lovely head of golden hair, taking in the room and its occupants without a flicker of fear. Her face was beautiful and stopped his breath when her deep green eyes finally came to rest on him. She sat up, stretching like a pampered kitten. Her body was remarkably full and sensual after being in hibernation for at least four Terra centuries.

It was only a matter of days before Pati had Carter Koble acting like an attentive suitor. He never left her side, granting every wish and whim she voiced need of, as if she was his Mistress. And then…she was!

He moved her from the medical complex to a condo on the seventy-fifth floor of his magnificent Koble Needle, a slender structure of steel and glass. He was a daily visitor to her glassy aerie, leaving the media to rave about the "romance from the stars!" Except, it was nothing like that.

After her first three months with Carter, Pati began to show signs of restlessness and displayed a rising level of discontent with their relationship.

"I am not your plaything, Carter! Keep your hands away from me if you want to keep them attached!"

One morning, after a particularly violent attack on him when he asked for a morning kiss, Pati came at him armed with the curved knife she's been using on her favorite Alaskan grapefruit. He had bent down to offer his lips to her and instead had his eye scooped out like so much pulp. He fell backward just as she was reaching for his silk necktie to take the other eye, ripping it off his neck in the process. She lurched backward losing her balance, falling onto a heavy chrome and steel kitchen chair on rollers. The momentum of her actions catapulted her toward the vast wall of glass, and its fantastic view seventy-five stories below. This view was much improved as she smashed like a wrecking ball through the glass, and without the benefit of a spaceship, landed once again on Terra Firma.

Carter, sans one eyeball, was taken into custody and charged with murdering his famous mistress, after an obviously vicious fight for her life. The courtroom was packed with media, and those who followed such events with prurient enthusiasm. It seemed likely Carter Koble would be found guilty after so much damning evidence of his obsession with the late space traveler came to light. But that was before someone among the courtroom visitors sprang to his feet shouting.

"He's innocent! I have proof that that woman was not what we thought she was."

The judge allowed this introduction of new evidence, since it was Koble's well-coiffed head that was at stake. The new witness was given the Oath of Truth and identified himself as Dr. Gunder Gritzwald. He stood in the raised witness box addressing the court.

"I have been researching the Archives of Interstellar Transport as requested by the Space Commission's high command. According to Pati's recorded interviews with the Commission's investigators, the ancient spacecraft she arrived in was named The Starburst. I discovered it was on its way to New Australia, a penal colony for extremely dangerous criminals, when it was taken over by some of the prisoners.

The deceased was the ringleader. Her name stamp read 'PATI, but I discovered that was an acronym. It stood for "Political Assassin Team 1". She was on her way to the gallows, along with her co-conspirators, two, three and four," he concluded counting off the numbers on his fingers.

Following his release, Carter Koble's life seemed frozen in time. His great love, his remarkable piece of history, was no more than so much space dust in the light of the truth. But then, so much of this universe is found in the dustbins of history.

He'd been told by the man who exposed Pati's sordid past, that if they didn't face extermination, the prisoners were sent to mine rare minerals of immeasurable value. The thought of immeasurable wealth seemed to break through his melancholy, and he decided to commit his vast fortune to finding the planet New Australia and claim its resources for himself.

His days blurred into years. He sent his personal space fleet out again and again at staggering cost, to search for the penal colony. His eye on the stars, he constantly repeated to himself, "One day the colony will be found, and Pati will have paid her debt to me."

Twenty years past with little notice by Koble. The ancient spacecraft, Starburst, sat in his personal space port, released to him after paying a king's ransom. His crews often saw the figure of the decrepit old man, hunched over in his air-chair as it floated around the blackened hulk while they worked. The technicians knew the star ship would soon be launched and Carter Koble would be inside. He ordered it totally refitted to make the journey into the endless night of the universe, where the stars awaited him. This would be the last attempt to locate New Australia and it would have a crew of one. A fitting end for him he mused watching the work near completion. His health and fortune were at an end, only is burning obsession remained.

His launch took place in the dead of night, the ship being small enough to remain insignificant as a star traveler he had no interference from the Interstellar Commission. Besides, he was considered a mad recluse who'd lost his sanity over a psychopathic killer who should have died centuries ago.

He sat in the specially built chair at the pilot's console and touched the microphone on his helmet. His voice sounded even weaker as it crackled over the radio to his ground control.

"Before I leave earth, know I won't be lonely on this trip. I had my lovely star girl Pati cloned from the DNA salvaged from her broken body. And here she is now. Say goodbye darling."

"Goodbye old man! Time for you to take a long, long nap."

The ground crew stood with looks of horror on their faces when the ignition and lift off of the space craft burned across their screens.

Never Grow Up

"I believe my baby boy is most adorable, Wizard, don't you find him so?"

The queen was cooing at the object of her intense affections, making the Court Magician twitchy to be free of her incessant burbling. *If I wanted to listen to a babbling brook, I'd go fishing*...he thought with a snort, covering it quickly with a smile.

"Your Majesty has truly produced a fair heir for the King and kingdom. Why, his chubby legs can barely hold up such a...sturdy body!"

The Queen looked pleased at his observations, though others of the Court saw it for what it was...a veiled insult to the stout, five-foot-one man-child sitting at his mother's dainty feet.

Prince Fenwick was born late in the normal span of child-bearing years. But then, Queen Scarla, was herself, anything but ordinary and predictable. She only conceived the Prince, after consulting the most renowned soothsayers, herbalists, two other Mages from distant kingdoms, until at last, settling on an old crone called the Red Raven. Even when her name was uttered in hushed whispers, the people of the kingdom shuddered.

The Red Raven was reputedly the oldest living witch in any of the five kingdoms, and surely the most feared for her powers. She could read a future by holding a twig from the yew tree over her petitioner's head, spitting three times on their outstretched hands. Though thoroughly disgusting to most supplicants, they still flooded her dingy cottage, requesting their future be told, and carrying clean towels.

Simply known as "Red" to the current Mage in the Queen's favor, he remembered days past when they were at least on nodding terms. Since the birth of Prince Fenwick, she had been elevated to the position of Sorcerer to the Queen, making the Mage a mere parrot to praise her skills. Their relationship soured like milk left on the barn floor.

The kingdom faced another challenge now. With Fenwick still crawling around his mother's throne like an overstuffed cockroach, whispered doubts circulated among the Courtiers. Speculation of how the runt could possibly succeed his aging father. The Queen had more or less assumed most of the running of the kingdom from her increasingly infirm husband, but this arrangement was no more appealing to most than Fenwick's ascension to the throne.

One day the Mage was mulling over the state of affairs, considering his own options to abandon all to the Red Raven, when the Sorceress herself materialized in front of his nose.

"Wizard," she croaked like a long un-greased wheel. "I've been observing your reaction to the Queen's son, Prince Fenwick. Mayhap we need to speak privately. Be at my cottage at the dark hour. Fail me not Mage." With that threat hanging in the air like a bad odor, the Red Raven vanished.

After he heard the guard announce the midnight hour, the Mage slipped through the side gate of the castle gardens where he'd been hiding. Stepping quickly into a thick gloom, with only a sliver of moon to help his aging eyes, his sandals did little to protect his toes as they were stubbed on lose rocks and pricked by thorny bushes.

"The old hag planted these damn things," he fumed into the unyielding darkness.

"Ah, I see you are prompt, old one. And a good thing too." She opened wide the door to her rough cottage. The Red Raven had put up a pot to boil and was pouring some sort of brew into two clay mugs, while the Mage tried to settle his old bones into a rickety willow bark chair.

"No need to fuss on my account, Red, I need no fortifying I can assure you."

"Spoken like a simpleton man. It's cold and damp, and you're an ancient old coot. Drink this!" Shoving the mug at him, the Mage was delighted at the aroma tickling the hairs in his nose. Sipping it cautiously, he couldn't contain a sigh of delight.

"I have decided to lift the spell I put on the Queen's son, Prince Fenwick."

"Spell! What kind of spell?" the Mage spluttered, after taking a big gulp from his cup.

"Becalm yourself, Wizard. The Queen had me place a Life Charm on her son, Fenwick, so her darling boy would never grow up in the flow of time. She desires to keep him as her babe forever. She cannot bear other children with the decrepit King, her husband, and her heart is only happy when there's a child scampering about."

"Scampering! Morgana's tits, woman! Prince Fenwick is now a young man of one and twenty! He needs to marry…and carry on the royal line! The Queen is unbalanced, clearly. Your spell is as unnatural as a kingdom without Magic! It must be broken immediately!"

They talked and planned into the early morning hours, refilling, and sipping at the delightful herbal brew. Hearing the first cock strut about proclaiming his own arrogance, the Mage hastened back to the castle to help carry out the plan they hit upon.

That morning, after they broke their fast, the Queen had Prince Fenwick hoisted up from his crawling adventure around the throne room and seated in his specially built min-fortress. Surrounded by sturdy fencing, and sitting on thick furs and bedding, he played contentedly with his own crown. He'd already tasted it and found it unpleasant. His guards looked on, rolling their eyes. Besides the guards, none other were in attendance. The Queen treasured her alone time with her baby Fenwick.

The Red Raven appeared in the chamber and strode purposely up to the Prince's containment crib. She held her hands over the child-man, and before the Queen could question her action, the Prince fell to his back.

"Wah!" screamed the Queen.

The Mage leapt out of the shadows behind the throne, casting his own spell. When the young Prince Fenwick regained his feet, he looked directly at the Red Raven.

"Witch, you have finally released me from the encumbrance of eternal childhood. For this I shall reward you."

Turning to his mother, he saw she was now contentedly confined to the pen he had exited. She lay curled up like a sleeping infant, a peaceful look relaxing her lined face.

Fenwick took his place on the vacant throne that very day, and ruled in a firm, mature, if chubby handed way, for many years. The Mage and the Red Raven often spoke of the wisdom he showed. A man in full, he married and sired many children of his own, assuring that all left the castle upon the age of self-sufficiency, so they would experience an independent adult life.

The Queen, after Fenwick had her released from her own infancy spell, played out her days in the company of scampering grandchildren, content to sleep in the sunshine until her calling from this plane.

An important lesson stayed with the Mage as his own mind began to shutter in advanced age. Never prolong youth beyond its natural cycle, but rather, enjoy the rewards, as well as the challenges, of maturity and age. After all, simplicity of mind and behavior can be the curse that can alter the heart of a man or woman, with tendencies too youthful for old bodies to sustain.

After witnessing the stunted growth of Fenwick before his release into manhood, the Wizard was content with his lot, and allowed the seasons to play out the natural course of all life well-lived.

The Fairy Doctor

"Tis but a wee bit 'o rattle in me chest, thet's stealin' me sleep away! Me dear young wife es haggard wit' it she claims, an' needs ta sleep apart. So, I been keepin' company wit ta sheep in ta barn, most nights."

Collin McFadden was sitting atop a ruggedly fashioned fence that encircled his prized herd of lovely Galway Sheep. He owned a clean baker's dozen by the time he married his second wife, who encouraged Collin to turn his eye to more prosperous farming of wheat and feed corn. The sheep served little purpose now, except for the mutton dinner he supplied to the village priest during the Yule Season.

Collin was remarking to his best mate, Peter Crenshaw, how his sole ram was faring these days, explaining the dwindling number of kids dropped by his ewes.

"Sad, but true 'tis! Ol' Boy ain't been gettin' any more ta' comforts of a female, den I 'ave these past days, an' ta weather be settin' in wit a hard chill now wit ta autumn nights."

His pal shook a full head of fiery red hair, the tight curls springing around his face like angry red snakes.

"Tsk, tsk...ye poor ol' sot! 'En yer Mary sech a dear soul she were. I ken recall 'er bakin' dose luvly cakes, en sittin at er loom, weavin' them fine woolies fer ya. She weren't no prettier than yer ol' ram, but sech a fine mate she were ta ye."

Now, all this rambling on about his first, now deceased wife, Mary, was rather off-putting to the newlywed, Collin McFadden. True as it was, that his Mary was as homely as the tufted ram browsing in the sparse grasses of the paddock, it was still hurtful to be reminded. He studied the shaggy beast more closely, snuffling loudly when he remembered his Mary even had a sprinkling of wiry hairs on her chin. Oh, she could cook, bake, sew, keep their cottage as clean as the Priest's vestments, but she was plain, stout, and as unattractive as she was industrious around the farm. They were only married a handful of years when a sickness roared through the village like a tsunami and Mary was swept along with it. Collin was not so bereft of her marital company in their bed, but he sorely missed the cooking, cleaning, baking and other domestic miracles she could work.

And then, he met Tessa! Slim limbs and fair skin, her hair a golden honey hue, her eyes blue as the summer skies. She stole his heart at first glance and he offered her the comforts of his sturdy cottage, and the steady, if modest income he made from his holding. He credited the new light in her eyes, to having such a fine proposal come her way, and her, only a poor potato farmers youngest daughter. Her father had already married off three such beautiful girls and was delighted Collin McFadden had made himself available so quickly after becoming a widower.

Tessa was everything his Mary wasn't...a bad cook, a poor seamstress, a horrid baker, and never took notice of the dirt and cobwebs gathering in dark corners. In short, she was lazy. But smitten to the quick with her scintillating beauty, Collin kept any complaints to himself, and went about the cottage in a constant state of lust. And this became something of an annoyance to the young Tessa.

When Collin came to their marital bed of an evening, he laid his head on the pillow his Mary had stuffed so lovingly with goose down, snuggled under the warm wool blankets she had woven, and taking in a deep, satisfied breath, he fell to coughing until his face turned an unhealthy shade of red. This rampaging wheeze, brought tears to his eyes, shutters to his body, and a wide-eyed look of disapproval to Tessa's lovely face.

"Well, ye can't stay 'ere, ken ye? I'll not be gettin' me sleep wit all that hawkin' en chokin' like a rabbit in a snare! Ye need ta take yerself ta the bern. It'll do ye, wit a blanket to throw down on ta hay."

This same routine went on for several nights, and then for nearly a fortnight. Collin, exhausted from lack of sleep, stressed by his enforced separation from his beautiful wife, took it in his head to fix his problem before he died of exposure and loneliness. He'd been aware of the neighboring hamlet's claim to a Faerie Doctor, a man with close ties to a Faerie clan living in wild woodlands in the valley. He took his old dray, hitched the plow horse to it, and set off to consult with the one who knew a bit of something never mentioned aloud...Magic.

"En, I tell ye sir, ta bouts o' coughin' en chokin' da breath from me body, comes only when me head is laid upon me pillow of a night. Me sweet wife can't bare ta hear me hacking me guts out, en banned me ta sleep in me bern wit da sheep."

The doctor was listening very carefully to this lament and felt an unnatural state had befallen poor Collin. He suggested he go home, and after he was sure his Tessa thought him asleep in the barn, as she would be in the cottage, he needed to creep back into their bedroom.

"It seems ta me ye are sufferin' from some unnatural trickery, me lad. Follow me advice dis very night!"

That evening, Collin kissed his wife on the forehead since she forbade her lips, as he might carry some sickness. He took himself off to the barn and settled in upon his rough hay bedding and watched for the candle to be blown out near Tessa's head. He moved as silently as a shadow, creeping back into the cottage. Just as he was beginning to move toward the tiny bedroom in the back, he heard unlikely sounds. Moaning and groaning and deep sighs tickled his ears, until he nearly fainted with dread. Going forward on ghostly feet, he peered into the moonlit room and looking down on the bed, spied his best mate, Peter Crenshaw, tussling about with his lovely wife.

He listened to them as they laughed low into those down-filled pillows, whispering how poor Collin never suspected his beautiful Tessa put a charmed black pepper into his pillow each night, to bring on his racking cough and choking.

"Ta Faerie Doctor is a wit, 'e is!" Peter snickered at the joke played night after night to clear her husband from Tessa's bed.

Collin crept back out to the barn, picked out his favorite pitchfork and returned to the enraptured couple. They were too distracted to hear him, until he fell upon them with such a vengeance, even he was shocked at the result.

With the first light of day, Collin took his prize herd of sheep to the neighboring farm and traded the lot of them for two brutish pigs; one sow and one boar. You may be wondering why he would divest himself of his prized sheep for these two, less noble creatures, but then, you must remember, pigs will eat anything.

The Christmas Kiss

The darkness closed around her like a fist. She felt her heart racing, pumping as hard as her legs, as she ran blindly through the woods. Her old leather boots caught on exposed tree roots and low, creeping vines, causing her to trip several times. She wiped her bleeding hands down the front of her torn skirts as she ran, not stopping to examine them for damage. *Is he still following me*, she wondered, tearing through some clustered saplings? Surely, he's given up by now.

Just then, over the sound of her heavy breathing, she picked up the noise of someone, or something, thrashing their way through the underbrush and low limbs of the naked trees. She dared not pause to listen more closely, but increased her pace, pushing against the implacable wall of darkness.

She nearly pitched head-first when the shadowy winter forest opened suddenly into the small glade she'd run through earlier. The moon spilled its light like cream from a jug, over short grasses and wild Rose of Shannon bushes that ringed the area. These shouldn't be blooming she knew, but this was an enchanted place after all. Even the heavy snow was absent from the rich earth of the woodland.

Her first instinct was to fall face first onto the cushy grass bed and close her eyes to the terrors she knew followed. Instead, she took a cleansing breath of the green smelling air in the bucolic setting, and sprinted across to the other side, closer to the forest edge. She took a backward look into the enchanted clearing, spying on her pursuer.

Approaching the center of the glen under the keen eye of the fat moon, was a young man. He was dressed in a richly made garment with the soft sheen of velvet in the moonlight. When he called out to her, she scrambled under the sweeping arms of the nearest evergreen.

"Imogene! Cease this reckless dash through this cursed wood. I mean you no harm, my girl. On the contrary, I only wish to offer you a special gift this Yuletide. Won't you show yourself; I know you are listening?"

She heard the stranger's words as he called out to her from the glade and crept forward a little way to take a better look. He definitely was richly attired; his manner and stance spoke of a wealthy upbringing. The moon hung directly over the spot where he stood, as if drawn the tall figure. He was looking directly in her direction. His face, being lit from above was mostly in shadow, but Imogene could clearly see he was tall, slim of waist and broad of chest. His hair was a lustrous black, its waves brushing his shoulders. He looked nothing Ike the monster she had just encountered. Her misery this day began with the first cock's-crow.

Just shy of the dawning hour that very morning, an impish looking man, entered Imogene's bread stall, while she set her loaves out for the day's selling. He said he was sent to find the fairest young woman from among the peasants, during the village's market day.

"My Master has requested I bring him this girl, so he may bestow great wealth upon her, in exchange for one simple kiss under this sprig of mistletoe."

The little man pulled the red berried bunch, with its waxy leaves, from somewhere under his cape, leaving Imogene to wonder if indeed, he was an elf of the woodlands surrounding her village. She was immediately filled with suspicion that he planned on taking her to some Troll. When he drew near, she recoiled, lest he touch her.

"I will nay go with ye, a stranger! En then, yet again, ta another stranger still! Ye mistake me fer a fool! Now, bugger off!" she'd told him defiantly in most direct manner.

The little man again reached back under his cape, this time bringing out a leather bag, tied with red cord and bulging. This he upended upon her table, next to her warm breads. Gold coins spilled their rich glow over the brown loaves, as they sparkled in the small light from Imogene's stubby candles.

"Are ye sayin' these are fer me?" she asked drawing a bit closer, her eyes fixed like flies on dung upon the coins. The little man smiled, showing a mouthful of pointed teeth, before locking his lips firmly in a kind smile.

"Tis all yours, Imogene the minute my Master is granted his Yuletide kiss."

He temptingly gathered up the coins and hefted them in his small hand as he exited the booth. She quickly fell in behind like an obedient lamb, leaving her breads unattended, and to the honesty of others.

They arrived at a cottage that looked as if a hermit might live there for all its simplicity and roughness.

"Why, tis not ta house o' a grand man," Imogene whined.

Just then, the door swung inward, and the little man gave Imogene a great shove inside. She was caught up in the strong arms of a hideous creature. He was greenish of complexion and lumpy in build, with a prominent hump. His eyes were the shade of horse dung. Before she could protest being restrained, the imp was springing up to the low rafters and hanging the sprig of mistletoe. The creature leaned in, and with his wet, rubbery mouth, planted a kiss on her lips. Imogene struggled free of his embrace and dashed from the cottage into the woods.

And here she lay, shivering as she hid for her life. The bag of gold was not worth the feeling of that kiss. It was as if she'd been kisses by the wide mouth of a lake trout! Or worse, a giant leech from the village healer's bag.

Imogene knew she was lovely, in fact, many of the handsome young men of the village sought to court her. Why would she allow a hideous creature to have her favors when she had her choice of lovers? Her mind had been wandering over the scene inside the cottage and she almost missed the soft rustle of the twigs and leaves near her hiding place. A soft voice made her heart studder with dread.

"Imogene, you have earned this bag of gold, and I am honor bound to give it to you. You have given me a great gift this Yuletide season, and I would repay such generosity of spirit. I hope this is a gift you desired as much as I did mine."

With that, Imogene heard the heavy bag of coins clink as it hit the hard ground in front of her hiding place. She watched as the glossy leather boots of the man, turned and left her, walking through the woods and disappearing among the shadows.

Scooting out from under the fan of fern branches, Imogene was nearly beside herself with joy at this turn of events. Not only was she safe, but she was also rich! Taking the bag and securing it to her girdle, she returned to the village square and her bread. Entering, she saw her neighbor's little boy pawing over her chilled loaves. Glancing up as she entered, he took one look at her, and ran screaming. This happened again when the mother came in to investigate her son's terror at Imogene's hands.

Finally, after a dozen villagers she'd known since birth, came and vanished as quickly as snow on a griddle, she left for her cottage. Running into the tiny alcove that made her bedroom, she snatched up the only possession left by her dead mother. The glass was veined and yellowed with age but showed clearly the face of the monster that had kissed her under the mistletoe.

After an hour of crying and sobbing and nearly fainting with disgust as she studied her new visage, Imogene opened the bag of coins. On top of the gold pieces was a small square of rolled parchment. Imogene lit the candle on her table and though she had no talent for letters, the picture drawn there was easy to decipher. It quivered upon the parchment as if a wind blew upon it. It was the handsome man and her sitting together under a gnarled oak.

Thinking he would cure her of this curse, Imogene ran like a deer through the woods until she stood in front of his battered wooden door. There was a light tap on her shoulder and she spun around to see the impish manservant.

"The Master has been expecting you Imogene. He has promised to restore your beauty to you, but there is one condition. You can never leave this cottage; else the curse be set anew."

Imogene was now confronted with a quandary, her beauty or her freedom. After a minute of deep consideration, she reached for the door. The imp smiled with his pointy teeth broadly showing. "Beauty does have its own price," he chuckled.

Creating Chaos

She suspected giving birth would be no easy matter. There was, after all, the matter of extreme pain, something she was loath to inflict upon herself. Then, of course, the matter of stretching one's perfect body to accommodate the ever-growing offspring, was quite off-putting. Squeezing an eight-pound, twitching, jumping, kicking human inside a svelte figure, called for a monumental lapse in one's reasoning powers. No, Queen Portia's method of conception, was far more civilized, eliminating the muss and fuss and most decidedly, the downside of stretch marks on one's smooth midriff and hips.

But conceive she must! The king was becoming agitated by her lack of providing him with his heir. And the Court was ever vigilant that she does not take a younger man "to seed her garden" as her spy delicately reported.

Though her royal husband was much older, and never quite up to the task in the royal bedchamber, his age didn't appear a relevant factor. Considering the number of royal bastards scattered around the kingdom like dandelion fluff, all eyes were on her own procreation abilities. Portia knew she had to act or be packed off to a dreary estate in the hinterlands, or worse, leaving her royal accouterments behind.

Climbing the narrow, chilled stairway to the top of the Black Tower, Portia entered the roomy workshop occupying the entire floor, and overlooking the castle and its surrounding grounds far below. This was the domain of Blazec, the King's Wizard.

She was greeted by a large black and orange cat who curiously followed her as she moved into the rooms, carefully stepping around iron pots bubbling with inky oils, heating over black, sooty flames. She crouched down, avoiding the possibility of her gauzy headdress touching the drying carcasses of wingless birds and bizarre, unearthly creatures. She smoothly negotiated a maze of racks, bowed under the weight of preserved body parts and bottles of potions, and all leading to the magic user's room of secrets.

This was where the Wizard would be creating his most magnificent work for his queen, a baby son, to place in the arms of her dull husband after the appropriate nine months. Until then, she would surreptitiously use pillows of varying sizes to promote her scheme of gestation. Not even her Ladies would be privy to her faked pregnancy.

Not wanting to disturb his work, Portia quietly watched him for a moment. Suddenly he spun around, her soft breathing alerting him to a presence.

"Your Highness," he said making a deep, graceful bow.

"I am here to ask after your progress in the delicate task I've set for you, Blazec. How goes it?"

"Ready for you immediately! It needs a single adjustment."

He stepped very close to Portia's upturned face. This close to him, Portia saw how very handsome the Wizard was. Broad of shoulder, thick, black hair, peppered lightly with silver strands. But it was his heated gaze that bore through her like a hot poker. Portia became alarmed at her response to this virile man, hovering so close to her, his musky maleness drifted warm and alluring around her. She could taste it on her tongue as her mouth opened slightly with small breaths.

"Your Highness must allow me a small interlude in my work. Follow me my Lady, to my inner sanctum, and I shall complete the task as quickly as your lovely eyes would blink."

That moment was the last thing Portia recalled, when she came to herself, sitting in the gardens behind the Black Tower. A tingly feeling of satisfaction and total exhaustion saturated her body. She felt as if she was glowing from the inside-out. She wrapped her heavy shawl around herself, taking the hidden passageway connecting to her rooms. She often used this to avoid the many courtiers milling about the main rooms.

Entering her chambers, she handed the shawl to her Head Lady, who immediately dropped the garment with a look of disbelief on her face. Portia looked around herself to see all of her Ladies were staring at her.

"What's amiss with all of you? Why do you look upon me so strangely, as if I've sprouted a second head!"

"But your Highness, you, you ..." her Head Lady sputtered like a tea kettle, until Portia grabbed her arms and shook her violently in her frustration, demanding an answer.

Another girl quickly stepped forward, saying, "Your Majesty has the look of a woman five months gone in pregnancy!"

Portia's face froze, her lovely mouth open in a silent scream, her bright blue eyes, smeared below, with dark circles of sleepless nights. Her hands slowly rose to touch the rounded bump, where her flat stomach should have been. Her breasts were tender and uncomfortably enlarged. She paled like a fading moon at dawn.

"Your Majesty, you shall give the King his heir at last!" her Head Lady said enthusiastically, finding her voice again.

"Your worries are over at last. We shall all pray that you have a son, and that he looks exactly like his father."

"No!" Portia screamed out, or was that imagined too?

In the Black Tower the handsome wizard busied himself putting away vials of muddy water and snuffing out the flame under pots of foul-smelling herbal teas. He smiled to himself as he worked, stopping long enough to look at his moon and stars chart and speaking to his only companion, the attentive black and orange cat perched on the worktable.

"The lovely queen should begin her confinement in three months, delivering a fine son soon thereafter. Speeding up the gestation period for the offspring was a stroke of genius on my part if I do say so myself."

Looking directly into the golden eyes of the cat, the wizard whispered, "My spell worked to perfection."

The animal looked as disinterested as any feline unless it concerned food.

"I realize it is time to repeat the charm in reverse to free you from your current state, but there's been a change in plans, or should I say…feelings. Forgive me your Highness, but your hissing is not warranted. I've provided you with the long-desired offspring, haven't I?

Over my time of service to your highness, I have been restricted to these shabby rooms laboring in secret, and never given the accolades I so justly deserved. Recalling the recent war with the Journeyers, I turned the tide of battle for your kingdom before they stormed the walls. I did it all from my Black Tower and received not even a nod of approval from you!

It is time to claim my reward for nearly a century of forced confinement in the Black Tower in service to you! I shall leave you here to eat the mice and rats that inhabit this foul place, while I see the result of the rest of my spell. The queen is under my enchantment and will easily accept me as her husband. I shall have her and my son and sit upon your throne!"

The walls echoed with the pounding of his boots upon the stone steps as the wizard hurried down the circular stairway to his freedom and glory. As soon as he reached bottom, he flung open the heavy door, stepping into the hot rays of a noonday sun. Raising an arm to block the unaccustomed blinding light, he choked on his next breath and crumpled to the ground.

"No!' No!" he screamed as his blurry eyes stared at his skeletal arm, the skin yellowed and sagging just as it did from the rest of his once virile body.

Wailing, and cursing his fate in loud screams, he didn't see the black and orange cat as it softly padded up to him. It began to rub itself on his boney shoulder, purring contentedly until the wizard rose unsteadily to his gnarled feet and passed through the dark entryway of the Black Tower. The cat followed closely behind the once more handsome man as he slowly took the first step upward. Flicking its tail, the heavy wooden door creaked loudly as it slammed shut. Looking back, the wizard knew the king had learned a few tricks of his own.

Poison Spring

They arrived at their homestead in the dark of the night, the wheels of the creaky buckboard scrabbling madly over the rocks and hard clumps of dirt. It was still a young spring and bitterly cold, as he prepared to stop. Maddie sat rigidly, as if awaiting the hangman's noose to envelope her slender neck. The pale moonlight painted her face a chalky white. If one peered closely, they'd see the slight tremble of her lips. She stared straight ahead at the looming shape of the small house where it pierced the darkness.

The reins were pulled to the left and Benjamin guided the horse to a stop near the front door. Maddie turned her head slightly, watching her new husband throw off his part of the heavy travel rug, and jump down lightly onto the frozen ground. She could see her warm breath curdling like thick milk in the dark air, shuddering at the thought of a true winter here. Benjamin's heavy boots scrapped loudly over the rough ground. He quickly secured the sturdy draft horse to a short railing in front of the house, patting the beast on a muscled flank as he past.

He was a large man, well over six feet. A shaggy head of thick, black hair made him appear even taller. He had shaved the beard he sported in the small tintype she'd seen. Watching as he walked around the tethered horse to her side of the buggy, Maddie realized she'd barely looked at this man when they met at the train station in town. He had seemed to have materialized like a phantom, his huge frame stepping out of the billowing steam, pouring off the idling cars and engine.

She waited silently as he came around to her side, and pulling back the rug, took her hand to help her down. His own hand was smooth and strong, the long fingers wrapping tightly around her own. She allowed herself to be swept from the hard seat, engulfed in a strong arm around her slim waist. For a moment, she was carried like a feather, floating to the ground.

Benjamin had barely spoken since collecting her from the railway station. It wouldn't have been difficult for him to recognize her, since she was the sole female occupant of the narrow platform. After installing her in the open buggy, she heard only the occasional clicking sounds as he encouraged his nag to hurry over the uneven country roads to her new home,

and her new life as his mail-order bride.

Now, with his arm clutching her slender body to his muscled bulk, his voice sounded rich and warm.

"Welcome to our home, my dear. Go inside and warm yourself by the fire, while I see to the horse in the barn."

Maddie felt a twinge of fear when he walked back to the buggy and began unfastening the rigging. She turned, and relying on the cold light of the moon, she walked up the short path to the front door. She stepped inside, closing the heavy door behind herself. Without warning, a roaring fire sprang to life in a hearth occupying the far wall of a spacious room. Maddie blinked, but the cold that seeped into her body during the long ride in the open buggy, drove her toward its welcoming warmth, blotting out the oddness of its sudden appearance. Standing with her hands held out like a supplicant to the heat, Maddie slowly became aware of another presence.

"I hope the chill has left you, Maddie," her husband said, his voice deep and caressing in its tone.

"I feel quite warm now, but...how..."

"Never ask questions of me, wife. All will be clear shortly. For now, rest at the table and let us have a bite."

Maddie turned her head slightly, wondering how she hadn't noticed a roughly made kitchen table, set with steaming plates of what appeared to be a stew and warm breads.

"Who...?"

"Maddie, remember what I just told you. I shall demand little of you, but you are never to question me!"

Benjamin's anger flashed from pale, gray eyes. He took her heavy coat and felt covered bonnet off of her, as if she were a young child. These he laid on top of a long wooden chest set against the far wall, before leading her to a chair at the table.

"You need to eat before it cools my dear. I shall look to the bedroom so you can retire after. I know you must feel exhausted from your travels."

Maddie watched Benjamin's back as he walked toward the rear of the small house. The aroma wafting up from the steaming food, made her mouth water with anticipation. She hadn't eaten since the morning, and it was now, far past midnight. As she spooned the thick, meaty meal, her mind wandered back to the circumstances that brought her to this place, while her eyes took in her surroundings.

She answered an advertisement she found in her town's local paper.

"Wanted. A bride to share my wealth and bounty and who will find everlasting happiness as my wife."

Her life had been nothing but drudgery and hardship up to that point. Working long, stifling hours in a cotton mill, she saw her future as clearly as if she'd read it on the paper she clutched to her chest. She knew this was her only way out of that fate and leapt at the chance. Her picture didn't do her beauty justice but did show her fine features and full figure as she stood near her deceased husband, Jack. Dying unexpectedly of a brain fever before his twenty-first birthday, he left her widowed less than two months after they ran off together. At twenty-two, Maddie considered herself little better than a spinster, but saw a glimmer of hope in becoming a mail order bride.

Not wanting to deceive the bachelor who might consider her for a wife, she fully explained the circumstances of her widowhood and desire to establish a new life. Her words must have moved Benjamin, who quickly proposed marriage, hiring a man to stand as his proxy in a hurried wedding.

Her spoon clanked against the bottom of the empty bowl, bringing Maddie back to the present. The fire still swayed in tall, red and orange flames, though Maddie couldn't remember her new husband coming back to tend it. She stared into the deep hearth, feeling the warmth radiate out and wrap around her whole body like a heavy quilt.

She snapped out of her dreamy state at the sound of something heavy scraping the wood floorboards. Benjamin was dragging yet another long, black box, similar to the one her things laid upon, into the bedroom he was preparing. She vaguely wondered why he wouldn't be joining her in their marriage bed. Why do they need the long box in there? *Perhaps,* she thought, *it's a wedding gift, filled with fine dresses and shoes!*

She leaned back and let the warmth caress her face. Without warning she was floating like a paper boat on a stream. Benjamin lifted her in one smooth movement into his arms, and through to the bedroom.

"It is time to consummate our marriage, dear Maddie," he spoke close to her ear. His breath felt cold against her neck and she shivered in his embrace. He laid her upon a narrow bed, barely able to accommodate her body. Maddie found both her arms slipping off the sides, dangling freely.

"This isn't...big enough...bed," she mumbled through the haze that had taken root in her brain since eating the stew.

"Do not distress yourself wife," Benjamin said smiling down at her from a great distance it seemed.

"Very soon, we'll have no need for it. You shall lie peacefully next to me upon a cushion of red satin, just as they all do, in time."

Maddie's eyelids felt heavy. They were drifting shut as Benjamin's mouth came down hard on the pulsing life in her throat. There was a sudden stab of pain, followed by the sound of her voice as she whispered her last question, "What are you..."

Dead Mail

There's no turning back, not now, not ever. My training kicked in as this mantra pounded through my head, jarring me as badly as the impact of my boots on the hard-packed dirt. I'd already come more than half-way, and if the pack of feral dogs hadn't stopped me, what waited at the end of this road was just another pain in the ass to me.

It didn't start out to be this race against time. I thought I had plenty of that when I picked up the heavy duffel bag at three this morning. It was so dark, I had to use my flashlight to locate the stuffed canvas bag. I hated wasting the battery on the search, but I took the opportunity to count how many bags I had left. Three. Only three and my work here would be done!

The building was as quiet as a tomb as the saying goes. Never was one for using euphemisms. My command of the language is more than sufficient to describe this new world. But, then again, how do you describe the end of the world? How can you draw a verbal picture of the demise of civilization? Yeah, well, that's why I'm doing what I do. To restore even this small bit of a lost society. What else can I do in this god-forsaken place?

The people died in their millions around the globe, some from the all-out insanity of men with itchy fingers, sending nukes sailing off like fallen heroes to Valhalla. The aftermath was probably worse than the explosive concussions the planet took when those speeding crematoriums smacked into Mother Earth. The poison rains, the nuclear winter, a breakdown in all civilized behavior, and so on, and so on...into plagues, starvation, the loss of hope, in a world suffocating inside a planet-wide bubble filled with radioactive dust.

I woke from my eight-year hibernation, jolted awake when the life-support system shut down. This was supposed to be a test of my ability to sleep in this state, enduring long journeys to far off planets. Instead, I found myself reborn into the last chapter of this hellish place, still fully expecting to find family, friends, colleagues. The bunker-lab was void of all, save me, in my hermetically sealed chamber.

I took the designated elevator to the surface, counting the floors slipping by, until I reached the egress point, one and a half miles later. When I stepped through the camouflaged exit, I thought it must be midnight. The world around me looked shattered under the stark glow of the halogen flashlight. The heavy growth old forest surrounding the lab, was reduced to charred matchsticks. The mountain I was standing on, was devoid of vegetation, any animal or human life.

Eventually, I made my way down that dead pile of rock, wandering for months through towns and neighborhoods, empty of people, living off canned goods I found in cupboards and drinking any bottled water I could scrounge. That's when I stumbled across a U.S. Post Office in what was once a thriving suburb of Phoenix. That's also when I began this, my last career in life, my last profession. Mail Carrier. Why not? It gave me something to do, and a purpose in life…what was left of it.

I dedicated my days to studying maps and locating addresses in the surrounding areas. The pledge of mail carriers, back to the Pony Express Riders, was to overcome all elements and impediments and deliver the mail! When I was sufficiently schooled in the layout of the town, I took up my first canvas bag, proud of the US Mail logo emblazoned on the front. It took me a long month to find all the homes and businesses before I emptied that bag.

And now, here I am, nearly two years later, and there are only three bags to go. I figure when I finish here, I'll move to the next big town and continue my work as a mailman. I can't allow this civilized communication to lapse. It's the last form of human contact I have, in all this bleak, lifeless landscape. It matters not to me! As a sworn servant of the government, my mail will be delivered, and not be consigned to the Dead Mail containers like the people who sent them.

Now I have to face what lies in wait down this road. From here the two of them seem to be standing on two legs. Zoo apes? Perhaps my next career will be rounding up the wild beasts and repopulating zoos. It would be more exciting than delivering mail to empty houses.

They're moving away from me. "Hey wait!" I haven't used my voice in so long it sounds scratchy and foreign to my ears. I'm yelling again to see if they'll turn around. I'm going to fire the flare gun I found last year in the marina. I have no trouble finding gas to fill my mail truck and can find another when I move on from here.

The apes…or whatever they are…stopped and seem to be waiving. This is a miracle! Life is fragile, but the will to survive is indomitable. I'm going to drive the mail truck over to them and find out if there are others.

As I get closer, the forms I spotted from far away begin to crystallize. People! I am stunned to see how well dressed and healthy looking these men appear. One is in some kind of uniform and carrying a side arm. I feel a little uneasy, but…I want to speak with them to find out where they came from. I'm going to get out of the mail truck slowly. I better identify myself and put them at ease so they don't feel threatened.

"Greetings fellow survivors! I can't tell you how happy I am to find you. I'm sure you've discerned from my blue uniform and the insignia on my shirt, that I am the mail man."

They seem perplexed so I'll explain what being a carrier entails after the Apocalypse.

"I've been delivering the mail I find in the Post Offices around the country for over two years now…since the end of the world as we knew it!"

I quickly reached into my mail truck to grab my letter bag to prove my words. The bigger of the two men is stepping closer. I'm holding my ground so I don't show any fear.

"Mr. Matheson. We're from the FBI and the local Sheriff 's Department here in Hanover, Arizona. We've been tracking you for some time now, and it's time to take you in and let someone else deliver the mail."

This guy is nuts! Might be radiation poisoning effecting his brain. But what about the other one playing a Deputy, and rather poorly to my mind? They've clearly mistaken me for this Matheson guy. I better bluff my way out of here, I don't need to get mixed up with these crazies.

"I'm happy to meet you as I said, but I'm afraid I need to get back to my deliveries. I still have three bags to go. And the mail must go through no matter what!"

"Mr. Matheson, you've been breaking into Post Offices at night and stealing bags from the Dead Mail bins. Believe me, you are not a mail man. You escaped from Billings-Dwyer Confinement for the Criminally Insane several months ago and we're here to take you back."

"Look. I am a simple postman and only survived Armageddon because I was in a cryo-sleep and protected from the nuclear blasts. I admit, I kind of appointed myself a federal worker when I took over as the mail man, but I'm serving the Postal Service's mission for hundreds of communities."

"You were never in a cryo-sleep! And the only thing you're serving is a life sentence for murdering your entire family when you were on a camping trip. After slaughtering them, you went through the campgrounds and butcher seven more people as they slept. No Matheson, you're anything but a dedicated mailman. You're a psychopathic killer. Now drop the mail bag.

I swung with all my strength, taking the imposter FBI guy out and got into my truck just as the fake Deputy shot at me. The rear window is shattered, but I'll locate another truck eventually.

I've learned an important lesson; people have gone insane and I'm not safe around them!

I've driven for at least two hours, and now I'm out of gas. Being on foot is hard in these rocky hills, I need to stop for a minute to catch my breath. What's that sound? Some kind of motor, but it's pretty low. Might be those two weirdos. There it is again, but much closer. Not an engine…

I think it's coming from under that rocky outcropping behind me.

"Hey big boy! Looks like you and I are real survivors, right?"

He's just stretching himself…I wish I'd stayed with my mail truck. He's moving down the rocks and crouching low. Does a twitching tail mean he's being playful? Oh my God, those teeth…!

A Fireside Chat

The two elderly men sat in over-stuffed leather chairs, placed side by side, at a slight angle to improve conversation. A well-trimmed fire lit the deep creases and sagging jowls of their age-worn faces in warm, rosy shades. Each languidly sipped from a delicate brandy snifter, the dark liquid spreading a warmth through their aged bodies. They relaxed deeper into the comfort of the moment.

"My dear fellow, while you may be a dyed in-the-wool skeptic of things of a mystic nature, outside of scientific explanation, I must relate a tale riddled with supernatural elements! I daresay that even *you* shall be persuaded, Smethwick!"

So said Lord Bruntly to his boon companion of many years, Lionel Smethwick, Esquire. They had been at university together and became fast friends, their relationship spanning well-over two- quarters of a century. Smethwick, acting as legal counsel to his Lordship, was privy to every major or nuanced happening in his friend's life. Lord Bruntly's holdings included vast tracks of land in the south of the country. His family castle, sat on a thousand acres, filled with orchards, wheat and barley fields, an extensive coal ore operation and a handful of fairly large hamlets. Smethwick was familiar with his old friend's penchant for outlandish storytelling, so smiled benignly, indicating he should proceed.

"As you are keenly aware, Smethwick, my villagers are like my children. As such, they are dependent upon my largess and good management for their livelihoods and well-being. I have taken this responsibility to heart, and they have responded with love and loyalty."

"Ahem," Smethwick interjected, feeling apprehensive with the prospect of an interminably long narrative, and the coming of the long, dark road going home.

"Oh, yes, I do ramble."

His Lordship cleared his throat, took a long sip to feel the warm liquid smother the cold that curled around his carpet slippers, even in front of the roaring fire.

"There was a young lad in the village of Marlsburry, not far from this very castle. His name eludes me, but he was a carpenter's apprentice, and a promising tradesman by all accounts. On a Sunday, before the Yuletide, the apprentice was sent to retrieve new logs for the Church bench I commissioned. The pastor having discovered, one missing from the back; likely pilfered for firewood by a local. Disgraceful! And likely one I paid for, being rather generous to the local parish and..."

"Ahem,"

"Oh, alright...stop your fretting, Smethwick. I'll get on with it."

Staring into the fire as if to collect his quickly evaporating thoughts, which, in fact, was the case, he sighed deeply and continued, finally remembering the details.

"The young man was directed by his employer to go off into the surrounding woods to fell the required trees. As reported by the carpenter, the boy prepared for at most a two-day venture, with food and drink, and packing his whet stone to keep his ax in sharpened condition. He'd have to go deep into the forest to find suitable trees to the need.

Besides the necessary chopping accoutrements, he also took along a companion to warm his blankets on cold nights. His wife of only a few months secretly accompanied him, not wanting to be separated for any length of time from her new husband.

As evening fell, after a full day of chopping trees, she helped him bundle the limbs as he removed them from the trunks, doing as much hard labor as the young husband. By all reports she was quite a robust girl of nineteen and..."

He stopped when his audience of one, made a deep groan in his throat.

"They slept upon a bed of soft pine needles it appears, for when the young apprentice did not return to the carpenter upon the following evening, a search party was deputized to seek out his whereabouts."

The speaker struggled to his feet and reached for the poker to stir new life into the fire before sitting down with a deep harrumph, and picking up its thread before it became knotted in his head.

"Now, there was a bit of gossip circulating at the time among the people of Marlsburry. Whispers that others from their village had gone missing over the past four years. The first was a surveyor, sent by me, to help lay out a plot for the new wheat growing. A few weeks later, two hunters were dispatched by my grounds keeper to cull-out sick or injured deer from the herds. He went searching for them after they failed to report back and found bits and parts of their remains and clothing scattered around, as if consumed by a frenzied beast.

The headsman from the village took the lead in the search for the carpenter's young apprentice, discovering bloodied blankets, and a woman's waist purse. The group of ten men separated to cover more ground, continuing their search for the missing apprentice, and who they guessed was his young wife, or more likely, their dismembered bodies.

The village leader and the four volunteers in his group discovered a cave, well concealed by trees and brush, deep into a hillside near a small pond. He used his signal call to bring the others, not wanting to face whatever creature that might lurk within with only a handful of men. He was quickly joined by the villagers; each setting alight a long torch carried for just such searching. The ten men quietly entered single file into the cave.

Deep inside, the torch light set the roof of the cavern to shimmering with movement, followed by hundreds of bats streaming out above them like a black cloud into the darkening sky. As they went deeper still, the thick odor of bat guano and heavy musk choked off any fresh air. They walked close together, taking some comfort in the friend at their shoulder no doubt. Suddenly, a long howl shook them in their boots, reverberating off the dank walls and stirring the hairs on their necks.

They stood in a tight cluster, frozen with the ungodly sound of yet another, answering howl, this one from directly behind the terror-stricken group. Half of the men turned to meet this new threat while the others, including the headman, faced the shadow taking form directly ahead.

A massive creature detached itself from the inky shadows at the back of the of the cave, into the flickering glow of torch light; It could very well have stepped out of a fevered nightmare! The creature stood man-like, at least seven-feet tall, its shoulders hunched over, as if the weight of the cave pressed down upon it. A powerfully built body was covered in a black pelt, its arms nearly trailing the ground. The long, pointed snout flared, as if deeply breathing in the scent of the men's fear. Blackish lips pulled back revealing jaws filled with sharp teeth and dagger-like incisors; saliva constantly drooled onto the coarse fur of the chest.

First two, then three more men at the back of the group made a mad dash for the mouth of the cave, leaving the others to face the beast. The movement of the fleeing men caused it to charge. It dodged the flames grazing its long arms, snatching two of the men, tearing them apart as easily as ripping the wings off a cooked partridge. The next minutes the cave echoed with the sounds of screams as the wolf creature tore the two men apart.

The three men startled when two of the deserters rushed in behind them. Nearly incoherent they spoke of a second monster tearing their friends to shreds near the opening to the cave. The cowardly men described the monster at the entrance, saying it resembled the other, but was decidedly female. The path to outside and safety, was blocked by a smaller, but no less dangerous creature.

The men became aware that it had become silent. The sounds of flesh being ripped and bones snapping ceased. The beast dropped a leg and stood. It appeared ready to leap upon the surviving men, armed only with their torches. It hesitated, stepping back as they waved their torches furiously, creating a wall of fire. During this lull in its attack, the beast howled once, long and throaty like some primeval creature. There was a scrapping sound overhead and the tight group of men looked up. The female wolf creature clung to the roof of the cave with long claws, moving like a huge spider over their heads.

Seeing their prospects for survival diming, one of the terrified men mimicked the actions of the earlier deserters, backing away until he could run toward the entrance. He could hear the male's roar followed by his mate's. He watched the walls behind him just long enough to see the light from the torches dropping like falling stars to the floor of the cave. The screaming stopped quickly, replaced by more howls. The cave walls amplified the unmistakable sounds of bones breaking and the sucking sound of flesh being torn away from what were once living men."

"Who was this lone survivor, Bruntly?" his friend asked in a somewhat quivering voice.

"It was none other than the carpenter, the young apprentice's employer. He told me he barely got away but knew he must survive to report to me their deaths on that horrible day.

In a strange twist of fate, two days after this atrocious incident, the young apprentice and his new wife returned to the village, which was, as you might expect, in full mourning. They seemed fit as two love birds, blooming with the vitality enjoyed by youth. When asked to explain their disappearance, the young husband smiled over at his sweet young wife giving a most unusual response."

"Well...what did the boy say?" Smethwick asked exasperated at his friend's long pause.

"Ah, yes. He answered that they were always within sight of the village but were doing a bit of rabbit hunting to help stock their larder for the winter days ahead."

The very long story concluded on this rather flat note, and Smethwick was disappointed in the outcome. He told his old friend he was still unbelieving of such twaddle, and it was time to return to his own hearth in any case.

As they stood together in the foyer, Smethwick, putting on his gloves and wrapping a thick scarf round the loose skin of his thin neck, stopped, looking around himself at the open door and the waiting night.

"What was that sound?" he asked looking at Lord Bruntly.

"Why, it sounded like a wolf howling, dear boy. You'll be inside your coach, so no worries."

They opened the door wider to see his driver standing by to assist the old man onto the snug cushions inside the coach. As the heavy door closed behind the age-bent back of Lord Bruntly, the coach horses became skittish, both pawing at the ground, and snorting. The full moon showed streams of steam coming from their flaring nostrils.

"Best get home, sir. Don't like the sound of them wolves prowling about tonight, so free like." his driver said nervously as he shut the coach door to his employer's worried face.

Smethwick moved the window curtain aside just enough to peer into the darkness swallowing his coach and team. He could tell it was picking up speed without the encouragement of his driver's whip. Unbeknownst to him, the driver began to panic at the horse's growing agitation, as they went from a controlled trot into nearly a full gallop over the rough roadways. There was a sharp bend in the road ahead of them, and he was unable to reign them into a safe speed. The wheels were flying now, the deadly curve moments away. The driver knew the fate that awaited them all. As they tore into the untenable curve, the last thing he saw was the two wolves running beside the careening coach and pair. He closed his eyes for a second when he heard the larger creature on his side, howl like the son of Satan himself.

A Christmas Goblin

"Nothin' tastes better, me dear, than a nicely roasted goose!"

The old man looked proud of himself as he plucked the plump black and white bird of its feathers, its head drooping like a large tear drop from his knees. He was careful to put the feathers into a much-dented washtub, knowing they'd to be used inside a winter comforter by his dear wife. He was quite pleased with this acquisition, newly made by him when he raided the nearby farmstead of Cormack Murphy. It was in the darkest hour of night, when he stuffed his squawking, squirming prize in the burlap sack he'd brought along.

It was his wife of thirty years his comments were being directed to between pulling great tufts of feathers. They began their harmonious union when very tender in age. He barely needed to shave; she, just learning the grave meaning of womanhood. They had many challenges over that span of time but stuck together like a glue pot and its lid.

"Benny, ye are a neat rascal, ye are! I been fussin' an' worryin' these past weeks, what victuals we'd be 'avin' fer the Yuletide! An 'ere tis! A goose ta size o' a cart!" she chortled loudly.

He loved to see the merriment on Megan's face, so bereft she was most days of that sparkle. Up before the first weak rays of sun, to make the fire in the hearth for her bread baking; then, after their meager pottage, helping her stiff-jointed Benny, to see to the four pigs and one milk cow. Late into fall, Megan could be found tending her precious garden plot on the sunny side of their cottage. Most days, with the exception of her wash day, which was much longer, his dear wife worked until the sun slipped behind the mountains, encircling the small hamlet.

They lost their only son in his fourth year, grateful they'd had the foresight to have him Christened, else he'd been buried outside the Church cemetery as a baby heathen. They called him Jamie, but he never heard his name, or any word for that matter; him being born without hearing or speech and suffering in his own well of silence all his short days on earth. He was as quiet as a passing cloud, and, as soft in the head the villagers said behind their hands. They reckoned his passing as a blessing to the very young couple. He would have proved a sorry burden in their life, and clearly, no help in filling their larder.

"Are ye certain this 'ere goose be free ta our needs then, Benny?" she asked again, still amazed at their great fortune.

"Oy, why da' ya' bother yerself so, my Megan? Tis a Christmas gift from dat young fella down in Baleyroost Haven. He were cullin' 'is flock, so ta speak, an' I give 'em a quick hand ta set 'em straight on 'is day. No use ye worryin' yerself. Let's jest enjoy our feastin' me lass!"

With that, clearly being his last word on the subject of the goose's provenance, Benny continued his plucking while Megan gathered the feathers, imagining to herself the fine comforter she'd be making.

That night was Christmas Eve.

A heavy snow fell persistently throughout the day, gathering the tiny cottage into the cold embrace of high drifts, skirting its two shuttered windows, and bringing a deep silence into the evening. Benny and Megan had eaten a spare supper, looking forward to the rich meal of fattened goose, stuffed with Megan's lovely bread seasoned with garden herbs and the little bit of garden produce Megan had stored in the root cellar. They would rise at their customary hour, and welcome Christmas into their dingy, mean world with their first kiss of the day. Meantime, the goose was hung near the crude front door of their cottage, keeping it fresh for cooking, Christmas morning.

That night they slept on their straw-stuffed pallet, curled around each other like a tea pot and its cozy. In the darkest hour, as the wind rattled the cottage door, and the snow was so heavy it appeared as a curtain of white, a shadow passed over the elderly couple. Never disturbing them, they were made to sleep even more deeply, when a vaporous cloud appeared, hovering over their gray heads. A pale shaft of moonlight was reflected up from the high snow mounds, filtering through a thin crack in the wall. The finger of light found the shadowy figure, and it took shape within its glow. The goose they had plucked earlier was now tucked under the arm of a very large and hairy Goblin.

This creature was not unknown to the sleeping couple, or the other folk of the hamlet. It occupied a prominent place in their colorful folklore, and was the subject of many a good tale, told by the roaming story tellers and troubadours. The dark-robed clerics tried diligently to dismantle or debunk tales of the Little People, and Faeries, and Hobgoblins. But over long eons, through many dark times, the allure of magic and mythical creatures clung to the culture of the people like dew to the morning grass.

The Goblin stood awkwardly, his hairy head grazing the low beams of the roof, listening to the couple's gentle snores and sighs. He had visited all of the villagers during their meager lifetimes and over several of his own. Always cautious, he only rarely frightened a waking child. For some reason, these two decrepit humans, touched something in him. Perhaps it was their generosity to others, even when they had so little themselves, and especially when it wasn't the Yuletide! He had witnessed the old man take the goose from his neighbor's pen, scattering a few tufts of red fox fur around the yard, disguising his part in the theft. At the time, the Goblin thought this clever, but was curious, because Benny never struck the Goblin as being devious and cunning.

You must understand, though they suffer a reputation for their terrifying appearance and ill-tempered nature, Goblins have a deep and curious nature. Sadly, it is often the case that judgments are made solely on the superficial aspects of a being. It was in fact, the Goblin's curiosity that compelled him to follow Benny back to the small cottage. Hiding in the woods, close enough to be privy to the conversation inside the cottage with his keen hearing, the Goblin heard Benny's explanation about the neighbor's gift of the goose, as payment for his help.

Goblins are not known to have any concept of selfless love, but it gradually dawned on him that the man risked his freedom, and possible hanging, to bring some cheer into his wife's dour life. While the theft would cost the other farmer very little, it gave the old man and his wife so much. The Goblin wondered at this moral conundrum.

Christmas morning dawned frosty and as clear as the bells from the Church belfry. The old couple shook the deep sleep from their heads. Benny stepped into worn woolen breeches, Megan covered her thin shoulders in a woolen shawl. They both suddenly stopped moving, sniffing at the chilled air.

"A beast 'as been visitin' us, Benny! I ken smell it I ken!"

Megan was thinking their goose would surely have been snatched by such an intruder. But Benny was on to something else altogether. Besides the pungent odor wafting about their small sleeping area, the breeze poking through the walls carried the rich fragrance of cooking goose!

They forced their stiff legs to the task, creeping from the back of the cottage where their pallet was tucked. A warm glow greeted their sleep-dulled eyes. Standing by the rough stone fireplace, looking as homely as a mud bog next to a rose garden, was the Goblin.

The fireplace was merry with dancing low flames and a thick bed of cherry red coals. The spitted goose was dripping fat onto the hot coals, sounding like the crack of a whip with each rich plop. The Goblin turned the spit, making minor adjustments to the goose's position. The old couple watched, without an utterance passing between themselves.

After a few good turns, the Goblin left off working the spit, and began setting the rough wood table nearby, with two dishes of battered pewter, knowing this was their best plate. Without acknowledging their presence, he then turned back to the fireplace where he shoved two large loaves of dark bread into their pots for baking. The vegetables were in a side iron pot, ready for cooking. The fragrance of the gastronomic feast of Yule goose, and the baking breads, made their mouths water in anticipation. While the old man was still overcome by fear of the giant, hairy creature, his wife took a different view of the situation.

"We be grateful fer ye ta be joinin' us, on dis 'ere Christmas morn, Goblin. En ye 'ave outdone yerself, wit all dis fine cookery."

The Goblin gave his shaggy head a quick shake and grunted, "Tis me first Yule feast, an' I've no place ta be, 'cept wit yuns. Benny, I've sent yer invitation ta the farmer, Cormack Murphy, down the way," he said in a deep, gravelly voice. "e'll be 'ere fer ta feastin' en' is grateful, seein' 'e's all alone like."

Being a creature of Magic, sending this message to Cormack Murphy was as simple as slipping a word into the sleeping farmer's ear. He awoke, believing he'd been asked to dine with Benny and his wife, and readied himself to do so, whistling merrily at the prospect.

This marked the first of many Christmas feasts to follow over the next decade of years allotted to the elderly couple and their new friends. The Goblin returned each holiday, with a goose tucked under his arm, preparing the feast and then going to fetch the farmer, Cormack Murphy, to join in the fine company of the happy couple and himself. The other villagers were curious about the large visitor coming every Christmas to the couple's door.

"Tis like magic I tell ye! We be blessed wit long, lost kin ta me." Benny would explain whenever this was brought up in idle conversation around the Yule Season. The villagers all agreed, the huge, shambling man, did hold a family resemblance with old Benny. And from the size of the goose he supplied for their table, he was both rich and generous.

Before he passed on, joining his Megan in eternal feasting, old Benny asked the Goblin to bring a second, live goose. He took it to the farmer Murphy's yard, adding it to his flock of geese pecking around in the dirt. Benny felt grand with this compensation for the old wrong he did. Another lesson for the rest of us who have read this tale perhaps.

"While your goose may be cooked, it's always better to share the feast with those whose life may be uglier and poorer then our own."

The Hidden Cost of Love

You may be tempted to view this story as yet another of my works of imagination, rather than the cautionary tale it's meant to be. I've exposed, herein, the hidden cost of love. Your opinions and critiques will be of little concern to me. Just as they were when I walked among your society I might add.

Of course, then you knew me only in the pale caricature of a human female, but I was a famous authoress, none-the-less. As I close on that distant horizon, that line between death and life, I need to unburden myself of a few of the ghostly chains I forged, as the illustrious Mr. Dickens would call these painfully remembered transgressions.

My life as a female was blighted, like most of my gender, by the all-male interpretations of every aspect of my life as a woman. From procreating, to schooling, to attire and ruination by fornication, with heavy emphasis on the latter. I was carefully indoctrinated in the beliefs of religious zealots, part of a myopic society of men, many having no understanding of the gender they so diligently crushed. What they tried to convey in their dictates, seasoned like a thick stew, with the grave consequences of sin, was that my sex had no original thought, only Original Sin, brought on by our innate wickedness!

Naturally, a man would have to beat the evil out of me, either physically or mentally, and I'd be expected to endure in the process. Instead, I took up the pen and began pouring out my womanly desires and fantasies upon the pristine, blank pages. I was like those clean sheets of paper, unblemished by the twisted ideas of others. My pen was filled with the ink of freedom. Freedom from the tyranny of a male-dominated society, through stories I've written clandestinely in the pitch-black hours.

I discretely funneled these lurid tales of romance, and conquest, into the hands of a publishing house under the pen name, *'Venus'* and, to my astonishment, became an overnight sensation. There was a hue and cry from starched-up husbands, finding their wives and daughters, panting over the pages written by the mysterious *Venus*. Village society was rocked when the Rector's own wife was discovered with one of my more daring stories. Appropriately, it was about a pastor's wife and the joys she found in cultivating cucumbers in her garden. I heard that particular book was a favorite topic for discussion at the Barrister's Club as well.

Have I shocked you with my double identity as dutiful wife and Author of Erotic Fantasy? No doubt. But I hope my stories reveal the hidden passion we all struggle to control like tigers caged inside our bodies.

Now, I face the high cost of expressing those passionate feelings. I sat in this jail cell after my identity was discovered by the authorities. I am among other women, of lower pedigree, but no less female. We all await our sentencing today by the Magistrate visiting our village on his rounds. He shall decide my fate. Yes, another man shall dictate the terms of my life.

As I sit under the small window so that I may feel the weak sunlight on my back, I wonder if the judge, in his dark robes, shall ever find his plump wife sighing over the pages of *Venus,* before turning down the bedside flame.

The Empty Chair

Fernella Osborne was a stiff woman. Wealth had guaranteed her place in society, and it was only by sheer happenstance that she had to deal with the likes of me. I'm as far removed from the rarefied air breathed up her Patrician nose, as Moses was from being a real Egyptian!

It was my reputation among the local coppers working in this gritty town, that brought me to stand uncomfortably under the sharp scrutiny of her cold, blue eyes. Consulting successfully on many unusual cases, gave me a certain credibility when it came to dealing with the unexplainable, or in my words, the supernatural. The case of Mrs. Osborne's missing husband, fell neatly into that box of mysteries, so, the cops called me in.

Living in the Bowery District of New York City, wandering its twisting, fetid streets after sundown, is part of my work. I don't need much sleep, and in my profession, that's just as well, since closing my eyes in the dark isn't a great idea, if you take my meaning. The particulars of the Osborne case were chasing around in my brain as I wandered toward the Flatbush Cemetery last night around eleven. It was the closest one to the Osborne residence, so I figured that was the place I needed to visit.

I started out, after a lengthy interview with Mrs. O, monitored by Captain Paddy O'Rourke, my buddy from the Fifth Precinct. He didn't want me upsetting the lady I suppose, slipping in a few words like 'necromancer' or 'possessed' into my conversation could set off an avalanche of denials and tears.

The case was laid out to me like this: Old man Osborne, described as a portly man in his late fifties, had been enjoying a late-night brandy with his wife, both sitting in front of a cozy fire in his study. Mrs. O said she must have dosed off, with the effect of warmth of the fireplace and the exceptional brandy. When she reopened her eyes, her husband no longer sat across from her in their compatible silence. The distraught lady described how she looked around, calling his name several times, before rising and approaching his vacant seat. That's when she spotted something extraordinary in her spotless home. Piles of sooty-gray ash rose in small towers on the brocade cushion of the seat, on the footstool where his slipper-ed feet rested, and the floor surrounding the empty chair.

I eyeballed the powder in silence, not wanting to give away my suspicions. Mrs. O assured me she'd have them swept up as soon as I left the premises. The sight was "most disconcerting," she emphatically stated.

I left in a hurry and made my way to the one place I hoped to find answers. When I pulled open the heavy wrought iron gate to the cemetery, I was sure the screeching sound of the hinges would likely wake the dead.

I already had a theory of what had befallen the Steel Magnate. Spontaneous Combustion! I was only going through a few formalities, to confirm my conclusion. I thought visiting the shadow-filled graveyard, was going to be a short visit, resulting in a quick resolution to the man's disappearance.

Even a sleeping city has its sounds. But within the gloomy confines of Flatbush Cemetery, they were muted like screams muffled under a soft pillow. I walked toward the farthest vault in a sea of gravestones, towering angels and leaning crosses. I spotted a slender shaft of light painting the stairs leading up to a remotely placed tomb. I was as silent as a hunting cat climbing the flared skirt of stone steps. Even the leather of my shoes didn't creak to announce my presence. Pulling the wooden door wider, produced another unwelcome squeal, but I wasn't overly concerned. She already knew I was there.

"You left poor Mrs. Osborne in quite a state!" I said as I stepped in. "The coppers suspect kidnapping, but I guess it's more a case of burn and snatch!"

I spotted the shade of Charles Osborne reclining peacefully on top of a stone sarcophagus. His once corpulent body was well-defined and translucent in the scant moonlight filtering into the vault from the open doorway. Uncrossing his ghostly hands from where they lay on his round mid-section, he sat up, smiling fiendishly.

"This one is mine, Ghost Hunter! He burned hot and long for me and is proving a most comfortable fit for my continued possession. He's no good to you, or his bland wife. Leave me before I make you sorry!"

"You know I can't do that Lucy dear. The fact that you keep visiting vulnerable men is bad enough, but now you're causing fires to consume otherwise healthy people; inhabiting the confused spirits of the newly dead for cheap thrills!"

I talked like a Dutch Uncle to the famously wealthy brothel Madame, who should have been the sole occupant in this mausoleum. She finally gave in, rising like dark smoke from the center of the ghost body of Charles Osborne. I was going to report back to Mrs. O that her husband died from the exposure to the flames of his toxin-riddled body. Sounded scientific enough and she'd be none-the-wiser. My pal, O'Rourke, would suspect paranormal activity, but not ask any questions. He really didn't want the kind of answers I had for him.

I was walking back through the graveyard when I felt a sudden stabbing pain in my back. I reached around, my hand closing on a long, cold shaft, just below my left shoulder. The stone Guardian Angel on my right, glared fiercely back at me, but now stood empty handed.

Lucy's voice floated into my ear, "This just got easier, Ghost Hunter!"

I knew I was a dead man, but I couldn't let this succubus creature consume my spirit for her own use. I'd been messing with her for years now, interfering with her schemes of seduction and possession. Old man Osborne probably fell for her, when she came to him in her sultry body form. I had to act fast if I was going to save myself from death and eternal control by the beautiful demon.

Only seconds from proving I'm mortal, I called out to old-man Osborne's spirit.   I figured he'd be hanging around the gravestones, looking for a different place to rest. He came to my rescue, smashing the stone lance to bits. He was glaring at the desirable female spirit who had lured him to his death. Wrapping transparent hands around her slim waist, he drew her into a tight embrace. They were swept away by a howling wind, toward her crypt. I heard the heavy door slam shut, the bolt sliding into place from outside.

"Oh, you ain't gonna like this Lucy! Locked for eternity with the old fat guy is not what you expected. Guess you shouldn't play with fire."

I left the dead to the dead and closed the gate to Flatbush Cemetery, already healing from the paranormal assassination attempt. With Lucy occupied inside the crypt with Mr. O, her power was no longer influencing the attempt on my life.

There was a new sound added to the night noise that my super sensitive ears picked out of the rest. The sound of sobs and maniacal laughter.

Winter Eyes

His world was covered in a crisp, white blanket of snow. There were no footprints, no animal tracks, no desecration of yellow to mar its pristine surface. Thom was a trapper of sorts. He never trapped to kill or sell the pelts of the beautiful animals he saw around his cottage. He was there to study them, using his non-lethal traps to get close enough to sketch them in detail. These renderings were sent off to a scientific journal that used them as illustrations. The journal was published once a year, so Thom had plenty of time to amass quite a number of drawings for submission over the long winter.

This winter was different from the last one he'd spent in this small farming community. Most everyone here over the age of seven had a gun, and hunted avidly not for the sport, but for the table. This was a poor rural town, and a number of the menfolk were not long returned from 'The war to end all wars.'

Thom knew mostly everyone by sight, forming casual friendships with several of the returned veterans. As an impressionable, untested twenty- year- old, he was in awe of their wartime tales, sitting for hours as they sketched in words, their own stories of death and near-death experiences that surrounded them in their fox holes and trenches.

He was most interested in their peculiar superstitions. Some of these were deep-rooted from childhood and transplanted in the mud of France. Others, were newly unearthed, like the channels they crawled through, and only spoken of in hushed voices. While he had developed an intimate knowledge of the wild animals that roamed the area, Thom didn't have the same understanding of the lives of these war-aged men he sat with over long winter evenings.

A small wooden shack on the edge of the town served as the local pub for those thirsty for the taste of throat-biting whiskey, and the companionship of other menfolk. The winds blew hard and bitterly cold moving down the narrow footpath, stirring the snow and masking the trail leading to the front door of the watering hole. It didn't matter much. The locals knew the way by heart, or as some claimed, by sense of smell. The sign, hanging from four nails bleeding rust above the windowless entrance, advertised itself as Winter Eyes. A stranger pub name, Thom never heard.

Inside, a roaring fire radiated welcoming waves of heat from the stone hearth taking up most of one wall. The hearth appeared to be the sturdiest thing about the rattling structure. Two rows of roughly finished wooden shelves lined the back wall of the pub. The few varieties of drink were stored here, along with glasses and mugs, all of which rattled, as if sending a coded message out into the night, whenever the winds buffeted the flimsy building. No polished bar ran the length of the square room. Instead, an old dinette table was used by the barkeep for his money box and order taking, and several round tables, wide enough to hold a few pints, were scattered over the uneven wooden floor. There were also two unpopular short benches lined up near the front door, where the chilled winds poked through like sharp fingers and stabbed at the necks of those unfortunate few. The benches were donated by the young cleric before he left the village to serve his country, never to return to his white-washed country church.

One of the fantasies carried from mouth to ear around town, was that the young minister had a vision, seeing himself in a trench filled with bodies. His own body was on top with a bullet hole through his left eye. Thom asked if the pastor had been killed over there like he foresaw. One of the older veterans answered after a deep silence settled upon the small group.

"He seen it all and faced his death with a cold stare of defiance, he did! We all saw how we would fare before we were taken into the army, for that matter. It was no mystery to any here, and a testimony to the bravery of those that went anyway."

"But how can that be, Macrae? No one can see their time of death."

"Well, Thom, boy. There's more than what you can see with your natural eye to be found, if you're of a mind. We all decided to follow the young pastor and look with dead, winter eyes, to find what future we had left. Step over to the fireplace young Thom and have a gander for yourself!"

Thom hesitated, something inside of him shrinking back from the challenge. But he was among friends, people with good hearts. Soldiers of a poisonous war, most coughing their lungs up every few words. He had to look, or they'd think him less a man than the young cleric.

He walked over to the great hearth, the orange and yellow flames dancing in a wild frenzy in the gusts seeping through the boards of the walls and the open chimney flue. His face became hot as he moved closer, staring into the frenzied flames. He blinked furiously as his eyeballs dried in the super-heated air blowing on him in waves of heat. He was about to turn away, ready to announce the sham they had all experienced, and sadly so, when a log shifted in the fiery nest, and suddenly…he saw.

He jumped back from the bizarre scene playing out among the flames and smoke but couldn't tear his eyes away. He saw himself, working on a sketch while lying on his bed in his one room cottage. A shadow passed by his window, blotting out the moonlight. There was the sound of heavy, shuffling steps outside, and suddenly, the flimsy cottage door was knocked off its hinges, crashing onto the floor near a few boxes and a suitcase. A huge bear let out a blood thirsty roar, plowing into the room and straight at the petrified Thom.

"Well, Thom boy, you are pale as a fish's belly, and your legs seem as rubbery as its tale. Tell us what you seen, boy. We're all anxious to know."

Thom flew out the door of the pub and didn't look back. He reached his cabin and began packing his art supplies and pads into two heavy boxes and a large valise that he tied with a rope to secure. It was too late in the day to try to get a lift to the next town over where the train station was located, so he tucked in for a long night.

Meanwhile, back at the pub, the once young men, leaving their youth on the battlefield, were laughing at the naive boy, so afraid of looking death in the face. Why, they'd done it themselves hundreds of times. Macrae took a long drag before taking a stubby rolled cigarette from the corner of his mouth. Two streams of smoke snaked through his large nose as he spoke.

"I'm guessing the young Thom is better off letting old man death sneak up on him. A surprise he'll never see coming!"

Back in Thom's tiny cabin, he was having trouble sleeping, so turned the wick higher, letting its flickering flame settle. He pulled out his sketch pad and pencil and decided to draw what he'd seen in the hearth at the Winter Eyes pub. It was an almost perfect picture, the pig-like eyes of the bear stared out at him from the paper. He spoke out loud, telling himself the men were just trying to spook him and reached for the hurricane lamp to lower its flame. The noise was so subtle at first, he doubted hearing anything but the moaning wind. There were two heavy thuds on the wooden planks of the small porch.

The breath caught in his throat as he squeaked out, "Who's out there?"

The front door was blown inward as if caught in a tornado. Standing on two legs, taller than cabin roof, was a grizzly bear the size of a locomotive. Thom looked into its black beady eyes as the creature studied him. *My vision in the fire was true…my God!* Rather than the headlong charge he expected, the bear dropped to all fours and entered the room. The bear snuffled and raised its massive head, appearing to be sniffing the air.

The young man began to have an uncanny feeling that he knew his dangerous visitor. Thinking back on his two years roaming the woods and mountain, sketching wild animals, it finally dawned on him. He found his voice and though it quivered, he spoke out loud.

"You are the young bear I found injured, with your mother nearby shot by hunters. You were orphaned and I brought you food and tended your wounded leg. I fed you until you were able to walk and you disappeared into the woods. I called you Hank after my grumpy old man. Did you come looking for me Hank?"

The bear seemed to be listening attentively until it let out a terrific roar raising the hair on Thom's head. It charged the young artist landing on his chest. During the short attack, before the bear could drag Thom out of the cabin into the woods, Thom's flailing arm knocked over the lamp and ignited the bedcovers and ran up the cabin wall, spreading quickly. The bear reared back and ran from the conflagration.

The next night, after word spread about the fire that claimed the life of the young artist, the veterans were gathered as usual at the Winter Eyes pub. They were all somber and deep in their fiery drinks. The older man stood from his seat, walking close to the fireplace and its leaping flames. He shuddered inwardly, thinking of their young friend's death.

They spotted the fire through the woods as they left the pub at closing time. As part of the volunteer fire brigade, he was with the others, trying to douse the flames, later, finding Thom's charred remains.   He turned to the men lounging around the quiet room.

"We never should've told the kid to look for his future in the fire. He was pretty upset when he ran out of here last night. Suppose…suppose he really saw something?"

"Nah! Sarge, it was just an old wives' tale! There's always been stories floating around here 'bout Winter Eyes being haunted by demons an such. Ever since the first owner was found hanging from the rafters. And we better not let the pastor know we made up that whopper about his predecessor seeing his future. Sounds like the devil's work for sure!"

The others were all nodding at their friend's comments. The older man seemed unconvinced, noticing as the evening wore on, how the other's avoided moving in front of the hearth to escape the drafts for a few minutes. His own inclination was to leave and return home to his own fireplace where the ashes were cold, but he could forget what he suspected about Winter Eyes.

This Seems Familiar

"It wasn't good enough that he worshiped her from afar. Herbert Grayson's desire for Clementine Hurley, reached a fever pitch, leaving him in a state incompatible with performing everyday life. As often occurs in crimes of passion, he allowed his fantasies to push aside all rational thought and acted like a mad man. As Chief Detective Inspector on this most unusual case, it fell to me to unravel the mysterious disappearance of the obsessed, Herbert Grayson. And, I had to do it before the case exploded publicly, with the supernatural-claptrap surrounding it from the beginning. For the sake of brevity in this interview, I'll give you the bare-bones of the case."

CDI Remington cleared his throat, stroking either side of his impressive black mustache, as if it was some kind of talisman. A stern look settled over his face, its normally flaccid cheeks, pulled down further, into a deeper frown. For a man in his early fifties, Remington had the look of a stodgy, sixty-year-old, retired banker. His great bulk nearly over-flowed the groaning wing chair, as he rearranged himself for his monologue. His only audience, the reporter from the Daily Gazette, sat behind his desk, pen at the ready.

"Herbert Grayson was unknown to Clementine Hurley, according to her solicitor, though they lived in flats situated directly across from one another. She is described as a quiet girl of twenty-two, and apparently, has no living family. Her only companion according to residents of the other six flats in the building, is a large black cat she keeps without the landlord's knowledge. Her closest neighbor, a woman named Bette, said Clementine had jokingly referred to the clandestinely kept feline as her 'familiar', though she never explained to Bette, the meaning of that obscure description.

Supposedly, unbeknown to Clementine, the flat almost directly across from hers, was occupied by a man consumed with lascivious thoughts and unrequited desire for her. An often-deadly combination."

The CDI puffed up with this piece of insight, shared with the bland, unresponsive reporter taking down his words. This case already had a long enough press-life, according to his Editor, but the young man felt there was something missing here, beside the missing weirdo, Herbert Grayson. Listening to the pedantic presentation of CDI Remington, he wished he hadn't been so persuasive with his Editor. He snapped out of his roaming thoughts at the sound of the Inspector's deep voice.

"Herbert Grayson tried everything to capture the lovely Clementine's attention, going so far as blocking her way in the hallway once. Witnessed by Bette, she told me this attempt earned him a swift kick to the groin, leaving him mewling on the floor. After all, to Clementine, he was a stranger trying to accost her, and she'd have none of it!

Herbert, who studied the object of his crazed obsession like a starving man does a steak lying in the butcher's tray, knew of the presence of the large black feline. He began plotting ways he might use Clementine's beloved pet to demonstrate his adoration of her. Kidnapping the cat was the result of this devious scheming. According to Clementine's Solicitor, the wily scoundrel broke into the girl's flat during her absence one day, snatching the cat and returning to his own flat, where he awaited her return. His plan, of course, was to miraculously rescue the kitty for its lovely owner, thereby becoming her hero. The plan went well, as noted by the vigilant Bette who testified that she spotted Herbert exiting Clementine's flat with a heavy towel wrapped around something large and squirming which he carried back to his own flat."

The reporter looked up from his notes and asked, "If Herbert was holding the cat, seeking Clementine's gratitude and attention, why do you think he disappeared after getting what he wanted?"

"Oh, he got what he wanted, alright! Bette testified Clementine went directly to his door, banging with the flat of her hand and screaming, "You've taken him! I feel him in there with you!"

Herbert opened the door. Bette, and two other flat occupants, testified that Clementine rushed in, only to find the heavy towel had gotten wrapped around the cat's head so tightly, he suffocated. According to the witnesses, Clementine's screams were like the sounds coming from Bedlam on visiting day. The door to Herbert's flat was thrown shut, and everyone in the hallway waited with bated breath after the screams stopped.

When the police arrived, called by the ever-present Bette, they found Herbert's flat torn to shreds. Herbert was nowhere to be found, however, and not one of his neighbors saw him exit."

The reporter stopped his story once more to ask, "Well, what did they find?"

"A towel, laying on his daybed. Clementine was the last person to see him and was charged with his disappearance and possible murder. Well, you've already reported that all charges were dismissed, due to lack of evidence and…well…a body! I did make one peculiar finding, but it only sparked speculation of paranormal happenings surrounding the case of the missing man."

"What was that?" The reporter saw the CDI's face go pale, when he answered.

"When I last interviewed Clementine Hurley in her flat, a large black cat wandered out of the bedroom and jumped into her lap. They both seemed quite content with one another's company."

Your Time Is Up!

My name is Detective Inspector, Martin O'Malley, Cork Constabulary. This report pertains to the disappearance of one Harold Pickery, Number 8, Creek Way, New Mill, Country Cork, Ireland. My investigation reached its conclusion a fortnight ago, but I am only now, in fit enough mind, to commit my findings within this document. The following will illuminate what would appear at first glance to be a tale spun by a deranged mind.

Harold Pickery was prissy to a fault, in the opinion of his extensively interviewed, immediate neighbors. He trimmed the hedges surrounding his cottage to within an inch of their life, tended a variety of flowers as if ten.

ding the Gardens of Versailles and kept a small stream running behind his house as pure and fast running as the River Shannon, allowing no refuse to be thrown into its crystal waters under his vigilant eye.

Now, while all of this may sound irritably time consuming, consider first, the size of Harold's dwelling. His cottage was so tiny, it could be mistaken for an overgrown playhouse for children to the unknowing passersby.

The Pickery clan had lived among the villagers of New Mill for countless generations. Harold inherited the homestead from his Great Grams, many times removed, who, like Harold, was reportedly one of the Little People. That particular jargon may seem insulting when describing a grown man, but is appropriate in this case, for you see, Harold Pickery was a Leprechaun.

No doubt at this point, you have an urge to throw this report onto the floor, but I swear, the balance of my findings will confirm this assertion beyond a shadow of a doubt. I therefore continue in hopes of your forbearance.

Harold lived quietly in this out-of-the-way village, where his only form of industry was caring for his cottage, with its beautiful grounds and crystal stream. The tiny house was no more than a single room, where a large hearth filled all of one wall, likely heating it to a snug comfort in brisk weather. Another cottager's house, sprung out of a wild field of golden rod, across a worn dirt track, set within a few steps of the surrounding woodlands. Two other rough-built, sod-roofed cottages, sat on either side of the Harold's own, with the width of their gardens and low stone fences, separating them. There was only a smattering of other mean-built homes scattered around the area and calling it a village was somewhat overstated.

None were close enough to peer into a single round window at the front of their peculiar neighbor's dwelling, but, in the stillness of a night, near enough to hear strange singing coming from the cottage. To a man, these neighbors swore the words were like no tongue they'd heard spoken in their village, or elsewhere they may have traveled. One old neighbor woman, reported how she was outside when darkness had just fallen, fetching more wood from a pile stacked near her garden wall. She heard a voice swept over to her on the night winds, and listening closely, was positive the words were old Druid incantations. She called these, *summoning spells*. When pressed by me, she swore that when the chanting ceased, she heard a woman's sweet voice, much laughing, and then silence. This old crone was the first to speak the word *leprechaun* to me, but not the last.

Harold Pickery vanished the night of the 31st, December 1899. The whole village was out in the streets, celebrating this auspicious New Year's Eve with fireworks hosted by the village Magistrate. Tables were laid with food and sweets donated by every householder. All but Harold, danced and celebrated under the cold moon that night. Harold's absence was not noticeable until the fuzz wore off their brains, and his nearest neighbors woke to something truly astonishing.

The hedges around Harold's cottage were full of spider webs and gnawing bugs, the leaves blackened and brittle. The beautiful flower gardens surrounding his tiny plot, were overgrown with noxious weeds, shoots of thorny vines chocking the stems of the once graceful roses. The stream at the back of his cottage had been transformed into brown sludge, festering with blow flies and garbage.

Alarmed by these horrid changes of a single night, the neighbors poked their heads into the front door of the cottage. The old woman, pushed to the front of the inquisitive group, being the only one to squeeze through and enter.

"I erd queer chantin' en moanin' like," she said to the knot of curious faces that morning, and again to me later.

"I erd it, loud en clear, as I were ta home ya see, bein' old en all. It went on, en on, till all night exploded by them drat fire works! I took a peek out me window, 'en I seen wee 'arold Pickery! Holding ta arm of a beautiful young lass, en she leadin' 'im inta Little Shire Woods, across ta way."

When questioned by me about hearing any conversation between the missing villager and the young lady, I swear the old woman's eyes took on an eerie light.

"Well, ta lass sed, "Yer time 'ere is up 'arold. Three hundred tis enough."

I conclude this report by mentioning the little cottage occupied by Harold Pickery, suddenly vanished from sight, the very evening I as trying to investigate. I was bent down at its threshold, my hand extended to push in the front door, when a low chanting could be heard from within. The language was foreign to me, but as I readied to confront the intruder, the small cottage disappeared from before my eyes.

I ran through the garden next door, to the old women's cottage, only to find she too had vanished. The closest neighbor swore he'd seen her heading toward Little Shire Woods with a small sack on her bent back.

I'll conclude my report with this witness's last words to me.

"When I called out ta 'er, sir, she said, 'er time was up 'ere! Can't tink what she meant. Anyway, 'appy new year ta ye sir, 'n hope yer own time runs long en free!"

Deadly Grits: A Dystopian Diner

The silver diner sat like a fabulous jewel in the surrounding ring of darkness. The sound of dry rocky dirt was magnified as it crunched under my boots, in the great void of endless night. I was lost, and knew I'd never find my way off as long as the deep canyon walls held me captive. I laughed cynically to myself, when the delusion of hope flared in me, seeing something other than rocks and death. Hope that I'd be rescued before I turned into just another desiccated creature lying on the scorched ground.

I'd gone off the grid along with my companion for ten years, long before the grid ceased to exist. If it wasn't love, it was the closest thing to it, and our commitment to one another was unique in my experience among my human peers. That's why we fled what was left of so-called society. I rejected the confines of their prohibitions and backward thinking, and we lost ourselves among the rocks and sand, the lava flows, frozen for millennia upon the face of the mountain we made home.

Our rough, though peaceful existence, ended when Champ was swept away in one of the fierce storms known to deluge the area as suddenly as they appeared. The gullies become fast moving rivers through the dessert landscape, the waters carving out new paths in a headlong rush. Champ never had a chance to escape and I couldn't find him for two days. He was wrapped partially around a boulder of lava that looked like a chunk of a meteorite. His arms jutting out from his sides as if trying to swim in the killing cross-current of gushing waters. When I prized him loose, I knew I could never repair the damage done to his systems. What was left of his wiring was ripped out of his chest and coated with the fast-drying sediment. One of his legs had been torn off in his passage over the sharp lava rockface, and I didn't bother to search because my tools were not sophisticated enough to reattach it. I'd seen vultures circling overhead, leading me to his mangled body. As I got closer, I saw even the vultures rejected the pile of metal Champ was reduced to. It hit home like a Planet Jumper's laser; I was alone.

This state of isolation was not new to me, not since the world imploded, withering into a greenish-black ball in the heavens, where once it was the blue gem of the firmament. The heavy cost of a ruthless, continuing war on the environment led by the multi-national conglomerates, contributed exponentially to the poisoning of the body of the planet. The oceans and waters pumping life into the earth were poisoned, the air turned into a miasma of gases and particles. This was followed quickly by whole countries, cultures, civilization itself, unravelling, until the face of humankind was nearly obliterated upon their home planet.

I went back after the cataclysm overtook life, visiting what was left of the university campus where I was a professor, before learning became irrelevant. Nothing but empty classrooms, overtaken by rudimentary vestiges of nature. Instead of looking out at the eager doctorial students in the Advanced Robotics Engineering class I taught, I saw prickly vines wrapped around chairs, with seats and desks filled with dirt blowing in from broken windows and cracked walls. A respected university for over two-hundred years, its beautiful grounds were filled with the detritus of war, famine, plague and every other Biblical curse found in that once famous book.

I stayed on the campus for a year, living in a room in a partially standing dorm. I took that time to scour the Robotics lab and finish my work on engineering a perfect, human-like robot. Why not? All my friends and family were dead or dying in craters on the pox-marked earth.

Some likely survived by joining the roving gangs of The Righteous Few, punishing any they believed created this

Armageddon. That meant anyone found teaching ideas conflicting with their own. They hated science because they feared it, like early men feared the lightening that lit their caves. The Few, ironically, rounded up the many. Every man and woman, every student advocate of learning and understanding the heavens, and they sent them to a hell many of them didn't believe in. I escaped by hiding among the most ruined buildings, and when they left off their hunts, escaped to this mountain of rock, waiting for the final curtain to fall on earth.

Champ was with me when I ran, leaving the university rotting like a corpse behind me. When he was destroyed, I began to search for the wilderness, spread out like a torn blanket, in every direction. That's when I saw the bolt of light, a cloudy gleam of smoky stars off a metal surface.

I was starving and cold, the vast night of the scorched land had sucked me dry of every ounce of energy. I felt devoid of the innate will to survive, but as a scientist my curiosity pushed me forward to investigate the unknown. Did my eyes deceive me?

I approached the curved, aluminum sided diner with caution, having learned several painful lessons about traps set by The Righteous Few. They were nothing, if not cunning. They nearly snared me in the university cafeteria once, where I scavenged the vendor food, left open for the taking. I began to reach into the shelves for snack bars, but instead used a ruler to prod them out onto the floor. When the wood touched the third bar, a sharp blade shot out of the side of the machine, slicing the ruler in two. I was able to disarm the innocent looking machine and foil their plan to collect hands from unsuspecting survivors.

The moon, like the stars, was nearly lost under a layer of clouds filled with ash from the constant fires consuming the husks of long dead trees and foliage, bodies. Like a single-minded beast, enriched by this fuel, the unchecked flames devoured anything that stood, stuffing its red maw.

In this Stygian night, I crept toward the diner. The lights from inside spilled into the darkness holding its gleaming body. As I got closer, I saw a sign hanging on the door, WE NEVER CLOSE! I backed away while keeping it in sight, scrunching under a nearby outcropping of granite, staying in shadow while studying the solitary form.

I tried to weigh the empirical evidence before moving closer. First, it looked brand new, resembling a bloated oblong balloon. Then, there was the light. Though only a dull glow came from inside, the view into the interior was obscured by heavy condensation on the windows. That moisture alone was enough to have me licking my lips. Lastly, the sign posted on the door was farfetched, indicating a never-ending cornucopia of food inside, and that wasn't remotely possible in a land barren of all growing life. Wasn't this one of mankind's hardest lessons...where there is no forest, no clean water, no fertile earth, there is no food?

In the end, curiosity and hunger muscled out the logical response that I was probably walking into a trap. I scooted out from under the granite shelf, moving toward the diner, I approached from the side, hoping to see through a patch of glass before committing to entering. Crouching under the window, I raised up enough to peer over the sill. The moisture was not as thick here, further away from the hot kitchen I assumed, and I began to scan the interior.

The table on the other side of my glass periscope, was empty, and so were the other booths. There were three male patrons, sitting at the counter on those old-fashioned bar stools that always looked too small for anyone's butt, covered in well-worn black leather. The floor of the diner had a pattern of black and white linoleum squares, the long counter was a freckled white Formica; the same material that was the rage over a few centuries ago. None of that was overly alarming; diners were supposed to bring feelings of nostalgia to their patrons. There was something stiff and unnatural about these customers though, something that raised the hackles on my neck. I read the *Specials for the Day* written in a neat cursive on a chalkboard: *Three eggs & Skirt Steak with Lou's Deadly Grits.*

Directly across from the counter was Lou's kitchen. Occasionally, small clouds of smoke drifted out of the open window between the stove and a ledge where prepared dishes were set to be picked up by the waitress. I had a good look at her as she stepped out of the kitchen with a full coffee pot, and began refilling mugs set in front of her only customers. A short, heavy-set woman, she might have been close to fifty. Her washed-out complexion was exaggerated under the dull lighting, as it deepened the blueish circles under her heavily made-up eyes making her appear unhealthy.

I suddenly became conscious of a rich, meaty aroma, mingling with the heavy air around me. My mouth began to water. I could almost hear the fat from a steak sizzling and snapping on the grill. Keeping low, I moved around to the front of the diner desperate to see if this was another sick devise of the Righteous Few to lure survivors to their cult, or to their death.

The waitress was nowhere to be seen, but now I saw all three men had huge plates in front of them, thick slabs of steaks dripping juices onto the counter where they hung over the sides. One of the men shifted on the stool and I saw a pile of bright yellow scrambled eggs besides a steaming scoop of cream-colored grits on the plate. It was too much for me. I had to eat and I'd convert to any religion, follow any phony patriotic mumbo jumbo, if it meant I could eat and survive.

I stood up, adjusting my torn jacket, smacked futilely at the dust on my pants and reached for the door. With my catastrophic needs fueling my actions, I jerked the door out of its frame, watching a thick stream of corroded metal disintegrate even as it fell. The glass shattered into a million yellowed shards. I froze in shock, until I felt the heat from inside the diner hit me full in the face. My eyes felt seared, automatically squeezing shut, while tears streamed uncontrollably from them. When I reached up to wipe at them, my hand came away with parchment like layers of skin, blackened like marshmallows over a campfire. A primordial scream filled my head, so intense, I fell to my knees, covering what was left of my charred ears. The scream went on and on until I felt myself being lifted under both my arms. Smoke swirled around me as if I was a candle, just snuffed out. My eyes were still screwed shut, and I knew I dared not open them to see what was happening. It would make it too real.

I felt myself being lowered onto one of the round stools at the counter. Dare I look? My face! No, I chose to remain blind to this reality.

"Evening, sir. Can I get you some coffee while Lou makes your dinner?"

My eyes opened like clam shells, ready to snap shut at the least bit of provocation. The waitress was looking patiently at me, a smile drawn in red lipstick on her shriveled mouth. Without answering her, I turned to the men on either side, seeing their featureless faces under the dim lights. My breath caught in my heaving chest as I caught a glimpse of myself in the glass partition that was now closed between the kitchen and the counter. My face appeared to be melting, sliding down the boney structure that formed my brow, cheeks, jaw. I felt oddly calm, watching a blank sheet of skin forming over what were once my blue eyes and prominent nose, my mouth sealed forever. There was no confusion at what I saw. Life without my face, living on a dying planet, seemed acceptable.

"Am I in heaven or hell?" I thought.

Somehow, the waitress could hear my panicked thoughts. And somehow, I saw her, her pencil at the ready to get my order.

"Well, now, that is the question, isn't it? Let's just say, it's of your own making, so whatever it is, you've yourself to look to for blame or credit. The cook won't take back your order if it's not to your liking, but he will try to make it more palatable with some good spices, and his secret ingredients, from time to time. Just no predicting how it will all mix together until you've tried it."

I slid off the stool, marveling I was able to see clearly without eyes, moving away from the counter to the entrance.

"I don't need heaven or hell right now. If this is my world, let me get on with living in it."

No one stopped me, or even called after me, as I walked out of the dim glow into whatever waited for me in life, I still felt worth living.

The Boy in the Basket:
A Tale of Redemption

"If yer gonna keep up dat caterwauling', yer gonna bring ta whole village down 'ere, boy!"

The small child lay on his side, his thin legs drawn up tightly to his heaving chest, while his arms protected his small head. Without warning the man's foot was swept out and kicked into his bony, rounded back.

"Now ye got sumptin' ta screech over!"

The boy Samuel, was a foundling, placed with the Clappers by their Minister, Thomas Pratter. He saw them at church on major feast days, unaccompanied by any children, though they were both of childbearing age. The foundling, he thought, might bring joy into what appeared to him, and the other villagers, to be a bleak home indeed. The day he showed up with the wicker basket that had been secreted beneath a church pew, only the missus was about the small croft to greet him.

"Tis a fine babe ye bring us master Pratter, but I'll not be takin' it in if ye please."

"But mistress Clapper, ye have none of yer own, and this un is but a wee babe, nary a day old he is!"

"Aye, and a sweeter babe I've never clapped me eyes upon, but…it's the mister…he'd none of it fer sure."

The preacher waited uncomfortably, shifting his rather substantial bulk on a hard chair, his elbows resting upon a rough oak table. He noted that the woman never left-off staring at the infant, her eyes, crinkling at the corners, making the dark circles under them almost vanish as she studied him closely. He smiled to himself, hearing the babe gurgle in delight when mistress Clapper ran a roughened finger across his tummy.

The husband finally showed up after spending another long day down in the dark, damp coal mine where he made a paltry living. His face was covered in black dust where it wasn't streaked in sweat ran down his cheeks. Every footstep shook off more of the ubiquitous coal trace, while he stepped across the swept floorboards leaving black footprints in his wake.

"What's dis then?" he demanded as he entered the tiny cottage, seeing his wife and the minister sitting at the rickety table, a large wicker basket between them. Pratter knew Clapper's reputation as quick tempered, and excessively jealous of any attention his plain wife might garner from other men.

"I am here ta bless yer home with a precious gift, Clapper!" the minister said with heartfelt conviction.

"Aye? En what be dis fine gift?"

"Tis a beautiful boy child!" Pratter answered with grave assurance.

With a grand gesture, he threw back the frayed, but clean blanket covering the baby in his wicker bed. "Jes as Baby Jesus would ha' been upon 'is birthing day!"

Clapper stomped over to the table, staring into the depths of the crudely woven carrier.

"A boy ye say?"

The minister and the woman both took heart with a response that wasn't composed of fiery swearing and pugnacious threats. Also, they noted how Clapper began to study the little chap, touching his fingers and counting toes, his mouth silently mouthing the numbers.

"I reckon e'll do. Do ye leave some milk ta feed da ting then?"

Pratter said he'd arranged for one of the new mothers from the village to bring her own mother's milk daily.

"The missus ken feed ta little one from a bottle she'll leave, jes' stopping it wit a clean rag fer 'im ta suck at."

The boy was subsequently named Samuel by his adoptive mother, when she tired of hearing him referred to as 'da ting from da basket.' Like most children, he did bring joy, but only to his mother. Clapper made it clear over the ensuing years, that the boy was a lowly foundling, unwanted, and unloved; at least by him. He railed against what he saw as demon possession; having witnessed how the boy would go perfectly still, no matter the circumstances of his activity, and his eyes looked like a dead man peered out of them.

"Ta' boy's been taken by dark uns, I tell ye," he would mumble into his tanker at the local pub, to anyone willing to hear his ravings.

Samuel was ten years and six months, when his hard father told him at their meager meal one evening, that the following morning he'd be accompanying him into the mines. His mother sucked in her breath.

"Time ye got yer scrawny arse at sum kinda work, boy. Tomorrow, we leave at first light. I warn ye ta be up, unless ye want an ear boxin'!"

The other miners were dumbfounded when the small boy stepped out from behind his father's back. He was wearing the only coat his mother could secure for him from among her neighbors. It was two sizes too large, and she'd rolled the sleeves several times around his thin arms. A moth-eaten scarf was fastened round his neck, lost inside the large coat, making it harder for him to turn his head.

Going down in the rickety bucket with his father and a few others, Samuel squeezed his eyes shut when he felt the familiar signs; he was going to have another vision. Something so remarkable, that he stood transfixed when the basket bumped hard to a stop. He opened his eyes and tugged on his father's sleeve.

"Da," he said in an urgent whisper. "I tink sometin' bad is gonna 'appen down 'ere. I seen it when we was in ta basket cumin down."

Clapper gave his head a shake, looking at the closet men, and saying his boy was a strange one. When the others filed into the wide, dark hole they were working, he turned to the boy and gave him a hard rap on the ear with the flat of his hand.

"Don't be spoutin' yer weird tales down 'ere! Mind me now! Bad 'nuff ye speak of future seein' to yer ma!"

They worked for five hours in the gritty air, with only short breaks for a drink of water. Samuel was picking up chunks of rock strewn across the tunnel floor, for the narrow wheelbarrow he pushed. The constant tapping sounds of picks gouging out the black walls stopped his ears to all else. Suddenly, in his unique state of isolation, he lurched-up from his hunched position, his arms flung out like a marionette on strings.

He stood as frozen as the church bell that hadn't rung in fifty years. This time his vision was intensely clear. He saw the men throwing down their picks, scrambling over tools and debris as they ran for the lift basket. There were shouted warnings to the other miners, and all were shoved into the basket, except his father.

The boy snapped out of his trance as quickly as he fell into it. When his father wasn't looking, Samuel dropped his shovel among the lumps of dirt and coal, brushed his scarf over his wet face to clear his eyes, and hurried through the snaking shaft to the front, to locate the foreman.

"I been 'earin sum loud creaks down in ta' hole, sir. I guessed best ta tell ye," he said in his high, sweet voice.

Just then, there was a shudder under their feet, and a loud sigh of alarm from the foreman's helper. The foreman made straight for the deeper part of the black hole, screaming out his warning and using a hand bell to punctuate his shouts. A groan of wood under too much pressure, and the sound of earth sifting through growing gaps in the tunnel ceiling, brought the miners running toward the basket; their only lifeline. All but his father.

"Get ye aboard Sammy" screamed the foreman over the yells of the fleeing miners.

"I need ta find me da," he said firmly, immediately running back into the deeper parts of the tunnel.

Dirt was coming down in larger clumps now, and the sound of cracking wooden support beams became like an underground symphony. His father was lying under a support brace that must have given way early on. His eyes were rolling around in his head, and there was blood wetting his shirt where the heavy timber crushed him. This too was seen when Samuel peered through the shadows surrounding this event.

Without speaking a word, the boy reached down and lifted the impossible weight of wood off Clapper, scooping a thin arm under him, helping to lift him to his feet. Clapper moaned, his eyes squeezed tightly against the gnawing, radiating pain of broken ribs and deep wounds.

The basket was gone when they got to the front, and the tunnel was reclaiming itself just behind them. Clapper gave a scream of pain, sinking to his knees. The boy held his hands over his bent body. Out of the darkness, a piercing light sprang up around the fallen man, as the young boy lifted them both into the twilight of the fading day.

None saw this miracle; none would have believed had they seen. All were busy in groups of family and villagers, coming to the rescue at the warning sounds of the earth's deep rumble.

When Clapper opened his eyes several days later, it was as if he had reverted to infancy. He began to mewl like a kitten, drool spattering his chin. The fearful experience had turned him into a dumb-struck child. His legs were badly injured and he could no longer walk. His wife spoon fed him his small meals, this being his only activity. Mostly, he stared off into space; occasionally a few babbled words erupted like urgent messages from his mouth.

Because he had been responsible for saving all the miners from the mine cave-in, Samuel was rewarded with a stipend from the village elders until he reached the age of eighteen, when he could then support his mother and invalid father.

Samuel never spoke of his visions again to his mother, and she assumed they were only fancies of childhood. But as he grew older, he would sit with the muttering crippled father and whisper visions of healing his broken body.

"All that is needed da, is a single, kind word from you. But tis not to be now, is it?" The silence was as crushing as heavy timber.

Samuel never had to enter the mines again. He grew in wealth and knowledge over a span of a few short years.

"Tis like a miracle, 'ow dat boy has made 'is way! First a foundling; now, a rich man," the much-aged Minister, Mr. Pratter was heard telling a few friends over a pint.

"Aye, en 'im jest a cast-off in a basket!" added one of his drinking mates.

Magic Waters: Another Tall tale

"Ah, yes. Ye 'n me 'ave survived yet anutter winter."

Or so thought the sheep herder, as he poked at the well-thawed ground with his staff, following the placid, dull-witted mob. They were making their way out of the flimsy pen enclosure where he'd been counting faces and looking for any signs of illness among them. He knew his sheep better than he would his own children, if he'd had any children. He recognized the oldest to the youngest, and grieved as deeply as a father, at the demise of any of his woolly charges.

It had been a particularly dreary and difficult winter, with four wooly head of his precious herd, falling victim to starving predators, or frozen stiff in the frigid blasts from the north seas. His cozy cottage offered his only solace in the cruel winters that visited his Emerald Isle.

"Cum along now me dears. There be a few tender tufts o' grasses, waiting fer ye up ahead."

This time of year, when the sun struggled to brighten the sky earlier, the world around him seemed to cling stubbornly to the scraps of night hidden in the shadows. The old man trudged in silence, with only the occasional word of encouragement to his flock, and an answering bleat of acknowledgement. With the melting of the snow from the earth, and the subsequent releasing of fresh fodder for his sheep, he prodded them after an unhurried grazing time, toward a sweet water stream nearby.

He never used this as a watering hole before, but at the urging of his neighbor, Jack O'Rourke, and given clear directions by the man, he now guided his small band toward its burbling and welcoming fresh scent.

He counted off his woolly heard, and then by habit, recounted while they dipped their thick heads close to the water. He murmured to himself, scratching at his winter's beard when he found there was one more than his last accounting. Shaking his own shaggy head, the shepherd went among the creatures standing knee deep in the cold, fast moving waters. He touched each one with the flat of his hand, calling out the number as a fail-safe for memory.

"Why, how ken it be?" he asked the dumb beasts.

"Ye, there!" he called as he splashed toward a face he didn't recollect.

"Ye 'ave a strange look ta me old eyes. Let's 'ave a better look at ye!"

He grabbed a fist-full of thick, coarse hair, tugging the unknown beast out of the chilly water. He was about to begin a closer study of the animal, when a sudden chorus of bleating filled the air. Looking over at his tiny herd, he stood with a stunned expression as their numbers had increased two-fold. Where once stood ten lapping at the waters, now twenty looked back at him making a ruckus as if he were a wolf. He blinked and two more appeared on the fringes of the pond.

He sucked in his breath whispering, "Tis ta work o' woodland elves, it tis!" his rheumy eyes, wide with amazement.

He stood and marveled as the herd continued to increase until the small watering hole was covered in bobbing white heads. As far as the old man could see, which wasn't very far since he was unquestionably near-sighted, the face of the water was covered in matted, winter weary sheep. This was surely a prank by the mischievous elves known for such shenanigans, but this huge mob of sheep presented a temptation hard to resist. Besides, he no longer could pick out those sheep that were his, from the interlopers, because each of his had an exact twin in every respect.

A panic fell upon the simple man. He lost his only herding dog two years past, and it fell to him alone to keep track of the once tiny group. How was he to round up this larger herd, let alone drive them back to his meager croft, with its small rickety pen? No sooner had he cleared that thought from his mind, then he was struck with another. He spoke his plan out loud as if to give it credibility.

"The new neighbor, what tol' me o' this place...I'll go ta him fer help in roundin' up ta lot o' em!"

With the challenge resolved to his liking, the old man set off at his slow trot. He'd kept hold of the one sheep who had set off the whole investigation. He dragged him along the narrow path, leading away from the crowded pond to the new farmer's cottage.

He banged hard upon the much-weathered wood door, its hinges groaning with the rough treatment. After several minutes of pounding this way, the old man was turning to leave, certain the new man was off to tend his fields. Before he could take another step, he was thrown onto the ground by a mighty shove.

He sat stunned, looking up at a short, plumpish man dressed in greens and browns, and wearing a cap adorned with feathers the same color as his flaming red hair.

"O lordy me! Tis ta elf 'is own self!" the shepherd said in a choked whisper.

"I be tinkin' ye need a good thrashin' ol' shepherd! Dragn' me along like a sack o' old goat turd!"

"Sir," said the old man to the newly revealed elf.

"I be dreadful sorry! I were tinkin' ye was no morn' a black faced sheep."

The elf laughed at this description, and thinking it would be amusing, cast a spell over the old man.

Later, when Jack O'Rourke returned home from his many farm chores, he found two black-faced sheep munching in the stiff grasses of his front yard; as if waiting there for his return.

"What's afoot 'ere?" he asked the two dull witted sheep, with the usual response from them.

"Baa, baa."

"Tis a blessin' from ta woodland elf I 'spect, fer me kindness ta the old shepherd. Well, me boys, ye look ta be identical twins, but I ken tell ye apart by eating one o ye! It's been sech a long, 'ard winter...."

His last words drifted off as he led his new sheep to the barn.

Steaming Up the Windows

The windows were fogged over with the moisture of their heavy panting. She could no longer see out into the gathering shadows and felt a tingle of claustrophobia unless she shut her eyes. It was close in the car, already overstuffed with a backpack, sleeping bag, books, and whatever else he deemed too important to leave in his apartment.

After dating him for a few months, she was getting used to his rather eccentric behavior. She accused him once of living in the tiny electric car. He purchased it at the beginning of their freshman year at Community, where they met. He blew off her comment about the cost, saying it was his "duty to try to heal the Great Madonna, whatever that meant. He was always making statements that sounded like they'd lifted off an ad for donations to Green Peace. She admired his dedication to an altruistic cause but had lingering doubts about its sincerity. Reflecting on all the money he paid for the tiny, environment friendly vehicle, she couldn't help but factor in how that amount could have paid for her next two semesters and more.

She began to get a little drowsy with all the closeness of the car and the way he was nearly absorbing her with his body. He'd pressed her back against her seat, his arms on either side of her head, supporting himself as he kissed her deeply. She pushed him back so she could take a breath. He smiled down at her, their faces only inches apart.

Suddenly, he was hungrily devouring her slightly parted lips, his tongue probing her mouth. She couldn't move if she wanted. He had both of her arms in his strong hands and held them down to her side. Her feeling of claustrophobia was replaced in an intuitive flash by a new feeling; fear.

His smile never faltered as the long incisors peeked through his sensual lips. He surely read the alarm in the depths of her wide blue eyes. He leaned back toward her now, his tongue running down the soft skin of her cheek and curving around the slim stem of her neck. The last thing she heard him say would be the last thing she'd hear anyone say.

"Delicious, and I'm so hungry! But don't worry, I won't waste a drop and this meal is fully organic!"

She Remembers Free Love

Loretta believed that her days as a free spirit were over. Gone like her waist-length hair, long gypsy skirts and the 'free love' she randomly enjoyed in her turn on-tune-out days. Now, there was only the echoes of the music, and a grown daughter to remind her of that once, vibrant interlude of her life.

She finished college at a small Liberal Arts school, known for its high academic standards and very conservative environment. She still had remnants of her free-spirited self, and partnered with her sharp tongue, she often entered into heated discussions with the less- enlightened, especially her stodgy Professors. Once, while arguing with the rather handsome professor of *Religion and Modern Man*, she was gesturing to emphasize her points. Out of the literal blue, a wet plop of bird poop dropped on her open hand. Mortified and surprised at the heavenly intervention, she looked over at the now smiling professor who had removed his handkerchief and began wiping off the offending excrement.

"Guess you've been told off!" he said with a dimpled smile.

These memories poked around in her head, while she lay in bed trying to fall asleep. She was lying beside that same handsome professor who not only removed the gift of a passing bird that day but managed to wipe away the false bravado of her youth and replace it with a forever kind of love. They married after she graduated; her life settling into a harmonious routine of perfect partnership. She transformed herself into a domestic diva and put away her deep thoughts for diapers and the kind of fulfillment she never thought possible.

Twenty years later, she lay upon their bed, watching the shadows move around the room in response to the shifting moon.

"Wake up darling. The moon is almost fully risen," she whispered gently in his slightly tufted ear. She knew she was safe from his murderous transformation since she and their daughter wore the scent of his pack.

He had been turned while they were on a camping trip in Main, a kind of last fling for them to enjoy total freedom. They swam naked in a small hidden pool screened by heavy green woodlands. They ate freshly caught Blue-Gill and Sun Fish and the occasional snared rabbit and stained their fingers and tongues on sweet wild berries. They made love often, spreading their blankets over spongy grasses. It was idyllic, until the stranger came one night to their campfire.

There was a haze clinging to the face of a moody looking moon as night closed in but would be full of yellow glory by midnight. At least, this is what the stranger told them.

"You both may want to seek shelter tonight," he warned. "There could be some wild animals stirred to move about with such a moon."

He left the warm glow of their fire soon after. They began to take advantage of their solitude and the warm night, shedding their clothes like Adam and Eve in the Garden. They enjoyed the brilliance of the full moon hanging directly overhead, watching as their intertwined bodies were wrapped inside its creamy touch. The sound of something crashing through the nearby woods interrupted the young man's momentum toward that sublime moment. Loretta was equally put off her rhythm as they both held their breath and listened. The man pushed up onto his elbows and that's when he was taken.

The beast was covered in dark fur, but that was all she mentally registered as it swept her lover off of her steaming body. Loretta had no breath to scream. No thought to run. She was rigid with shock. The young professor was gone until sunrise, and Loretta knew his fate, and hers, was sealed.

All these years later, they lived like other families, except for two slight differences. Loretta and their daughter always wore a slight musky covered over in perfumes as much as possible, and the professor was always locked away in his padded room, secured by silver chains to its walls. Not that difficult really. But Loretta sometimes longed for the simpler days of free love and arguing about God's existence, before finding one of His Demons!

The Halloween Scarecrow Murders

"And whatever you do, Bart, don't make the Scarecrow mad, alright?"

Bart and Alec were both nine, and Alec's big brother Stevie, was giving him yet another annoying order. Bart thought he was being his usual bossy self, trying to tell people what to do all the time, but he bobbed his head in agreement so he wouldn't miss out on the night's fun. This was to be his first time to "Trick or Treat" without his mom whispering, "Say thank you," every time some neighbors put a Whistle Pop in his bag...he hated those things!

Tracy Hamilton had given Bart permission to go out on Halloween night with his best friend and his older brother, when her bad cold turned into bronchitis. She was exhausted from the deep cough that left her body feeling like she'd been hit by a bus after running a marathon. Because Tracy was a single mom, she decided to reach out to Stevie's mom to arrange for the boys to Trick or Treat together around their quiet neighborhood.

"There's only our development Tracy, and a few farms nearby, so they'll be fine. Stevie is almost twelve now and knows the rules of keeping together. Oh, and I've given both my kids flashlights, so you might want little Bart to have one too."

After struggling to get her son dressed as a pirate, she handed him his treat bag, the usual old pillowcase. Tracy watched apprehensively, as Bart stepped out of the small hallo of porch light, into the darkness of a country night.

"Stevie, when are we going to see the "Sacred Scarecrow God"? Alec asked his older brother. There was a small quiver n his voice, but the older boy didn't notice.

The brothers were both dressed as Zombies, their favorite scary creatures. Stevie was thinking he was getting too old to be out Trick or Treating, but figured he'd do it one last year. Besides, the little guys needed his help to show them the way to get more stuff.

"We can't go to the old Cranker farm until we have enough to offer to the Scarecrow God! If we don't please him, he'll just take one of us, and make himself another servant."

They went to every house with a light on, to beg for candy. Bart's pillowcase was heavy, dragging slightly over the ground by the time they finally approached the long-deserted Cranker farm. It was like a smudge against the clouds scudding across the inky night sky. The trees closely hugged the two stories its wooden siding looking as if it was covered in old scabs from the peeling paint. Branches scratched menacingly against the few windowpanes of the second floor still unbroken by vandals or the wild storms that roared through the town occasionally.

Bart didn't like the looks of the decrepit old farmhouse but didn't want to admit he was afraid to go closer.

Instead, he quietly announced to their leader, "I have enough stuff, Stevie. Let's just see the Scarecrow next year."

"We want to go back, Stevie 'cause we got just enough candy for ourselves and it's cold out here," Alec added, quick to back-up his friend's suggestion.

"What a little whiner you are, Alec. You begged me to let you guys see the Sacred Scarecrow King, and now you're just gonna' punk out on me!"

The two young friends gave each other sideways glances. While they were shoulder to shoulder, they were barely able to see one another in the heavy fog that was settling over the farmhouse and the barren fields surrounding it. They shrugged their shoulders at one another in a tentative consent to continue.

"OK guys. Now we have to walk through this stupid corn field and keep going till we see the old silo. He'll be standing in near there somewhere. We gotta be as quiet as ghosts so he won't get upset with us disturbing his sleep."

"How do you know he'll be asleep?" asked Bart, turning toward the direction of Alex's voice and vague shape.

"Because, knucklehead, scarecrows always sleep until the noise of the birds wakes 'em up. That's when they scare 'em away from the corn and stuff. Geesh, you guys are dummies."

They entered the stubble of the long past, harvested field, each boy hauling their bags of candy treats over narrow shoulders. They skirted the brooding shape of the farmhouse, heading out toward the center of the field where the promised the Scarecrow King would be standing watch. Stevie raised his free hand at the stop signal. The younger boys collided with each other with the sudden command that neither had seen in the thickening mist.

"Up ahead...he's waiting for us to drop our gifts for..."

Bart and Alec only saw a blur of movement within the fog, as Alec suddenly became airborne, sweeping like a scythe across the empty rows as he gripped his candy bag. At first, he was totally silent, speechless with the shock of being hoisted bodily into the air. Then, it was too late to scream. His head was quickly detached by two straw arms jutting out of a tattered jacket. The headless body dropped like a felled tree to the stubble below.

Bart and Alec's brother were electrified into moving, and screaming like banshees, high pitched squeals of terror. They gave voice to their horror, but they couldn't give enough power to their legs. They stood rooted like the old farmhouse inside the moon-painted fog. Stevie was the first to gain control over his limbs, but just as he turned to run back to the road, the form of a headless scarecrow came bounding after him.

Bart would never forget the bloodcurdling screams as the straw man tore him limb from limb. He didn't actually see the murders of his friend Alec and his brother Stevie, because the fog was thickest there in the middle of the field, but he knew, without a doubt, they were victims of the Sacred Scarecrow God.

As the attack on Stevie went on, Bart took off like a rabbit in sudden flight; his short legs pumping like pistons, his treat bag lost among the rotted corn husks. He ran until the stitch in his side made him slow to a jog. The porch light was on at his back door, inspiring him to gulp some air and run again.

Just as he reached the cement step, he heard something behind him… something crinkled like stiff straw being dragged across the stones of the driveway. He frantically looked over his shoulder, trying to peer through the swirling mist. The Sacred Scarecrow God stepped out of the fog, an apparition holding a pillowcase under a tufted arm.

"I thought you would want your Treats" said old man Cranker.

Stepping out from behind the old man wearing coveralls and an old jacket, were his friend Alec and his brother. They all started laughing, the old man wheezing and coughing and bent over, slapping his side with tears running down his white stubbled cheeks.

The backdoor opened and Bart's mother stepped onto the porch. The shallow glow from the small side light, struggled in the clinging mist of fog, but it was enough to show the fangs and blood dripping off them. Tracy Hamilton's eyes were bright red and her hair, normally a neat blond ponytail was matted with blood and what looked like freshly butcher meat. It dripped unnoticed by her down the front of her prime dress and apron.

"You fellas want to come inside for a bite? Just made a fresh batch of meat pies."

The two boys and the old coot took off running pell-mell down the driveway. The mom and her son could hear their screams piercing the thick fog like eerie messages from the long dead.

"Mom, this was the best Halloween ever," Bart said smiling at his mother as she leaned down for his kiss.

"Glad you had fun sweetie, but your friends and that old fella are sure skittish." She said as she slipped off the wig and wiped off the fake blood with her apron.

Francesca Quarto

Blood of My Blood

She screamed like a banshee; caught in the trap I so carefully laid for her. The high piercing wail of agony and frustration ran through my ears like shards of shifting glass. I had to cover them before my eardrums burst. The suddenness of the quiet return warned me that she was either dead, which was unlikely, or she was working on the escape plan used again and again, over the past twenty-four hours. The same twenty-four-hour day I already lived through, to the same point in time, every time, without a minutia of difference. This meant I would be dead in another three minutes.

My throat would be slashed open, and my limbs decorated with my own eviscerated body contents. Not a thing a mortal should have to endure, let alone relive, over and over in some kind of evil time loop. We just don't have the stomach for it, unless you can count the gut spilling, I was about to experience.

I waited for the inevitable massacre. I felt the same terror and frailty, as I was about to face my termination, yet again, at the hands of Beatitude La Pierre. I would again witness my own gruesome slaughter by the beautiful Bloody Beady, as she was known to the exclusive club of mercs hunting her.

I usually call her "Bloody goddamn Beady"! She had a bounty on her lovely golden head, of one hundred thousand sutans. Enough to buy my own stellar city or roam the universe until I was several more centuries older.

The High Order of Paranormal Policing, had every available agent hunting for Beady. They were sent to every remote corner of the planet once Hopp had confirmation of a sighting.

Me, I'm what was romantically called a bounty hunter many cycles ago. In these times it's Demon Spawn-Interceptor. The label makes no difference. I'm a hunter and making a damn good living bringing in Hopp's most wanted, dead or alive. I admit, sometimes dead, because all the squawking and curses hurled at me and my progeny, tends to unsettle my temperate nature, causing an occasional overreaction. Not that I have any progeny, or even the potential for any, but it doesn't make hearing the threats about baby monsters appearing on my family tree any less worrying.

Being female of the species, I have a distinct advantage over the mostly male agents that go on a hunt. Their sole purpose is to subdue the demon spawn and haul in the evidence of their success in a garbage bag. Me, because I have a female's tender hardheartedness, I at least make an effort to capture the paranormal nightmare, so they can be studied by our docs.

Many of the demons we bring in, have already contaminated some of the mortal population with their attacks. There's no "Once bitten, twice smart" either. Once bitten you are dead meat on the roadside. And so, I wait once more to become roadkill for Bloody Beady.

This unending nightmare, began when I discovered she was holed up inside a caved in building, used in the Bleak Bygone for those stiff-winged flying machines, called air-O-planes. None of the other trackers would think to look for Bloody Beady here, because like all the others air-O-ports still dotting the planet, it has long been swallowed by the ever-encroaching jungle, and home to wild beasts. These ancient sites proved perfect breeding grounds for creatures mutating over hundreds of cycles, adapting to the pollution spewed unchecked into their breathable atmosphere. In our time, without interference from my own species, these jungle denizens, have grown into huge, and very lethal creatures.

Any fear I might have of the four-footed beasts was forgotten. I was certain Bloody Beady was using this over-run, crumbling structure as a perfect camouflage for her home base. From here, she could infiltrate the outside world of mortals, as easily as slipping out of her skin. Knowing where to find her was simple for me to puzzle out. I looked over the numerous maps distributed by the High Order to all hunters, and quickly discovered what they had overlooked. The past holds little interest to most mortals, unless they use the past to learn from. They are constantly looking ahead, trying to peer into an unpromising, uncertain future. I like to view the world in reverse, so I won't be caught in traps that had been successfully employed in the past. I learned from yesterday, so I can live today and maybe into tomorrow.

Sitting on the rusted, vegetation covered engine of one of the flying machines, I listened as the silence filled the space around me. I knew it was almost time to die again. This was becoming too repetitive by far, to continue. I caught the movement of the same huge beetle I'd seen over and over and had a eureka moment!

Jumping off my perch, I decided to interject one small thing into the continuous coil of actions and reactions. I reached into my backpack lying on the ground beside me. Instead of shooting the unarmed bug, as I'd been doing endlessly, I used the laser knife and made a quick pass over my thumb. It bled like a dark fountain because the cut was deep. Pressing around the wound, I made it bleed even more profusely, catching fat drops with my index finger, I drew the totem symbol of my clan on the bicep of my left arm, the quick movement of my hand sent sprays of droplets flying into the heavy air.

With the rush of frigid wind, like countless hundreds of times before in this damnable, endless web of time, Bloody Beady made her appearance. I stood in the same position she always found me, only now, the long incisor of the Saber Tooth Tiger was clearly drawn on my arm.

Beady lunged at my throat, teeth bared and sharpened to fine points. Before she could tear out my jugular, I whispered, "Blood of my blood!"

I could smell her fear as the circle of life in this moment was shattered. I raised the laser I held in my palm and shot a bolt into her chest. Pulling back, I watched as the hole spread and I could see her beating heart.

Our clan had protected a wealth of secrets over the eons, most relating to our lineage and powers. I knew there were family members who ranged the many galaxies, plundering other life forms in their lust for blood. We were, after all, Vampires.

My branch of the family tree had taken a sort of spiritual purge, ridding ourselves of the need for blood drinking from unfortunate innocents. Instead, we survived by seeking out a bounty hunter's bloodletting to quench our blood lust.

Bloody Beady was my distant Aunt on one of my clan's far-flung branches. She ruled an underground Vampire colony for centuries, in the conclave of Old Orleans. She had used its decrepit collection of burned-out buildings and hovels as her own fiefdom. All living creatures owed her blood, taken over endless years of torture during their servitude.

Surely incredible to her now, she was looking down at her throbbing, black heart; seemingly fascinated by its mechanical workings. I took this self-absorption as an opportunity to speak.

"You are mine now, dear Auntie, and since you know of our relationship, I will need to stop your tongue before it can divulge that truth to the High Order."

Her lovely blue eyes began to shed tears as fake as her silky skin transplants, but my laser spoke once more, and she no longer wept. As she dropped away from me, I saw dark marks like a tattoo on her right shoulder. I never noticed it before, but she fell too quickly for me to study it, and I was too excited with my success to think about it.

The bounty money was assuredly mine. I began to pick up my pack from the ground, when it disappeared into a mist that rose from the ground and quickly began to obscure everything around me. Out of the unnatural fog I heard the voice of Bloody Beady.

"Blood of my blood, are you ready to begin?"

As soon as this cycle ends, I must find my mistake. Something small and insignificant no doubt. The mark on her arm? But for now, I must prepare to die yet again, knowing I have inadvertently stretched the time loop by several painful minutes. Her golden head is leaning in through the mist I brought into this endless circle game and I can feel her teeth graze my throat. It won't take long…at least *this* part won't!

The Little Queen's Tale

"Beauty is *not* in the eye of the beholder!" Lucinda screamed. All the palace was awakened because she'd been screeching like a cornered alley cat for the past hour without letting up.

"Don't you dare quote such drivel! As if a ridiculous platitude could make me feel less pained!"

Lucinda was losing some of her caterwauling power, her prodigious chest heaving like twin mountains suffering quake tremors. Her mother, Pauletta, Dowager Queen, was doing her level best to quiet her daughter, the *Little Queen*, as all knew her behind the fatty slope of her back. Yes, there was the matter of the hump... a slight hill actually...an imperfection that would never be openly acknowledged in the polite society of the Little Queen's Court.

Among their monarch's entourage, there was a singularly odd man, rumored to be a Sorcerer, but hiding his dark magic behind the Jester's facade. Unfortunately, Lucinda overheard the Court Jester taking extreme liberties, naming the slight deformity that none other dared speak of, and including it in his newest limerick. Her attention was first captured by the jolly sounding recitation as he began:

"I'll prance like a ninny from the bloom of the sun, till the curtain of night crashes down. For crumbs from the table, I'll spin like a top, or juggle the apples my Lady has munched. I sing for

my supper, a tuppence to feed me, while I'll whirl like the devil's own clown. For the Little Queen's fancy, I'll stand on my head, until her broad back is un-hunched!"

"I shall not be mocked by my own Court, Jester! I'll have the Royal Guard cut out his offending tongue, string him up by his twiddling thumbs..." and so it went on, long into the graying of the day. Alas, the Little Queen wore herself out with all this emotional outpouring, finally taking to her bed to recoup her strength. Her exhausted Ladies hoped she would also recover her senses during her rest.

As she lay upon her downy bed, she thought better of removing the Jester's tongue, or hanging him by his thumbs. *Too cruel,* she thought dreamily. Her eyes drowsed shut and she dreamed of having a beautiful, straight back. No hump to ruin the line of her gowns, drawing unwelcome stares and whispered comments behind silk fans. In her deep slumber, she saw herself as free of the hunched-back and when she awoke, she made a vow.

"If the odious Jester is in truth a powerful Sorcerer, he will be made to repair my back, and I'll allow him to live."

With this resolve firmly planted, the Little Queen called the offending Jester into her presence, while she was still abed. He was covered in whip marks and filth from the dungeons, but his appearance was more remarkable still, when the Little Queen noted the large hump upon his narrow back.

"What manner of taunt is this?" she screamed, thinking he mocked her still.

"Look only to yourself, Majesty, and see the truest love I bear, that I would take your pain upon myself."

The Little Queen leapt from her bed, tossing the down-filled comforter to the floor. She ran to a large mirror and saw that the hump no longer marred the beauty of a truly voluptuous form.

She stood straight and perfect, beautiful in her own eyes. While she stared in wonderment, she heard a deep and growing wail of grief and sheer terror begin to rumble and roll like thunder through the castle keep.

"What's this then? What is amiss? Guards..."

But they too were screaming out in dismay and clutching at their faces and rubbing their eyes and moaning! Over and over the words flew like swords..."I can't see! I am blind! Oh, gods help me! I am stricken without sight!"

The entire Court was struck blind except for the Jester and the Little Queen. He was smiling slyly and she...well...she was screaming with fear and frustration.

The moral of this story? Be careful what you ask for from the Dark Jester!

The Only Road Home

She believed she was invincible. The goddess had given her that impression after all.

"Here, take this stone and you shall prevail" she had told her cunningly.

But goddesses have been known to manipulate the truth to suit their own ends. Was this to prove one of those times? Her life depended upon the answer.

Clutching the smooth gray rock, she stepped out of the shadows where she'd hidden, waiting for the moon to be lost beneath the storm-heavy clouds. She let the darkness engulf her like a wave, not moving so much as a flutter of eyelids. Dressed in the black robes of the Acolyte, its hood concealing the glossy mass of coppery red hair, she melted into the night.

A low rumble, like snow gathering into the teeth of an avalanche, began to ride the incessant winds. It grew louder, overwhelming all other senses until it filled her head. She fought the urge to reach up to cover her ears. Behind the churning sound came the thud and tramp of heavy footsteps. The weight they carried surely crushed the very earth beneath, marking it forever with its passage. The moon hung desolate and alone under its mask of inky thunder heads, waiting and watching just as she did.

The goddess had only relinquished the stone after she had proven herself the Acolyte of Merit; the one chosen for this delicate mission. Though she understood this was an undertaking from which she might never return, she believed it defined her very existence. She, and the others of her kind, named the *Original Sinners*, had been locked away in this bleak and dying world, for crimes committed by faceless, nameless ancestors. The Ancient's outrage was deemed so great by the gods, that any of their progeny would also suffer their fate. Of these, only a handful remained.

Late, in the blast of the red summer, she had become the last female. There were now only six of the *Original Sinners* left to roam the barren wastes of their dark prison world. The others, all madmen without conscience or pride, stalked her like the sexual prey they viewed her to be. The goddess only intervened because she was bored watching the same game of hide and seek, day after night.

Her instructions to the girl were easy enough, "Follow the path that shall be revealed to you by the stone's light."

She was gripping the hard edges of her gift, until they pressed painfully into her palm. She wondered how its dull surface could ever show the way to the only road home, back to a place of light and life. The path back was through this narrow gap of time.

The sound of a low growl, like a stomach crying out to be filled, another heavy thump upon the parched, dead ground...*Here he comes.* She tossed the stone ahead of her so she could follow it to freedom. It made a shallow sound as it skipped like a rock over the flat face of a pond. But there were no tranquil ponds here, only brackish waters to quench a burning thirst.

It stopped several yards in front of her. She stood mutely rooted to the spot, waiting for the light. Suddenly, a shimmer of yellow began to pool around the tossed stone. The glow began to seep into the desiccated ground and shot back out like a bolt of lightning in reverse. This was the road home, illuminated for her at last.

Breaking her statue like stillness, she began to sprint like the fabled hart, to wherever this road would lead. *I am going home,* she kept thinking, as she pumped her legs and panted her breath into the eternal night.

The goddess watched from her marble throne as the creature ran into the oblivion of imagination. It still shone with the intensity of belief, beckoned with a voracity of freedom, but sadly, was only the mirage of a path out of her current existence. It was only a stone after all, not a gem. She had taken it, even knowing at face value, it was nothing but a stone. Smooth to the touch, sounding of promise when it was tossed, but still, only a rock.

"Ah, how silly these humans can be. They chase after illusion every time," she sighed to the scudding clouds over her marble head.

Her hands lay upon her knees, each palm up. One held a precious gem, the other, empty. Not unlike the promise of the stone the girl had chosen. The goddess continued to chuckle as she watched the girl follow the promises, until she faded into the distance. The female human would know the truth in the end. There would be no road back home, but then this peculiar being seemed ever hopeful and optimistic.

"Such a waste of your limited time," she mumbled to the girl who never heard. She was too busy trying to get back to a past that didn't exist, and to live a future that was only a dream. For her part, the goddess decided to divert her attention to a new supplicant, the wandering man in the dessert. He'd been stubbornly stronger than the rest, never falling for her promises, but she could be very persuasive.

The Alien's Mother

It was a typical Mother's Day in the small outpost of Glimmer Roost. They still celebrated long-remembered holidays from Earth times, only now, they did it in zero gravity. No bunches of roses and boxes of chocolates. Just the hand-made cards that could be erased and reused for the next holiday. There was no shortage of shiny baubles to be given, they were as common as road gravel back on Terra Uno. After all, the brilliant stones gave the very name to the mining town.

Mother's Day wasn't that big around there anyway, what with the lack of any women. And usually the only time the word "mother" was spoken, it was quickly followed with a profanity; a word likely to be around human settlements until the end days! This Mother's Day seemed destined to be marked like hundreds before it on Glimmer Roost…they broke out the Alien's Mother.

The female of her species landed on the remote planet, several months after the Pilgrim Miners. Workers living bubbles, a medical and research lab, and weigh stations for the far-flung outpost, were already installed and scattered over a large area. In a quick ceremony in the red glow of a second moonrise, the mining post was dubbed *Glimmer Roost*. The post commander figured it was shooting off the flares in celebration that caught the attention of the planetary rover.

The alien announced her arrival by blasting a group of unarmed surveyors and building engineers into space dust. There was no provocation on their part, unless you count their aggressive reshaping of her planet's landscape. One particularly enormous mound was flattened early in their terra forming process. Unfortunately, as they learned later, this particular geographic feature was the alien's domicile. The hive-like structure of connecting tunnels and chambers was subsequently shattered and buried under the weight of the debris. At the time of its destruction, the hive sheltered the Alien's entire family tree, from oldest to youngest.

She responded as any mother would, with unchecked rage and righteous lethality. She entered into a running skirmish with the Pilgrim Guard Unit, called in by the lone survivor at the mound killings. Her eradication was assured. They were human mercenaries, trained in the finer points of killing an enemy. She, as they discovered, was a mother, and the last defender of what was her home planet.

The body of the alien mother was to be kept for further study by the scientists that would follow one day. She was perfectly preserved, but as time went on, the Pilgrims realized the corporation funding Glimmer Roost would not waste resources on studying anything that couldn't produce a profit. Being human men, offspring of mothers all, they were collectively moved after the first one hundred years of keeping her in cold storage, to celebrate that most honored holiday, Mother's Day.

Forthwith, the preserved body of the alien mother was brought to the communal feasting shell, where the children of humankind could lay hand-made gifts around her blueish feet and short, whip-like tail. They had taken this mother of another race, co-opting her as their own. Over a span of many hundred cycles, the stories, along with the petrified shell of the last mother on Glimmer Roost, was dramatically transformed. She gradually evolved from death bringer to life giver, from alien, to familiar. Mother's Day became "The Great Mother's Day," proving, even in dying, there was eternal life for the love of an Alien Mother .

The First Love-Match

"It's no matter, pet. One day you'll find yourself besieged with offers of marriage. A dear girl like you, with a heart as big as the sky above! Here, have another honey cake, dear. "

Her mother's answer to any challenge in life was a sweetie of some sort. Plagued by worries of her continued spinsterhood, Corina feared her girth might soon match her dark moods.

"Mother. I am no longer willing to sit about, waiting for a suitable man to come banging on the gate, asking for the opportunity to bring me flowers and candies and pallid conversation! I shall no longer spend my time trying to entertain braggarts, brutes and banal bumpkins!"

She stormed out of the room leaving her mother with mouth gaping, and the lady's maid snickering behind her hand.

Corina went straight to her rooms, asked a servant to bring her paper and pen, and began writing on the creamy parchment in her sharp and practiced hand.

"Seeking Gentleman for Potential Loving Relationship. My description as follows:

Highly intelligent, good wit, patient beyond sainthood, tolerable storyteller, intolerant of fools and braggarts, loving of the Creator's natural world, respectful of all persons, no matter their gender. Appearance NOT relevant...Demeanor is all. The Lazy and Arrogant need NOT apply."

Lady Corina Forthright

Handing this off to the waiting serving girl, she gave her a small coin, along with the notice, "I want you to post this in the village square, where other news items are on display."

Then Corina sat back and waited for her replies to come in.

The first, as predictable as storms in spring, came from the town dandy. A lay-about heir to a vast fortune, he was seeking a new thrill to brighten his dull days as a budding cretin. He presented himself to Corina, two of his toadies in tow, ready to praise him to the heavens if called upon as character witnesses. His puny overtures were easily deflected by the robust young woman he desperately tried to charm. Any interest faded as quickly as his perfumed wig under her scrutiny and questioning. Corina scanned his frills and curls, noting the touch of powder on a pale face that never saw a walk in a summer field. She turned on her heels, left the room and smiled to herself when she heard his gasp of disbelief.

Suitor number two was not as obviously mis-matched to this fine young lady. Sir Ralph Longstreet was a self-proclaimed intellectual, with several papers on history penned under a fictitious name, and a penchant for stirring controversy with his unpopular rants on societal woes at dinner parties. His interests, however, were narrowly defined by a rather blind egotism. He would brook no differing opinion, as he alone held the defining one. Corina thanked him for contributing his views of the world that existed in his very small mind. She left him pacing, mid-lecture, on his unique insights regarding a woman's place as a mere muse, in the world of letters.

This parade of sad excuses for a man in full, went on for nigh onto a year. The parchment fixed to the wall on the Village Square was tattered and faded and nearly illegible from the elements. Naturally, few had the gift of reading, but word circulated quickly around the countryside and beyond, of this novel effort to find a potential husband. The Lady's quest soon morphed into urban legend as the months passed like wind driven clouds.

One day, a few days before Corina's thirty-something birthday, a caller came to the gates seeking entry for an hour still under the cloak of darkness. His insistent clamor raised half the residents within the manor; the others, being over the age of either hearing, or caring, or both. Corina was immediately roused by the clanging of the gate as it swung inward. She peered out her tall bedroom window in time to see a hunched figure ride through the gate. He swung himself from his magnificent stead with the grace of a boulder racing downhill. His arms appeared rather longish for his seemingly short stature, swinging like loose tree limbs from a stout tree.

"Oh, sweet Mother!" Corina moaned.

Feeling obligated to meet any who answered her peculiar manner of seeking a mate, she snatched a comforter off her bed. Wearing it like a queen's robes, she set her jaw for confrontation, and her heart for disappointment. She found the man installed in her smaller, intimate sitting room. The stranger had his back to her as he stood in front of a warm fireplace. Corina studied him from behind, noting the slope of his shoulders, the stubby bowed legs, and a mop of hair that sat on his head like the foam on a small beer. She cleared her throat. He turned.

She sucked in a breath when she saw his eyes were a deep red, glittering like rubies in a dead-white face. He smiled, and for a flash of a moment, his eye teeth gleamed long and sharp in his mouth. He had pushed his long cloak to his hunched back, enlarging its deformity.

"Good evening, Lady Corina."

His voice was like the feel of silk upon her skin. She gave a small shudder as she sensed, more than saw him move toward her. Suddenly they were within touching distance. He stared into her light gray eyes so intently, she nearly forgot to speak.

"You come calling at an odd hour, sir."

This sounded silly even to her ears, and she smiled back at him when he laughed.

"Yes, but this is one of my favorite times; when all is still, but the beating of our hearts."

Corina found this explanation totally logical and gestured for him to take a seat. He joined her on the brocaded love seat she favored in this room, and without asking her leave, took up her free hand, while the other clutched tightly to keep the comforter closed around her. She looked down momentarily at the long fingers and his very pallid skin. It seemed natural that he held her hand. He slowly raised his free hand to her slightly heaving breast, and then up to the pulse, hammering now, at the side of her neck, and lingered there for several heart beats.

His eyes never left Corina's during this intimate exploration. For her part, she only sighed with half-lidded eyes, at each contact of his roaming hand. The fire began to burn low by the time the stranger opened the door to the sitting room. There were no servants about at this hour, save the gatekeeper, lying inert once again in his room at the back of the gate house.

They exited the murky hallway as the stranger threw open the heavy doors with a flick of his wrist. Walking silently under the velvety dome, and bathed in the moon's creamy glow, everything appeared filtered by heavy gauze to Corina's eyes. She was aware that the stranger had a tight hold of her hand as he led her to his untethered horse. The horse snorted in recognition and the stranger patted him to silence. Turning to Corina he spoke again, his voice calm and soothing.

"I have come to claim you, dear lady. You will share all my years of living in this world. Know all that you want shall be yours, in me as my station is equal to your own."

He lifted her effortlessly, placing her gently onto his saddle, springing like a deer to sit behind her. The comforter she hung over her shoulders had long dropped away, but she felt no chill as he wrapped his long arms tightly around her, pulling her into the curve of his body.

She seemed to find her voice as they cantered out of the courtyard.

"Your station you say, is equal? What then shall I call you sir?"

"Count will do, my dear."

Death By Mummy

"Are ye proud of yerself, ya ninny?"

James Dunner was livid, and not about to let his mate off the hook for what he saw as his total lack of good sense.

"I specially told ya NOT ta open da caffin, until Matilda got 'ere ta keep tings on track. Now, 'tis awake en on da loose."

He would have said more, but Matilda McDonough poked her frizzy gray head into the shed.

"I cum as fast as ever I could, lads."

She was panting like a newly run greyhound, her thick body throwing off waves of heat as she bustled into the dimly lit out-building belonging to old man Dunner. He held a tiny croft near the village of Bailycline. Not much by way of a farmstead, his only livestock, a few motley sheep, a dozen barren chickens, one lazy rooster, and a milk cow he called Bertie, after the Queen's adored husband.

"Now, what's all dis I been earin' from da gossips? 'Bout yous two boys findin' a caffin in yonder woods? En why have ya sent fer me old bones? "

"Yer our onlyest hope, Matilda, at findin' dat ting as got out; afore it does some wickedness 'pon the village folk," James answered with sincerity spread across his face like butter on warm bread.

"Stuff 'n nonsense ye speak, James Dunner! I aint no sort a magic user, 'n dare's da truth a it!"

James opened his mouth to respond to her denial of having extraordinary powers, but his partner, Paddy O' Laughlin, jumped into the verbal fray. His high-pitched voice causing the chicken that had followed Matilda into the shed, to flee.

"Tis nay only us sayn' ye use dark arts, Matilda. Nay! Tis whispered 'ear 'n dare, 'bout ye sailn' ore' cottage 'n woodland, like a wee boat on dark waters! Tis said, ye sit astride a black cat, screechin' like a horny owl!"

This lively conversation was only interrupted long enough for old Dunner to retrieve his jug from his cottage adjacent to the shed. This required shooing away the broody looking sheep Bertie, the cow, as she wandered back to the dusty barnyard along with the other sheep, returning from their day of munching on his neighbor's garden. He kicked at the frustrated chickens and the lazy rooster, that seemed to sleep through every sunrise since he was hatched.

Returning to the shed, it became much warmer with the bodies sitting close together on stools and barrels. The fiery liquid was most welcome to their animated discussion.

"I ken see yer in a right nasty perdikment lads, 'en because I know a wee bit o' folksie remedy, I ken lend a bit a help. Firstly, ye 'ave told me naught regardin' who ya found layin' in yonder caffin."

The long wooden box in question, leaned precariously against the back wall of the shed, which was also leaning precariously. It was obvious from the shattered lid; it had been pried open none-to-gently. This occurred during Paddy's haste to retrieve any rings or baubles buried with the deceased. The story he related to Matilda went like this; though he did leave out the part where he was scavenging for valuables.

"Tis like a bad dream, Matilda," he said with a wispy voice.

"James 'ere, left me wit da caffin, while 'e went ta look fer a pry bar, or da like. We planned ta take off da lid, ta see who twas rattlin' round in dare! Whilst 'e was off searchn', I taught I heard a scratchy kinda noise comin' from da box! It scared me plenty, I tell ya! I woulda run ta fetch James back, but I knew it might be better ta see if 'twer a livin' bein', buried, afore e's time!"

Paddy took a deep drink from the jug as it was passed to him from Matilda, who herself had quaffed a good bit of the heavy brew during his story. James sat on his stool, looking over at the empty coffin while listening to the tale. He was shaking his head slowly from side to side, as if in denial of the story as it unfolded. His eyes were only slightly blearier than the storyteller's.

Paddy wiped a line of liquid from his mouth on his rough woolen shirt. "Well, I used me brute strength 'n tore open ta lid, ta let in some fresh breeze don't ye know. I looked inside ta hole, and me breath clogged in me troat like mud on a pig! Ta bloody body were wrapped like a rag doll as far as I could see! I pulled away them other pieces 'n afore long, I was lookin' at a giant, wavin' long, rag-covered arms about, en pullin' 'is own self out da caffin! I near pissed meself I tell ya true, en only me 'ere ta stop ta raggedy brute!"

His two listeners were nodding their heads, making sounds of alarm and fear, but that was mostly due to the level of brew left in their jug.

"Ah, Paddy," Matilda finally said, leaving a loud hiccup to finish the comment.

"We need ta find da rascal afore it can do a mischief!" James was slurring a tad, so the words sounded foreign to his friends who merely nodded knowingly.

"It appears ye do need me wee bit o' magic knowing, lads! I'll be back in da shake o a lamb's tail."

Matilda rose from her perch to her plump, unsteady legs and exited the shed. Good to her word, she was back in thrice of a wag, cradling a round iron pot with a heavy felt for a lid.

"Dis 'ere is me own magic brew, lads. It'll bring dat livin' dead creature back 'ear ta 'is caffin. When 'e cums, we put 'im back into 'is box, en carry it back ta where James found it."

They all nodded agreement with this fine plan, and Matilda proceeded to remove the cloth cover. The contents of the black pot let off an odor so pungent the three gave a collective gasp. Matilda studied the faces of the two friends, speaking as from a pulpit said, "Praps we'd best test a wee sip afore dat ting returns."

The villagers were holding their own search the next day, because three of their folks seemingly disappeared in the night. They scoured the countryside, avoiding the deeper parts of the woods. No sense was seen covering ground none of the missing would ever have gone. A few searchers reported seeing flashes of white floating through the woods and thought again about chasing after such an enigma. When one of the search party returned to the village for two hunting dogs to aid in the task, he passed directly by James Dunner's old shed. He was taken with a vague, but unpleasant odor wafting out of its partially opened door. Approaching to investigate the source, he threw open the door and let out a scream. Many of the other villagers were nearby, not wanting to leave the village unmanned entirely. Upon hearing the cry, they came pelting back to Dunner's croft.

James, Paddy and Matilda sat on their barrels and stool, surely stiffer than the boards around them. Each clutched their drinking cups like an owl would a mouse. Their eyes were wide, fogged over with the vacancy of death, for which there was no outward cause. The village constable and a doctor from two villages over, were sent for post haste. Both agreed the trio "...looked like they'd seen sum kinda monster, or ghost." Besides the bugged-out eyes, their mouths were all twisted in silent howls and screams.

The only bit of evidence found at the scene of the mysterious deaths, were pieces of white rags clinging to the rough wood around the door. The constable named it a case of poisoning by a putrid batch of spirits, but the local crofters had a different take on the deaths.

Late in the day, when the sun colored their fields purple and crimson, many a farmer reported seeing a human-like form shambling through the surrounding woods, wearing long white rags around its body and limbs. If anyone knew the truth of the deaths, they were certainly keeping mum!

Cosmic Truths

Standing erect as any of the guards surrounding the hall, his white and gold threaded gown glittered and shifted like a flame in the soft breeze created as his floating platform moved through the arena. He towered over most of the Cosmic Guard standing at attention in their body covering of titanium armor, reminding him of the Tin Man from the fable of Oz.

"Greetings, followers of the One Cosmic Designer. As Mindful Guide and First Law Counselor to your commanding officer, General Rad-He, it falls to me to speak against the base behavior of the General, and his chosen Light Bearers!"

He stopped speaking until the uproar died away to a few hushed whispers among the assembled cadets and Junior officers.

"I'm uncertain General Rad-He understands the full implications of his current orders regarding the prisoners taken in the last sweep of the outer sectors. His decision to use any means necessary to abstract information from these captured beings flies in the face of every accord struck in the treatment of other-world prisoners. But worse still, it goes against the heart of the First Law, the very basis of our civilization! I ask you now...think upon that law! Think about what it means to the fabric of our society. Think!

This aggression has been pursued far too long, fraying the better inclinations of our people. But it is our military leaders who are in the fore when it comes to its execution. It falls hard upon them to win the battles, while keeping faith with One Cosmic Designer! It is in this Divine Directive, I emphatically state... the Generals have failed! The prisoners taken into our camps, have been systematically reduced to quivering *things*, huddled in pens barely larger than an infant's pod carrier. These creatures don't speak our tongue, they don't understand our ways, and they surely do not follow the One Cosmic Designer, Blessed be his Luminaries.

I beseech those of you who have interaction with these prisoners, remember, they *too* are creations of the Cosmic Lord. Puny and hideous as they are to behold, they too have been imbued with the sacred fire of life. At times in their evolution, they have been productive, creative, following a higher order of conscience.

Scattered around their world, many leaders of these *Hu-Mans,* as they are named, displayed the total loss of morally guided power over the many cycles of time we observed them. They are quarrelsome, petty, and often self-serving beings. It is our responsibility as superior beings to aid their development and bring them to their own light of understanding and principled action.

For the love of the One Cosmic Designer, let us strive to educate and inspire this weaker species! They will never meet our intellectual prowess, but their innate curiosity has led them into our midst. Perhaps, after many cycles have drifted back into our own history, our own species will be remembered for our magnanimous gesture. A Hu-Man is yet another life form. We must judge their corruption and ultimate destruction of their home world, as an act of inferior competence in understanding of the Designer's plan. It is not our place to punish the ignorance that forces them to abandon their Earth and seek out a new home."

A voice was raised among the listeners.

"These beings may have left their home world due to a collapse in a sane use of its resources, but they brought with them that ignorance as proven in their settlement on our world. They spew unclean particles into the atmosphere above their domes, the living waters nearby, are filled with poisons from the installation of aqua farms to feed them, and they have shorn the verdant ground of our vibrant flora to install their domes in greater numbers, and greater numbers, crowding out any natural growth. Just as they did on their planet Earth, they repeat here on our home planet! These Hu-Mans surely will be the ruin of any planet they infiltrate."

The cadet who spoke turned to those in the crowds around him.

"What, say you all? Preserve our home world and others from these destructive parasites, force them to leave our planet before they can do more permanent harm to our world!"

The man on the floating stage, raised an arm, sending a laser bolt into the cadet's chest, evaporating him on the spot, along with both cadets seated nearby. A collective gasp rose from the shocked on-lookers. His voice boomed over them as he rose higher.

"There can be no transgression greater than questioning an anointed power! These strangers have much to learn, and apparently, so do some of you."

Floating behind a curtain, stiff with anger at being challenged, the Guide had the feeling his authority was more than challenged, it was in danger of being overthrown.

"Is there nothing sacred in the universe when the power of the enlightened can be questioned?"

He could hear the cadets whispering among themselves as he slowly exited. He was thinking it might be time to refurbish his old transport ship for possible quick extraction.

It would be many long cycles before the Hu-Mans encountered any of the population on his home world. Their population was located in the deep valleys beneath the towering mountains. However, the protesting cadet identified how they seemed to be expanding in numbers, noting their ruthless use of resources, while turning a blind eye to the future this created for the planet. He finished his disturbing thoughts aloud, being the lone audience as he often was.

"But this is, after all, their new home, their chance for rebirth of their kind. As they increase their population, and spread over the face of our planet, they must surely remember the lesson of the devastation they left behind in their old home world. Surely…"

An Inconvenient Death

"Why is that bird in my bird bath so selfish?" she asked in that strident tone that locked his jaw, making his teeth grind. "Where is that wretched servant? I need more tea! Likely off with my steward. I've spied the two of them sneaking about the kitchen gardens. Disgusting!"

He listened with only half an ear; he was gratefully deaf in one ear, and nearly so in the other. Of all the infirmities he could have while living with this hectoring woman for a quarter of a century, he thanked the gods this was the one bestowed on him late in his middle years.

Harold had not always suffered thusly. He was once considered a dashing charmer by the fairer sex. In truth, he made a tidy fortune living off their many generosities and allowances. Giving each in turn, his undivided attention in and out of the boudoir was never much of a challenge. His wavy flaxen hair and riveting blue eyes, a look he practiced daily, added mystery to the magnificent figure he cut. His broad shoulders and muscular frame filled out a doublet like the breathing Adonis he always imagined himself to be.

It wasn't the size of a woman's bosom that captured Harold's attention, but the size of her estate, properties, and titles. He might be seen dancing a demure minuet with a frumpy old hag, but if her diamond tiara flashed brightly enough, he'd ask for the next dance as well. The ladies from the Great Houses around the quaint countryside and the teaming city, fell all over themselves to garner a mere smile from his perfect lips. Any other men within his orbit, were so overshadowed by Harold's magnetism, they might just as well be the stable hand or potted plant.

He'd been making some headway toward his final goal of Lord of the Manor, with a particularly odious woman, ten years, six months his senior. She was recently widowed, and heir to a huge estate and fortune. Rich within her own rights as well, Harold deemed her worthy of a more persuasive campaign, immediately launching into a whirlwind courtship.

A parade of unique gifts, fantastic bouquets, sumptuous sweets, marched like fife and drums in quick succession, to her plump, bejeweled hands. Most of these were either given to him by one paramour, or another, or purchased with their money. In the end, it turned out to be the poetry he penned during his siege campaign, that finally captured the bird; more like a large hen turkey to be precise. His words were like frothy milk or spun sugar glaze. They coated his sly mouth with the sincerity of deep emotion. The Lady agreed to marriage after the fifth recitation of a luridly romantic sonnet, that almost made his own teeth ache, as he recited it into her bejeweled ear.

He recalled, after being installed as Lord of the fabulous estate, how his new, albeit, slightly used bride, had given him his first view of her nagging ways. They were working on the accounts together, as she explained in a haughty tone, the management of her vast holdings. He was taken aback by her steely resolve and understanding of commerce, surely not a Lady's purview. His wife became irritated with his own deficiencies in that arena, going so far as to call him dull, regarding how business should be done. Finding this major flaw in her new husband, she asserted her will in other corners of his life, increasing her influence over time, and wearing him down to a mere nub of his former glamorous self. The days turned into months of hectoring, finding fault with his every choice, decision, even wardrobe.

"You shan't embarrass me by wearing that color of breeches!" "Your boots look foppish. "That ring is far too gaudy for an afternoon tea." And so on, and so forth.

He believed he'd enjoy being addressed as Lord Harold by the minions staffing the manor, but they merely ignored him, taking all their commands and directions from the great Lady of the manor, circumventing even that small pleasure for him.

The months rolled by like the heavy trundling of oxen and cart, an analogy Harold felt fitting for his now, quite substantial wife. It seems her appetite for sweets never abated after the courtship of many years ago. Harold was often sent to the kitchens late into the night, to retrieve a certain pudding or sweet cake for his wife, who took her cravings to bed with her. He, to his great relief, was not one of them.

The day dawned when Harold and his Lady wife would recognize twenty-five years of marriage; a day set aside for festivities honoring their conjugal bliss. Before these were set to commence, his wife sent her servant to fetch him to her study. Peering at him, still trim and fit, bright eyed and skin a healthy pink, she motioned him to sit.

"I believe it is time, husband, to sign this," she said handing him a document. He read it over carefully, it was brief enough to quickly gather its meaning.

"Why, my heart, this is your Last Will that I hold. What does this mean?"

"It means, you ninny, that when I die, all of my estates and fortune belong to you! There is but one caveat; that you must not marry again, until I have been gone one year."

That sounded easy enough to Harold. He had twaddled about long and hard over the twenty-five years of his marriage, he could wait, or better, might never entangle himself legally again.

So now it became crystal clear; he was to be Lord of the Manor at last. He was much younger than his beastly wife. He took care of himself, he ate sparingly, leaning heavily on the fresh produce served at table, taking only the leanest cuts of meat, foregoing the endless array of tempting desserts. He walked or rode his horse endless miles to stay fit and strong. He was still youthful in his eyes, and never failed to notice even the most innocent smile in his direction by other women.

Yes, this would do nicely!

His over-weight, over-bearing wife, would precede him easily. He'd likely find her face down in a cobbler before the winter set in. Ah, that frigid season in the manor house might even be her death knell!

Thinking these freeing, rather ungenerous thoughts, Harold got up from his chair and watched as his wife signed the document, blotted it, and placed her seal upon the folded sheet.

Harold made a deep bow to her saying, "I shall await your presence my dear, downstairs in the ballroom. We shall dance as we did so many years ago."

She smiled weakly at his attempt to be romantic, saying she'd be with him presently.

Harold made haste to leave, fairly running toward the circular marble staircase. He was almost light-headed with giddiness at the prospects that lay so near at hand. Unfortunately for him, his distraction and perhaps to some degree, his new shiny boots, made him take a misstep on the very first step. The leather soles slid like ice off a hot roof, when he touched them to the highly glossed stone, his feet flew out from under him and he was airborne as quickly as a startled pheasant. His surprise was so complete, he uttered not a word, nor cried. He watched with mouth agape, eyes wide with disbelief, as the crystal chandelier flew by like a giant ice cycle, the candles winking back at him like naughty maids. His ears picked up a cry for help, but it wasn't his.

"Help! The Mistress...the Mistress... is dead in her study!"

The Necromancer's Lament

I ran through the howling night, battered by a piercing sleet, tripping on slick rocks along the river's edge, my hands filthy and cut by the stones.   My mind raced with my feet. *She can't be gone...She can't be gone.* Thunder boomed around me, a few heart beats later, streaking bolts of lightning lacerated the inky blackness that pressed down upon me like the weight of a dark sea.

I stumbled headlong toward the last place I held my darling Corine. Her beautiful face unsmiling, the luminous eyes closed to me, her delicate ears deaf to the outpouring of my everlasting love. Her hair, each strand glowing like spun gold, cascading over my arms.

Arriving at the graveyard, I wended my way through the ancient burial grounds. Gray angels, arms outstretched as if to embrace my living body, peered down as I passed. Gentle doves followed my movements with beady, stone eyes. I wiped the wet away with my sleeve, now as sodden as the earth beneath my feet. I paused, waiting for celestial illumination. A finger of lightning scratched a path to ground, showing me clearly where my beloved was held in death's sway.

I arrived at the crypt, determined that this was not to be our ending...this wretched death would not severe our bond. Ours, was now a connection forged in the devil's own fires. I had pledged my oath to the Soul-Taker, to make it so on this very night, this Hallowed Eve.

I went up three narrow steps, standing uncertainly in front of the heavy door into the crypt. A deep red light seeped out, framing the door like the portal to hell. I stared in disbelief. I left my darling girl lying in the cool, dry place, without the benefit of candle or flame. This blood-red glow, oozing out into the fury of the night, brought me much alarm and disquiet. As I was reaching to pull the solid iron ring and enter the tomb, there came a soft, rustling sound behind me. I spun round. Leering up at me was Soul Taker himself. The lower part of his body was goat-like and astonishing, as he stood on hairy, bent legs, ending sharply in gold-tipped cloven hooves.

"Why are you come?" I asked with alarm gripping my throat like two strong hands.

His own voice was a battering ram against my tender ears. "Have you already forgotten your solemn vow to my service, mortal? You will become one of my own, gathering the dead, and with my help, raising them into a new existence. You have pledged to me an army of servants to my ungodly cause. This, in exchange for new life for your lost love."

He stopped speaking and I realized he had already ascended the three stone steps. He stood so close I could feel his hot fetid breath upon my face.

"Shall we enter and see to your beloved, Corine, mortal?"

I unconsciously moved aside, and using his hand like a fan, he drew the immensely heavy door open as if it was a sheet of parchment.

The eerie crimson light diffused throughout the small chamber. I inhaled deeply with the shock of seeing my love. She stood in front of the stone casket where she was lying, its heavy lid lying upon the floor nearby. Her back was turned to me. The white burial gown flowed around her body as if little flesh existed beneath. The once glorious mass of golden hair, reflected the blood red of the strange glow.

The light within the crypt abruptly changed color, when Soul Taker entered the chilled vault. From the garish red, it morphed into something akin to a dazzling sun. The tomb was awash in this unnatural brightness, scouring the shadows from their corners and searing my eyeballs with unfiltered heat.

The Soul Taker moved to stand beside Corine. She appeared to be gazing raptly at an array of dead flowers and the small mementos of our life together; placed there many months earlier, before I struck upon my plan to save her.

Reaching out to her, Soul Taker covered one slim hand with his scaly, clawed one, turning her ever so slowly to show herself to me at last. Suddenly, a horrifying, blood chilling scream was reverberating around the chamber, bouncing off the damp-encrusted stone walls. It seemed like it would never end. I covered my ears with my hands. When it finally stopped, they were both staring at me; Soul Taker smiling like a King Cobra, and Corine giggling, until bloody tears ran down her cheeks.

It was I, who shattered the quiet of the crypt, screeching my very guts out upon seeing my beloved in the hot light of reality. She was putrefying even as I watched, unmoving while pieces of her sloughed off onto the stone floor. She came toward me, as fluidly as a shadow over the face of a pond. When she was near, I smelled the cloying sweetness of rot and death.

"You have served my Master well, and now, we will serve him together as we gather others to his cause. Do not look so distraught dear one, you have been granted your soul's desire. You are now the Necromancer who sleeps with death."

The Yeti: A Tale of Liberation

I'd been a Research Anthropologist, working in the field for eight grueling years. In my Post-Doctorate days in England, I snatched at any assignment the University threw my way, like a hungry dog under the dining table. Too often, these were well-below my capabilities as a researcher, smacking of male chauvinism as clearly as an auto-repair shop's wall calendars! Yet, I slogged on through the crappy assignments, waiting for the one that would establish my name in a male-dominated profession. Two months ago, I was certain the gods had finally smiled upon me!

I was sent to the rugged mountains defining the Tibetan borderlands, to investigate an uptick in rumors of Yeti sightings. According to random climbers, and a few academic types coming down from the rocky aerie, the epicenter of these reports was a small village located in one of the region's most inaccessible areas. At our base camp, I managed to hire a local guide with a smattering of English, paying him a month's wages as an enticement, before embarking in his ancient Land Rover.

From what poor English I could decipher, it appeared my destination had the odor of death around it, and few were willing to travel into the remote territory. My guide found a driver of a sturdy vehicle, and two other men to act as pack mules, carrying whatever field equipment couldn't fit into the vehicle. They followed behind during a tortuous climb over roughly carved-out trails.

It took almost three full days of grueling travel and rough campsites, before my guide pointed out smoke rising like pencil marks on a flat blue sky. I was greeted with suspicion the minute we entered the center of the village, no more than a cluster of rudely constructed huts. I had carefully packed my vehicle with a generous load of staples for the villagers. The food stuffs quickly disappeared into the head- man's hut, presumably to be divided-up later among the families.

After the Land Rover was emptied, and all my equipment piled into a small mound in the middle of the huts, the carriers got into the empty truck and rattled back down the trail and out of sight. I was left standing like a lost suitcase at the rail station. The villagers seemed at a loss to have me in their midst and began to move back into their huts. I was only able to attract the attention of these extraordinarily shy people, by shouting my introduction.

"Hullo, to all of you! I am Pamela Martindale-Hunter. I've been sent by the University of London's School of Anthropology, to look into the reported sightings of the Yeti."

They were unimpressed with the entire introduction, but when I pronounced the word "Yeti," there was a great in-drawing of breath among the people who backed even further away, their eyes wide and apprehensive. Suddenly, initial curiosity about me, turned into a palpable fear among the adults. The children clung to their parent's trousered legs, in response to the instant tension.

The head-man stepped closer, saying something totally unintelligible to me. I turned to my well-paid guide for translation. He was squinting at the wizened face of the village leader like he'd suddenly become near sighted!

"Don't you know what he said?" I asked brusquely, annoyed that he was straight away falling down on his job.

He didn't reply at first, but turned a rather ashen colored face to me, saying in halting English, "The head-man, he says, "Yeti already take woman from villages near his. Three, four, women and girls. He not speak of monster...might bring him to this village too."

I distilled his report into a few facts. They didn't want to draw attention to their village, and my searching for the "monster" as they called it, might bring undo notice of their village to the creature. I rattled off some quick instructions to the translator.

"Tell the elder, that I will not need to involve any of his people in my search. Tell him I will only need a map of locations where the Yeti was spotted."

Obviously, this was translation over-load. After several minutes of back and forth between them, my interpreter crouched down and made a map in the hard dirt with a sharp rock. It was crude but did reflect the boundaries of the village. He stood and turned to the head man once more. Spitting out more gibberish, he handed over the rock, indicating he should mark the locations the Yeti had been seen. It was getting colder by the minute the longer we stood outdoors. The head man gesticulating wildly, and stabbing at the ground, while I was copying into my notebook, the crude, and only map, I would ever get out of that lot!

I was settled into a guest hut after the chickens, various mongrels and one goat were removed. The translator was housed with one of the families. The night was long and dreadful. Low, growling sounds, like a pack of feral dogs, road the night winds almost constantly. I had been in some primitive settings during my time in the field, but this village, clinging to the side of a blue, mist shrouded mountain, was proving the most challenging for my peace of mind.

The next morning, after eventually falling into a fitful sleep, I rose, bleary-eyed, but ready to make my first foray into the surrounding mountain villages. The sightings seemed to have occurred randomly, until I realized they followed the lose circle the villages sat in, one after the other, like a string of prayer beads. Earlier reports had the Yeti coming in the darkest, pre-dawn hours, kidnapping the females, and carrying them off as quietly as the clouds enveloping the mountain's summit.

I took the translator with me and we hiked over the rough terrain to the first village struck by the creature. Here, we discovered the head-man of this community had lost his wife, in what, to his mind, would become a kidnapping spree by the Yeti. The translator told me how the wife had been beaten severely many times, for disobedience. The head- man said she deserved her fate to live with a monster and casually spat upon the crust of dark earth. We left when the headman seemed more interested in the heavy blanket, I gifted him, then the whereabouts of his wife.

Following the rugged trails worn into the earth and connecting the villages, I heard much the same story from every village leader. Women who were constantly being beaten for their many failures or infractions, and girls, just about to enter into marriages arranged by fathers for profit, or status, were suddenly taken from their sleeping mats by the Yeti. The consistent belief of the villagers willing to speak with me, was that these women were being punished for their insubordinate attitudes and defiance of their husbands, or family elders.

I returned to my smelly guest hut that evening, having visited half of the eight villages, exhausted by my excursions, my mind filled with the most extraordinary stories.

The Yeti was described at every village as seven feet tall, robustly built, and covered in a downy pelt of reddish-brown hair. The stories never varied, but when I probed more closely through my translator, sadly, I found no one had actually clapped their eyes on the beast.

"How did they come to this description," I asked him while we trekked back that evening.

"Women go up mountain, gather berries, wood for cooking fires. They see beast, jumping like sheep, with taken women and girls in..." Here my guide made a circle with his hands and continued.

"They are laughing, singing, very happy with hairy man."

I had to witness this outlandish scene for myself. Finding the Yeti would provide another link in our own evolution, I told myself as a scientist. Truthfully, I wanted to see why these women were supposedly so happy and agreeable to their captivity.

After midnight, I moved aside the heavy leather hide covering the doorway and exited my hut. The constant groans of the wind would cover any slight sound. I was halfway up the irregular trail leading away from the sleeping village, when a figure stepped out onto the path directly in front of me. Its long shadow covered me where I stood paralyzed with fear. I watched, fascinated as it glided like a graceful dancer toward his partner. A strong, musky odor radiated off its body, but rather than being offensive, I found it strangely alluring.

I shook my head to try to clear it, allowing the "fight or flight" instinct to kick in. The beast was standing close enough to me now, that I could see its muscular form was well proportioned, the covering of rust colored hair glistened like smooth seal skin under the hazy moonlight. I looked up, until I found its eyes studying me like an artist would a portrait he just finished. Suddenly, the heavy silence was broken by a beautiful, lilting voice that caressed my ears with its sweetness.

"Welcome to my mountain, English Lady. I was coming for you at this very hour. Do not fear me. I am blessed by the gods with abilities of discernment. I am aware you have not suffered from a brutal husband, or overbearing father, but your own life has been limited at every turn by heavy-handed males. Among the women, you will be a servant no longer to male egos. Among our family, you will find acceptance and honor. I know all these things about you and offer you this gift of freedom from a narrowly defined life. What say you?"

I knew instantly, I could never allow this remarkable finding to be released into the world. The Yeti was female. She was both intelligent and sensitive, destroying all the long-established theories. Introducing such a phenomenal creature to the human conundrum, would only worsen the myth of females as inferior, minor players on the world stage. She was, after all, still a beast. I turned around, fleeing back down the trail.

She never pursued me into the village. I was packed and ready to leave later the same morning. The interpreter looked perplexed when I told him my mission was complete but seemed content to be relieved of his duty.

Now, I sit in front of my fireplace, watching the wood crackle and smoke, wondering how life would have been for me up there, in the pure mountain air, answering to no man, needing no male in my life. No romance, no lovers, no husband, no yin and yang. I knew the loss of these things would outweigh a life of dancing and song. My own freedom was too precious a commodity. Even if it was blunted by the men who called the tunes, I could still choose if I would dance.

A Body Beneath The Snow

"I do believe this storm will last a goodly long time, Albertson."

"Yes, sir. It does appear so from the bleak look of the sky."

The Lord of the Manor, Sir Peter Halls-Bigsby was standing at the large arch framed window of his study, with his man servant, Albertson, a step behind his right shoulder.

"Let's get together for a sleighing party, Albertson! That would be jolly good fun for village folk and lift their spirits now that the Yuletide season is past, and they've little to comfort their meager lives. What do you think?"

It really didn't matter a wit what Albertson thought, but his Lordship tried at least to keep up a more democratic appearance. He knew that the turn of the century would herald social changes that would have lasting consequences on the Royalty and upper echelons of society. There was a new age of thinkers making noise about social inequities. Class systems were about to burst like dams, with raging waters pushing at their underpinnings.

"I think your Lordship has hit upon a fine idea! Shall I begin to instruct the staff to undertake the task of creating such an event, sir?"

"Yes and do it at once! I want to see sleigh races, apple bobbing, and snowball forts erected for battles. What jolly fun!"

Though this was to be a relief for the villagers from unrelenting cold, and scarce food in their larders, Sir Peter grew excited at the prospect of such a break from his own winter doldrums. As a widower of some fifteen winters, without heir or issue he could claim, publicly at least, he lived a narrow, regulated existence, broken only by bouts of depression and the occasional visit from one of the women from the village brothel. These visits were made in the dead of night, and not even his man Albertson, was aware of the arrangements. The women, girls mostly, would be contacted by Sir Peter himself, dressed in wig, beggar's rags and false beard. He would play the intermediary of Lord Halls-Bigsby, bringing the chosen female through a hidden tunnel in the nearby woods, and into the Manor house cellars. There, he revealed his true identity and sadly, for her, his true nature. At first, the girls were awed to be servicing his Lordship thusly, but when he reverted to his true form, their screams were lost in the bowls of the earth and thick stonework of the dark cellar.

It was an ancient family condition, inherited like blue eyes, or money. It was known only to the few who also suffered its claim over their lives. Sir Peter was a Lycanthrope. For the poorly informed among you, the Lord of the manor was a Werewolf.

His life had long consisted of hiding away when the full moon rose, using every excuse he could conjure to throw off any suspicions of his absences. The rooms beneath his manor house where he brought the village whores, were barred and reinforced with iron girding around the doors, so they couldn't be breached by his brute strength. He carried on his ravishing ways from the days of his earliest manhood, finding that easier, and less messy than involving someone who might actually be missed. The brothel was kept well supplied over this long period, by a secret benefactor who paid the Madame to secure the most beautiful young women she could lure, or drug, into service. In fact, the only time Sir Peter strayed from his hard-and-fast rule of only preying on the whores, was when he failed to get into the cellars in the early days, after his first, and only wedding. Sadly, it was a brief marriage. He disposed of his wife's remains, few as they were, in a peat bog on his vast estate.

But his spirits soared now, at the thought of the winter festivities being planned for the villagers. Being free of his normal melancholy, later in the day, Sir Peter decided to take his own sleigh for a jaunt, bundling up forthwith. He took the young stable boy along as helper with the twin blacks he harnessed for his lordship. The horses looked splendid in their silver and tooled leather tack, and Sir Peter felt invigorated at the snap of his long whip.

They'd been racing along at a clean clip, when the stable hand looked up and then over at Sir Peter.

"Looks like we be avin' a fine, fat moon t'night, yer Lordship."

Sir Peter, in his enthusiasm for the sleigh ride, had lost track of all time and place. In fact, he had driven the sleek sleigh a great distance from the main house, and the sky had grown dark, a full moon sailing before them.

"Boy! Stop the team now!" he shouted, giving the reins to the young man in obvious distress.

"Sir, wha' ails ye? Yer face 'as taken on a strange look, it 'as." He said bringing the ebony pair to a panting halt where they blew and snorted at this sudden halt.

Sir Peter didn't answer. He began to hunch down on his seat, the thick rug slipping from his lap onto the floor of the sleigh. He bent over, hiding his face and head with his arms.

The stable boy jumped out of the sleigh, leaving his master curled around himself like a mewling kitten, odd noises and grunts coming from under his arms. The boy backed away from the vehicle, slipping a long knife out of his high boot. He watched Sir Peter's back, seeing it ripple and twist and bunch under his heavy cape coat.

The young man inched his way around to where his master still crouched. When he got within a foot of the sleigh, he fell on his master, plunging the knife in deeply, over and over until the handle became too slick to keep hold of, dropping from his hand into the red stained snow.

"That's fer me sister ya bleedin' monster! She were a sweet girl, an' she were only thirteen when ya took 'er to yer hidey-hole. I seen ya sneakin' off plenty o' times, en' followed one night. Them cellars is me favorite place ta stay in winter, en' I knows every cubby down there!   When me darling sis went missin', I guessed ya had a hand inta it. I couldn't save 'er as ya locked thet great door behind ya both, but I heard 'er screams fer help, ya bastard! I ran away when it got all still like, fer fear ya'd do me the same. I found 'er head en' parts under the snow near ta' stables. Ya didn't dig her deep enough, but I will."

The stable hand pulled the body up in the seat to find half-man, half-wolf staring back at him. He lurched away, but soon regained his resolve and dragged the stiffening body from the sleigh. He reached behind to the compartment behind the seat where he had stowed a shovel, traces of horse manure frozen on the blade. He worked well into the night trying to clear enough snow away to bury the body, but as quickly as he worked the hole filled back in. Finally, in desperation he flipped the body onto its back and shoveled heaps of snow onto it until it was transformed into another deep drift.

This plan would have worked well, the boy told the Magistrate that charged him with murdering his Lordship, except for the spring thaw, when it popped to the surface, lying in perfect preservation for all the world to see.

The boy was to be hanged three days hence and the horrifying tale of the Peer of the Realm being a Werewolf would be lost with the snap of his neck.

That was until the body of Lord Peter disappeared from the family vault the night of the first Harvest Moon. The villagers all wondered what winter would bring and sharpened their knives.

A Turn of the Wheel

Aunt Margaret was not my favorite relation. In fact, I barely knew of her existence before she had me tracked down by her solicitor, offering me a position as her companion and care-giver. That was seven months ago. Naturally, she didn't recognize me as kin, her poor- as-a-street-beggar great niece, Lettie, but I accepted this crumb from her rich table, never-the-less. I moved into her mausoleum of a mansion, finding it stuffed with mildewy furnishing, and enough curios scattered upon every surface to open a china shop. My relationship with my Aunt-Employer, subjected me to constant ranting and badgering, from the minute she opened her piercing blue eyes, until her wrinkled lids drifted shut, after what felt like interminably long days. Fortunately, I occasionally found excuses to escape into another part of the rambling house, away from her harping and complaining. The money barely helped to dull the verbal abuse she inflicted upon me daily, with her wicked tongue.

My obnoxious relative was totally bedridden, when I wasn't moving her about in her wheelchair. I was told by Miss Jameson, the middle-aged housekeeper, my late Uncle Freddy, fulfilled this role before I arrived on the scene. In her severely tailored black dresses, Miss Jameson looked every inch a head mistress. The numerous house keys hung like a jailer's, dangling from her belt, announcing her whereabouts in the vast mansion.

Over tea, during one of my disappearing acts, the housekeeper filled me in on the details of the accident, "that put madam in her rolling chair." While I listened to her story over a cuppa and a warm scone, it became apparent she had little regard for her demanding employer. In fact, she looked down her sharp nose at my Great Aunt.

"Mr. Freddy was driving his brand-new Gold Bug Speedster… like the one owned by the famous boxer, Jack Dempsey; a man Mr. Freddy admired greatly, don't you know." She said this with obvious pride glinting in her eyes.

"It was a gift from Miss Meg to Mr. Freddy, on their first Wedding Anniversary. Naturally, it was paid for with his money."

I knew then, Uncle Freddy was a rich old bugger, and Aunt Margaret spent his fortune freely.

Before the automobile accident, according to Miss Jameson, Meg was a beautiful, vivacious woman. She wore her golden-brown hair in the stylish "Dutch Boy" bob of the day, cut straight along her chin line, with thick bangs brushing her fashionably thin brows. She always wore the latest in make-up, applying her powders and lash Kohl, as expertly as any aspiring movie ingénue. But all her fashionable wardrobe, make-up, hair styling and money, couldn't save her from the fate of a broken body. The housekeeper described the scene of the accident vividly, likely using some embellishments as servants tend to do.

Uncle Freddy, quite a bit older than Meg, and with very poor eyesight, pushed the Speedster to its limits. Sadly, he wasn't aware of a dangerous hazard around a slight bend in the road, likely thinking himself as invincible as the famous boxer. Unseen, with his near-sighted vision, he came barreling around the gentle curve in the roadway, and with no time to correct his rash speed, slammed head-on into the neighbor's thick-sided Bessie, newly escaped from her paddock. The cow was stunned but managed to get back to its wobbly legs and cross over the road, before succumbing to fatal injuries.

Miss Jameson said his only passenger, Aunt Margaret, was hurled out of the racing vehicle like a ball from a cannon. Uncle Freddy was fortunate to have the steering wheel in front of himself, and therefore was not ejected from the now ruined vehicle. But his bowels were never the same the woman revealed, and he died within the year, leaving his wife a very wealthy invalid.

Aunt Margaret never forgave Uncle Freddy for her condition, and with advancing years and ill health, she became increasingly afraid of how that would affect her after-life. She confided this fear to me one day, in a moment of self-pity no doubt, as I pushed her chair through the gardens. I had used this fear of hers as a perfect excuse to get her out of the house, and out of sight of the housekeeper and other household staff. I suggested we visit dear old Freddy's grave site.

Rolling her down the garden path and deeper into the less-tended park setting of the family plot, I knew exactly what I needed to do to rid myself of the wretched woman and gain a fortune in the process.

We had to climb a long incline to reach the square mausoleum, set on the hilltop like a beacon of death. Pushing the much heavier Margaret uphill, had me sweating like a racehorse with effort. My scheme was simple. I planned on giving Aunt Margaret a last shove at the top, so she'd roll downhill, picking up speed until she careened into one of the many trees below.

Finally, we reached the goal. Aunt Margaret told me to open the door with a large skeleton key she removed from a chain I'd never seen before, that held another key of the same cut. The lock turned easily and I pushed the door wider, so the interior was better-lit.

I heard my Great Aunt give a small laugh, more of a snort, like she knew something funny was about to happen. I had my back turned to her where she sat, curiously peering into the shadowy interior, when I was shoved hard from behind. I fell across the sarcophagus where I presumed Freddy was laid to rest, banging my shins hard against the rough gray stone, and rubbing my forearms raw on its gritty surface. I was gathering myself after the shock, when the door was slammed shut. I clearly heard the lock being turned into place. Stunned, and standing in total darkness, a voice suddenly came out of some kind of hidden speaker. I could hear Aunt Margaret's curious words from just outside the door as they flew around my head like bats in the inky air.

"You are my last relative, Lettie, and you thought of murdering me and inheriting my fortune. Many others have tried before you, dear. Now you can tell your pathetic story to Freddy while you await your own end. But you must admit, I had you fooled, playing the invalid. I've been able to walk short distances since the accident but kept the truth from everyone as it served to punish that dolt, Freddy, for what his stupidity did to me. Anyway dear, it's time to leave you with the others who tried to kill me off. Oh, yes, they're all in there with you, relatives who crawled out of the woodwork to get to their grubby hands on my money. Their company will help to pass the time until...well... you know!"

She was laughing outright, now. "Oh, and the key you used on the crypt door...its mate is to unlock it from the inside just in case I fell afoul of a drugged cocoa some night. Such a shame you weren't clever enough to have discovered my little secrets, but then, none of you were."

I could hear Margaret struggling to get back into her wheelchair, cursing as she hauled her substantial weight onto the cushioned seat. I pressed my ear to the door, hearing her begin to roll away over the loose gravel covering the ground.

The next sound was most gratifying, considering the end she provided for me. A high-pitched scream, lasting several minutes, fading in and out as it became more distant. Seems this mausoleum will shortly have one more occupant.

The Traveling Death Mask

"Auntie's dead, I tell ye! She took ta sittin' up, 'n fell off 'n 'er bed. Silly ol' biddy!"

He was shouting his news to me. I had stopped by Healer Charlotte's cottage to see to her needs. As a Healer myself, in my Lord's employ, I had to be certain this was not the beginning of another Red Scourge among the peasants on his lands. The door was flung wide by the wild-eyed nephew, and I determined the truth of his statement.

Martin, Charlotte's unpleasant nephew, was in a near fit of anger, mingled with a touch of anxiety. I'm guessing anger, because his elderly relative, had inconveniently passed out of this realm, and worry, because he had wasted precious time caring for the old witch only to have her die before he could uncover her secrets.

We left Charlotte stiffening on her pallet, since nothing more could be done for her in this world. I calmed Matin's head with a cup of strong ale from the local tavern. When his sputtering finally ceased, and the ale took control of his tongue, Martin shared a tale of his Auntie that piqued my interest and perked my ears.

Charlotte was held in high regard throughout my Lord's lands, and even well-beyond. Over her eighty and six years, she was acknowledged by most as possessing extraordinary talent in her calling as a Healer. Her fair-sized village of Locknear Cove, had dozens of folk wandering its lanes, who owed the old woman their fair health. When there was a tooth to be pulled, a baby to be born, or a scourge ravishing the country round them, Charlotte always had a cure or method to safeguard all.

Her nephew, Martin, wanted to take her place as the sought-after Healer, earning the same fine fees that kept Charlotte, and him, her only kin, living comfortably in the small cottage. Before she succumbed to the sharp scythe of the Reaper, Martin stayed by her failing body and wizened head, waiting for her to reveal her guarded healing methods to him. He tended her day and night, for what felt like an eternity of months, though in truth, was a mere fortnight. According to him, he even prayed to the gods, old and new, to make her lucid enough to speak her secrets.

"I did all 'er necessaries fer ta ol' hag, 'n even fed 'er like a babe! She only looked me in t'eye en smiled…in dat evil way she 'ad."

I remonstrated against such strong words in describing the kindly old woman. "She surely devoted her long life to others," I protested, looking sternly into his bleary eyes.

He was not to be swayed from his twisted fury at her death. Into his third mug of the strong brew, he shared a family story about Charlotte, one that traced her Healer's gifts to her own grandmother. His voice became lower and necessitated I lean in. His breath roiled my inners like an oncoming purge with its foulness, but I was too intrigued to lean away.

"Er granny's name were Midge. She were famous round 'ere, fer 'avin' ta power ta look death in ta face, en scare 'im away like mornin' sun do ta moon shadows. Charlotte sed Midge 'ad a fearsome face ta behold. Wit eyes dark as pitch, a great nose like a huntin' 'awk, en 'er dead-white skin creased like a dried bog. Even 'er 'air were ugly, lookin' all wild, en stuck out, like twigs from ta squirrel's nest! She scared any young'uns in 'er path wit a look o' dem black eyes."

I listened attentively as I could, though I found the man dreary as company, and the day was growing dark.

"Listen ta me when I tell ye dis tale. Charlotte, me blood kin, told me she were hidin' a *Travelin' Death Mask*, give her by dat witch granmutter, Midge! It were made frum ta death face o' a more powerful witch, what died near two 'undred year past.

Ta mask 'o thet dead witch's face were passed down, en outright stole, by lots 'o utter witches what know'd 'bout it. It 'eld all dat ancient witchy power, en' after Charlotte got it frum Midge, it give 'er ta power ta heal. She did lots 'o profit from it, I can tell ye! When she went ta attend one 'o the village folk, she'd wrap ta mask inside 'er shawl, afore she took 'erself off. I seen it only ta single time, when I followed 'er down ta widow Morley's, as she were dyin'. She opened 'er shawl en put somethin' on 'er face. When she turned ta where I hid meself, I seen ta face o' ta death mask, just as Aunt told it ta me."

It was now full dark outside the scruffy tavern. I became anxious to return to the comfort of my Lord's Manor, and a warm bowl of stew from the kitchen. I couldn't dissuade the bumpkin that no such thing as a Traveling Death Mask existed, and he must have dreamt the whole incident. I paid the barkeep for one more ale for the grieving nephew and took myself off.

A short while later, my wagon being pulled by a slow, dispirited bay, I spied some sort of movement at the side of the lonely road ahead. The horse became nervous, whinnying and snorting, her flaring nostrils shooting long vapors into the chilled air of the dark night. I halted the beast in the traces, not wanting to proceed until I could identify what manner of night walker was about. I heard a raspy, woman's voice, hallooing me from just ahead.

"If ye be fearful o' me, know I'm but an old woman, returnin' from a dear friend's bedside, I am. No need ta be afeared o' me."

I snapped the reigns slightly, to rouse the bay to her task. She stepped reluctantly forward toward the stranger who grew visible in our path. The horse continued to snort as if smelling something foul riding the breezes.

"Good evening, Mother. I would offer a ride to your door, but my direction is forward, while yours, behind."

"Ach, no worries. I'd be delighted fer yer company, en ken make me bed in any direction of me choosen'."

With that, snagging her long black dress into a bunch with her gnarled fingers, she leapt up as spry as a ten-year-old girl and settled down beside me.

While the night was indeed as pitch black as the bottom of a well, there was a sliver of a moon, and I strained my eyes to peer over from time to time at my new companion as we plodded on. For all her garrulous greeting, she had gone very still. I waited for a scudding cloud to pass across the tiny strip of moon, hoping to catch a clearer glimpse of the crone.

I easily saw a beak of a nose, wiry hair, bushed out around a long, narrow face. She must have felt my scrutiny and turned slowly in my direction. She wore a sly look around her mouth and her eyes were two orbs as black as two pieces of obsidian, and as cold and hard in their glare.

"So, 'ere we sit, me lookin' at a fit, young man, whilst I be in need o' jest sech. I know ye been wit that daft nephew o' Charlotte's, en him tellin' tales 'bout a Travelin' Death Mask, he was. What ye need ta know, tis only this."

And so, the old hag explained the workings of the Traveling Death Mask, as we plodded along. She explained it was worn for good, but only after taking the life spirit from a living being. Whoever donned the hideous thing was able to suck off the life force of others in tiny amounts, leaving them weak, but alive. These forces then, were given to the ill, so they could be cured of most any malady.

I was relieved to know no one died under the power of the Mask, because I now understood, I was to be its next victim. I knew I couldn't escape as the woman's power was already drawing upon the life surging through my body. She became very rigid as I felt my own body go limp.

I must have gone unconscious, for when I roused myself, I lay supine upon the bench seat, the horse, grazing among the weeds beside the road. The sun was beginning to rise with determination, and it would soon be full day. I was frantic to get away and whipped the horse to gain its cooperation and moved forward toward my Lord's Manor. When I arrived at the front entry, I was handled roughly.

"Get yer ugly face offin' ' is Lordship's property! How did you come by this wretch?"

I tore myself from the guard's rough hands, running back toward the stables. I stopped long enough to peer into the water trough for the beasts. Looking down I saw the face of the Traveling Death Mask. My mind was undone.

To this day, I search for the old hag who now wears my face and lives in my youthful body, leaving me her own decrepit form and a face that makes the birds fall to earth with one look.

I do some healing from time to time during my search of the villages and towns. I keep body and soul together with the pittance I can charge. My reputation is spreading as a Healer of some talent, but it matters little. After all, this is not my body, but as long as I wear the Mask I must keep moving. She may be in the next village and my time shortens.

The Wind Mill

The Wind Mill

Because I deeply desire my tale to be told, though my own voice be silenced, and I am as dead inside as my legs, I begin this written memory of my life.

Mathias Lundgren

Thus, I began this thin journal, long months ago. I continue to read it now, so I can relive what soon will be gone like the dawn's promise of a new day. I am compelled to write so I may hold the slender thread connecting me to reality.

Growing up in the shadow of the mighty windmill, I spent endless hours watching it turn lazily in the light breezes, or seeing it transform, becoming a demon-possessed creature, spinning madly when capricious winds bore down from the open plains. The sturdy wooden paddles were painted a gay yellow and green. The colors blurred into the muddy color of pond scum when the blades whirled like a fantastic dervish. To me, the spinning arms appeared to have sprouted from a thick trunk, resembling a massive bloom in a giant's garden. There were strange symbols painted all over the robust stem. But these signs have become all but invisible, succumbing as they did to the elements, and the creeping vines that began to climb the base when I was still a small boy. Now, their leafy shoots have reached close to the housing of the blades, as if determined to strangle its life, its very reason for being here.

I haven't missed a day, in the ten years of days, until today, without noting the subtle changes occurring around me on my family's dairy farm. It's easy to become an ardent observer, when you are confined to your own wooden wheels. Mine move reluctantly over rough ground, where dirt clots and cow pies litter the worn paths. Often, I was forced to cry out for help, when a wheel became lodged in a deep rut. Embarrassingly, there were times when I'd roll too far and exhaust my slim reserve of energy, unable to negotiate the return trip. In circumstances such as these, I relied upon the forbearance of my half-brother Larse, to fetch me from my hindrance. Larse is two years younger than I, his father and mine, being one and the same. My stepmother, Nora, came into our father's life, after my own mother fell like a freshly cut stalk to a winter fever when I was still toddling. It ravished many of the farmsteads among our neighbors, taking some of the youngest and fittest, in a torment of heat and twisting of once healthy bodies.

I was almost seventeen, Larse nearly fifteen, when Death walked like a shadowy presence among us, once again. It swung a sharp culling scythe, gathering many into a burning pyre. Our father was among the last to be taken from his bed of torment, leaving my step-mother to fend for herself and two near-grown boys. I was stricken more than a week earlier, but still lay wrapped in a phantasm of life, when my father breathed his last on the cot next to my own.

Larse dug his hole deep, he reported to me, when I could fathom his words once more. I took little nourishment thereafter, for my grief was as deep as my father's grave. Only this diary book, and the windmill's whisper comforted my weak mind. But the day came when my body ceased its shuddering, and my skin no longer burned to the touch. A few days on, Nora declared it was time for me to rise from my narrow bed and resume life.

"We have a dairy farm to see to, Mathias. You need to help me and your brother to tend what needs tending!"

Nora was a stern and sturdy woman. A winter fever was no match for her resolve, once it was set. But even with harsh threats poured upon my head like scalding water from this hard woman, I was unable to comply with her demand that I vacate my bed. Every time I sat at the edge of my cot trying to stand, I would topple over onto the rough planks, flailing about like a yearling colt after birthing.

Nora's ire rose with every futile attempt on my part, until frustrated after her haranguing, she would leave me in peace. Thereafter, I laid upon my bed for hours, trying to will some life back into my useless legs. Larse, being a loving brother, saw my loss of heart with the futility of my efforts.

"Stop wearing yourself down, Mathias. You can't move your legs and that's an end to it."

Over the next months of enforced confinement, I laid abed, watching the old windmill spin outside my window, listening for the sweet hum of air, turning its heavy blades. I studied it in every conceivable light as the day moved from early dawn to inky darkness. I listened for every creak and subtle chirp of the wood, while the old, flat blades, warped and expanded, shrunk and cracked. *Freedom,* I would often think. Movement came naturally to the wheel, while I, almost a man grown, was paralyzed, immovable as a limb fallen from a tree that has shaken it to the ground.

Nora eventually relented enough to release me from further obligations on the farm, and gratefully, from her harping at me. But she hated idleness so much, that she soon ordered Larse to fashion a crude rolling chair for me, saying, I could certainly be mobile enough for light chores around the dairy.

He scrounged a legless chair from a shed and some wheels from a broken pushcart. After several attempts at fastening one to the other, he came to my bedside to present his finished design.

"Mathias, you are now free to move about the farm and can leave off staring for hours at the damn windmill!" he laughed, proud of his gift to me.

After nearly a year of marking the weather with the turning of the wheel, I rolled outdoors to feel the soft wind on my face. It took no time to become proficient at wheeling myself about, gathering eggs from the coop, carrying milking pails on my lap, and myriad small, but meaningful chores around the farm. Even Nora was pleased, or more precisely, relieved I wasn't a mere lay-about any longer. In fact, she and Larse felt so secure in my powers of self-motivation, they decided to make a long- overdue run into town for needed supplies. They also planned to deliver the churned butter, eggs and urns of milk, to various customers before they spoiled.

"We'll need to be gone this evening and at least another full day, Mathias. I've left you sufficient food in the larder for your meals, and there's plenty of milk in the icehouse if you've a taste."

With that, Nora and Larse packed up the heavy wagon, harnessed Heidi and Clara, our two draft horses, and set off. That was ten days ago, and my fears are overwhelming me as night draws closer on the eleventh day.

I wheel out to the milking sheds to care for the cows, throwing hay and watering them as I've been doing of late. I must be vigilant not to overturn my rolling chair on the uneven dirt floor of the barn. I release them into their pasture, because they are conditioned to return with twilight for a feed, but I have proven inept at milking them and they grow agitated with discomfort. I've fed the chickens, snatching up eggs as needed for myself, which I enjoy after a good boil. I'm not concerned about food, but I feel the creeping panic set in with the coming of each dusk, and during the day, I feel a thrill run down my spine as if I'm being watched while I roll carefully through my chores.

It is now twelve full days since their departure. I am dreadfully fearful for their safety. As a young child, I heard stories whispered among the adults and older children, about how some men are affected living on the plains, with its winds and howling creatures stalking the night. Some of these men supposedly abandon all, as the isolation grows too much for them. Others, go mad, and become lost in the wild country surrounding us.

The darkness has settled in now. The only sound I hear besides the night birds, is the slow spinning of the windmill. Its creaking matches my own wheels as I move to watch out the window, searching the horizon for the wagon, and the stout-hearted draft horses pulling it behind.

I saw something dart around behind the cow barn earlier, before I rolled up the incline board Larse installed for me. Whatever it was, I think I heard it scratching at the front door. I've been sure to drop the bolting board into place but can feel my palms grow wet on the wheels of my chair in apprehension. The pages of this book are smeared with my fear as I cock my head to listen. Oddly, the windmill has gone still, even though there was a fair wind blowing from the north. I was comforted somewhat with its familiar sound, but now I feel even the great wheel is holding its breath until something is revealed from the darkness.

I have counted six separate times the door has rattled and I hear a deep growling from the other side. From the window, I see the windmill reaching into the star-hung night. A fat moon spills a warm glow over the tall structure, pooling like melted butter upon the ground beneath. As I watch, I spot something large hanging off one of the long blades. A bird? No! Some kind of creature! Its long arms let it dangle like fruit on a branch. I can't make out a face, but this thing makes guttural sounds that put my hairs on end. I have heard tales about such demons roaming the plains, picking at the dry bones of those that came here in canvas-covered wagons. It is said they come to harvest the spirits of the dead.

But I won't surrender my own easily. I have taken my father's old shotgun from over Nora's bed and will put an end to this nightmare. I must be careful with the loading, as it's not been used in nearly twenty years. I would have to hold it very still to get off a sure shot at the creature. I'll add my thoughts into this book when I return, but for now, I must stop to cradle the long gun between my dead knees and tuck it under my chin for accurate aim. This won't take long.

Walking in Darker Shadows

The day opened like a shadowy closet, dark and uninviting, but I ignored the unwelcoming feel and proceeded with my plan. I would begin a highly illustrated story book for my thirteen-year-old daughter, Felicia. As the middle child, set like a bridge between two, rowdy brothers, Felicia was most endeared by me. Indeed, she was unique to my family, having been taken as a foundling babe from the wild woodlands bordering my estate, when my boys were still quite small.

That was a day, not unlike the day of my gruesome discovery, dark and foreboding. The winds drove needle-sharp rain, to break upon the winter hardened earth, while black clouds scudded low, exploding with jagged lightning bolts. The thunderous roars from the heavens, like to set my teeth on edge. I was sitting in front of the wide, flagstone hearth in the kitchen, surrounded by the comforting aroma of baking breads. Cook had fitted me with a cup of tea and biscuit, leaving me to my pre-dawn incursions upon her domain.

Staring into the frolicking orange and red flames, I began to conceive a new story book to write for my young son, Todd. He was not yet five, with a quick mind that needed constant nourishment. Though a wealthy landowner, I had begun a clandestine career as a writer several years ago under the pen name, Henry Blest. As an author and illustrator of considerable success, I had already proven adept at stimulating the imagination of young readers with my fanciful stories of knights and dragons.

I hadn't begun a new storybook in over a year and felt inspired to begin at once. Never one to be dissuaded from a goal by the mere circumstance of bad weather, I told the cook to pack me a watertight repast, as I would be off to my small cabin for the day. This shelter, located a fair distance from the back gardens, was built for tools and such. I had it converted years before, to use as my island of inspiration, a space for my Muse to come calling, away from the clatter and interruption in our lively manse.

I packed up my writing materials carefully into a seal skin duffel. Quills, India Ink, creamy parchment paper, blotter, and naturally, the leather-bound sketching portfolio. This was to be an excursion of a solitary nature. A welcome escape for me from the enforced confinement of a particularly brutal winter.

I was out in the battering rains, moving briskly down the narrow path toward the shed, when I heard the distinct wail of an infant. Thinking it only the howl of the wind, lashing out among the trees, I trudged on until the shed came into view several minutes later. Stepping quickly to the door my hand was on the latch when another muted cry floated on the wet air around me. This time closer and more distinct. I opened the door with cold, fumbling fingers in my rush to enter. Throwing my dripping bundle on the floor near my writing table, I returned to the bitter rains, determined to discover the possible source of an infant's cry.

Walking as quickly as the sodden path allowed, I headed in the direction I believed the cry originated, going deeper among the water sodden branches of the trees. All around me was silent, except for the pelting, chilling rains, smacking against the trees and the black earthen floor of the forest. Out of this muck, I heard yet another disheartened wail, this one so near, I feared I might tread upon the babe hidden in the green gloom. Searching, while turning in a tight circle, something moved within a pile of dead leaves. A small foot, a tiny grasping hand, shot out of the autumn debris.

Scooting on hands and knees, I found a beautiful baby girl as naked as the day she was born, except for a fine coat of silky, golden hair, covering her from head to foot.

I jerked back from her tiny body in my shock, but the babe merely looked upon me with a mild gaze and honey brown eyes. She had no fear of me, and in fact, seemed to be waiting for me to discover her, swaddled as she was in brown leaves and a golden pelt. I scoped the tyke into my arms, managing to wrap her securely inside my woolen coat. She was content in this new cocoon as I rushed with my new burden back to the house.

We named her Felicia and my wife was beyond herself with joy at her new daughter. Even her fury body couldn't dampen the love ignited in her heart for the beautiful child. As the years passed, Felicia lost all of the yellow fleece on her body. We believed all was well, as she passed through this rather strange morphing of her body. Our contentment was shaken only of late, as Felicia entered womanhood.

Inexplicably, she began to vanish from her bed some nights, only to return with the dawn, drawn and exhausted, as if she'd run madly through the woods. After several such incidents, and fearing for her safety, I set a maid at her bedroom door, telling her to detain her young mistress if she attempted to leave. We believed, then, she was walking while in a deep sleep, unknowing of her circumstances.

Thinking to divert her attention by presenting her with an illustrated book dedicated to her for her thirteenth birthday, I went out into the storm, making for my writer's cabin. I walked rapidly until I spotted the old Wishing Well and near-by gazebo. Tiring of the wet running off my slicker like a fountain, I changed course and wandered over to the shelter. Placing my duffel upon the stone bench, I stepped over to the well. I knew this to be pure, sweet water, and the hike had brought on a nagging thirst. Leaning into the mouth of the deep hole, a wretched stench filled my nostrils, smelling like an open cesspit. I leaned back, gagging and covering my mouth and nose. I had to discover the source of what was clearly poisoning the well's water.

Taking in a deep breath and holding it, I began pulling on the rope to bring up the bucket. As it came closer, I closed my eyes, leaning away for a second to take another clean breath. When I turned back and opened them, I saw the rotted remains of a head staring back at me. Dropping the rope, the bucket and its gruesome contents, plunged back into the putrid waters. I ran back through the woods, forgetting my pack where it lay in the gazebo.

In due course, I rounded up some ground keepers, returning to the polluted well with its ghastly secret. The three of them covered their faces with rags so they wouldn't inhale the detritus of death below. There were five heads and several bones, clearly gnawed upon, brought to the surface by the men. I had to promise to pay them each a pound over their wages, else they would have left the hideous task.

Though the men were all sworn to secrecy at the time of this discovery, tales of a werewolf on my estate continue to fill the air like blistering rain. Now, whenever dear Felicia disappears toward the woods at dusk, my household holds its collective breath, and when she returns, we count heads before we retire from another day of watching.

Hardly Love

"You have no idea what you're saying, Marjorie. Why you scarcely know the man."

Marjorie's sister, Alice, was a self-assured, successful attorney. She was opinionated, and usually right about her take on people. She and her sister were well into their forties, and sliding fast into the firm grip of spinsterhood as their mother so often reminded them.

"Alice, you may be great in a court room, but you know nothing of love," Marjorie said firmly.

This discussion centered around the young man who moved into the apartment across from theirs, six months earlier. To Alice's mind, Marjorie had formed a deeply delusional notion that he and she were meant to be together.

"He's just biding his time, so we can get to know one another more…intimately. He's already alluded to his feelings for me on numerous occasions."

Sadly, this misconception was based on the handful of times the dashing young man had smiled, or held the door to their building, or greeted her, before her sister. His feelings dramatically escalated in Marjorie's mind, when he came over one evening, asking if she'd like to go out for a late supper.

"I'm in the mood for a light bite, and thought I'd see if you were available."

He smiled, and his adorable dimples popped out on either side of his smooth cheeks. Marjorie felt her knees knock together. Throwing on a clean sweater and underwear, brushing her teeth and hair vigorously, she came out to the front room where he sat. He boldly appraised her full figure and smiled again.

That evening seemed to stretch on forever in Marjorie's mind. Rather than go directly to the local restaurant, her dream date suggested they work up a real appetite and walk through the nearby park.

"It's a lovely evening," he said, though it was chilly and promising rain.

Marjorie would have agreed it was like the Caribbean, as by then, she was so totally under his spell. They entered the park through a break in the thick bushes surrounding it, so there was no chance of being spotted going in he told her with a mischievous smile. Marjorie was not alarmed by this precautionary measure, but tightened her grip on his beautifully muscled arm like it was the brass ring.

They walked silently, without a word passing between them. Marjorie daydreaming the whole time that this must be what it felt like walking down the aisle on your wedding day. He heard her deep sigh and placed his strong hand over hers. She sighed again.

When they reached a point on the grounds that was poorly lit, with only sporadically placed light poles, he stopped. Cupping her upturned face in both his hands he smiled into her eyes, and then he smiled more broadly, and she saw the fangs. He pulled sharply on her hair, forcing her head back and exposing her long, slim neck. There was a quick movement as he pulled her to the ground, his hand still clutching at her head. Her sweater was being ripped open for better access to her pulsing neck. Marjorie felt herself drifting away, just like she always did just before she shifted.

Her body twisted and sprouted a thick pelt of black fur, while her delicate face elongated into a rough snout, filled with more teeth than she brushed earlier. Her would-be-lover froze in mid-bite, too shocked to understand what was happening to his meek prey. The last thing his super hearing picked up was the cracking sound of his spine as she pulled him closer.

"Damn! I really thought this was love!" she murmured softly.

A Dragon's Story

"Oy! Listen up goodly! Dis ain't ta' kind 'o tale told by ye granmutter of a stormy night! Dis 'ere is as true as ta' face yer wear 'round dis sad village 'o our'n, day en night!"

The old man squinted rheumy eyes sharply upon his listeners while he squirmed on the woven reed chair, searching out a comfortable spot for his skinny bottom. He sat close to the hearth, positioned so he could feel the soothing warmth on his gnarled hands and knobby knees. While his feet barely touched the floor, there was something robust about his presence. It might have been the thick clump of snowy white hair encircling his bald pate like a slipped hallo just above his ears. The hairless dome shone in the firelight, and whenever he bobbed his head, it was marked by dancing sparks of light.

He was called Liam Corkoran, like his father before, and his granddad before that, but the villagers only knew him as 'Ole Corky.' This suited the old man well, as he had never seen his name written down, and wouldn't have recognized it in any case, since he didn't have the art of reading.

Ole Corky finally settled back to begin his story to an attentive trio of village children, their upturned faces anxiously hungry to feed their imaginations. The storyteller looked above their heads into a distant past.

"Twas a day thet started wit' meself goin' ta me favorite fishn' 'ole by ta Sleepin' Dragon rock. Ye knows where dat is I 'spect!"

The three children, likely no more than seven or eight, nodded their heads in unison, the flames reflected in their bright eyes.

"Well, I trew me fishin' line into ta deepest part o' ta water, en' set meself down on ta Dragon's back, so's ta rest meself a touch, after me hard work. Ta sun were climbin' high-like in ta sky, makin' me drowsy after a bit. Seein' as I 'ad me woolly coat on meself, I peeled it off, en rolled it like a sausage fer me 'ed, en laid back on ta Dragon's haunches fer a wee nap. Since ta day were pleasant like, en no utter fishin' were goin' on nearby, I must 'ave fallen inta a deep sleep. Suddenly, me fishn' line went flyin' out me 'ands! I were 'bout ta jump up ta see ta it, when a great roar near broke me 'earin'! It were sharp as a pick pushed trew ice on da pond t'was!"

The three children huddled closer to one another now, their eyes gone wide with fear and thrill.

"It were like a trumpet blast, en' meself, alone ta face whatere' twas made sech a sound! I were about ta slip off ta back o' Dragon Rock, but I takes a look down en' sees ta ground been moved forty feet below!

The children inhaled their great terror at this revelation, not letting their breath out until the old man continued his tale.

"Aye, t'was most disturbin' ta see so much air 'tween meself en' ta land below. But I gathered meself enuff ta grab at ta neck o' the Dragon's 'ead. Fer sure as death beatin' down yer door one day, ta Dragon were flyin' like a great bird! Ta beast seemed fine wit meself sittin' like a Lord 'pon 'is back, so I scooted meself forward a bit, ta keep a better seat upon ta scaly creature. 'Ee flew like ta wind, ore' treetops, en plots o' farmin', en ta Squire's own lands, en' great stone 'ouse! We flew o'er ta the next village, en twenty more besides.

Twere beginnin' ta cum on dark, when ta great beast turned 'is great green 'self 'round, ta return ta me fishin' 'ole. It were wondrous, dose tings I seen wit me own eyes, but I tell ye, t'was good ta set shoe 'pon dirt agin! When I slid off'n ta Dragon's back, 'e looked me over wit great, yellow, cat eyes, 'en opened 'es huge jaws, en meself standin' jest ta foot from teeth ta size 'o a butcher's chopin' cleavers, dey were! "

By now the three tykes, sitting like a clump of arms and legs they were so close to one another, seemed to shrink into themselves. A long, collective murmur, trickled out from their round mouths. Their reaction spurred Ole' Corky to even greater description of his encounter with the mythical Dragon.

"Ah, ye wee lads (for they were all boys), ye have ner' seen ta like 'o ta monster what I rode thet day! But me tale ain't near done in ta tellin'. Whilst I be starin' into thet great maw, filled it were wit teeth enough to grind a tree in one bite, ta Dragon began ta speak."

At this point in the story telling, the boys imaginations became stretched to the limit. They could clearly accept a Dragon's flight over their land, but a Dragon that was able to converse was out of the realm of possibility, surely! They began to smirk at one another and whisper behind their grubby hands.

"Ah, me ol' eyes can see ye doubt ta Dragon could speak, but 'e not only spake 'es words ta meself, 'e toll 'es own tale 'o how 'e come ta be made 'o stone fer so long. Twas a curse put 'pon 'im by a witch, twas. Ta' ole hag found ta beasty as a wee egg, in 'ta woodlands. She took it ta her cottage and kept it warm and cozy like, waitin' upon it ta hatch. When ta Dragon popped 'is ownself out ta great egg, ta ol' hag were quick to feed him, else he looks upon er as tasty don't ya see.

Well, she fed him fine beef, en mutton, 'en chickens, she did. Now, she' weren't no farmer, but ta hag stole from the barns en pastures round 'ere, till all da folk were up in arms at ta mysterious goin's on wit all ta livestock. A trap were set ta snare ta teefs. A cage were placed outside a barnyard, 'en a fat Billy placed inside. When ta teefs came into ta cage ta snatch dat Billy, a gate twould drop like a stone behind, catchin' em clean and fer good. But ta Dragon had grown as big as a cottage by then, 'en 'e took one step and broke ta cage ta splinters, snatchin' up ta Billy goat as he flew off. When ta villagers discovered ta ole witch in 'er cave, she were taken ta be hung from ta crooked apple tree, where sech miscreants were done fer.

She begged 'n pleaded fer mercy, 'en made the village leaders a solemn promise, ta put ta Dragon ta sleep as deep as a statue, en only a king could waken 'im again ta fly. So, that's 'ow she come ta turn 'er pet Dragon ta stone, and he were sleepin' like a babe…until I set meself upon 'es back."

At this conclusion, Robbie, the ringleader of this little cadre of boys, piped up, his quick mind digesting all the information. "Be ye a King den Ole Corky?"

"Aye, but me Dragon needs fed, en though yer but wee morsels, ye'll have ta do."

Just then, a dark shadow passed across the light filtering through the doorway. The fire wavered in its grate and was neatly blown out when the Dragon poked his anvil shaped head through the doorway, snorting upon the puny flames. Each boy was taken in a mouthful and swallowed with much alacrity.

When the Dragon was finished, he turned to his only human friend and asked, "Are you ready to fly King Corky?"

The old man was in his sagging reed chair when the villagers found him. The young boys reported how he was telling his story about the flying dragon and when he got to the part about being a king, he seemed to nod off. But this wasn't the sleep of a drowsing old man, for he was as cold as a rock figure when they found him.

One village wag commented to the curious onlookers, "Looks like Ole Corky is on 'is last dragon ride."

They heard the sound of thunder off in the distance and the man added, "Could be thet dragon's comin' fer the king."

No one laughed with him at this poor joke, but one or two looked back toward Ole Corky's favorite fishing hole.

𝒯he 𝒲itch 𝒲ho 𝒞ame to 𝒟inner

"The guest list must reflect our lofty place in society. We must invite only the high-born and well-connected, or our own standing will be diminished and in question."

Their "standing" as she named it, was already in question as far as her husband was concerned. He was reluctant to add more phony, posturing, narcissistic peacocks to their already long list of such. If these represented the "cream of society" as his wife was constantly reminding him, he believed the cream had long ago curdled!

"My love, haven't we sufficient to fill our table by now? I do believe every Lord and Lady from within a fortnight's journey, has received an invitation."

He knew full-well, his wife would never let off her adamant pursuit of even the lowliest of creatures, if they had a title attached to their name. She merely gave him one of her steely looks, and he quietly withdrew to his study. Sitting at his empty desk, its gleaming walnut surface held only his dark reflection. He had turned all household affairs over to his young wife. He was twice her age and looked like the fool he supposed to all his contemporaries. But she was beautiful and filled with an extraordinary appetite for life. These were qualities his first wife, Corella, lacked in equal portion. While he sank deeper into the cushions of his leather chair, he did what he did best; daydreamed.

Corella was a plain woman, well past her prime, if indeed she ever had one, when they married. With her frumpy style dress and shy demeanor, there were more than a few occasions when visitors shoved their cloaks at her, as she came to greet them, mistaking her for a servant, and not the Lady of the Manor. It always galled her husband, but Corella never seemed to take notice of the slights. Her staff, on the other hand, all adored her. Though their union brought no children to bear his name, her husband lived a quiet, if predictably unexciting life, for the better part of eighteen years. It all ended in a mystery that was yet to be resolved to his satisfaction.

Corella went to call on an elderly villager who worked as their grounds keeper's assistant. His health was failing, and true to her caring nature, Corella packed a large hamper with provisions and set off alone in their small carriage, not wanting to take the stable boy from his tasks as he later reported to his Lord. It was a blustery day in February, and she covered her legs in fur, telling the boy he needn't go along, as she'd be back before sunset.

They waited the noon dinner for her, then the evening meal, and still, she didn't appear. By full dark, her husband had staged an extensive search for her, arriving at the old man's cottage first. There he learned his wife had never arrived. All believed Corella had fallen prey to a wolf, or other such predator, as not a trace of her could be discovered.

That was two years past, and her husband's loneliness put him squarely in the sights of his second wife, along with his vast estate and fortune. The older man welcomed, even enthused, over the attentions of the beautiful young woman. When she suggested her deepest desire to care for him in his declining years, he tripped over his tongue asking for her hand in marriage.

Leaving off his unsettling musings, he wandered about the huge manse until he found his wife by the sound of her unhappy voice. It seemed the dinner party lacked one female attendee to balance her carefully strategized table. His wife interrupted his less-than helpful suggestions about removing a male guest, saying he needed to think of someone who could add "amusement and perhaps a touch of mystery," to the party.

"Well, my dear, there is that strange woman that lives deep in Farley Wood. She's a widow I'm told and enjoys a reputation for having the ability to commune with those that have passed. Total rubbish, but..."

"She'll do nicely! Have your man deliver this invitation to her immediately!" she said imperiously, her sweeping gown giving finality to her command. He sighed and left to do as he was bidden.

The following two days were hectic with activity, and the evening of the dinner found the Lady of the House deeply caught up in her toilette and picking and discarding gowns like fallen fruit in a colorful orchard. Her elderly husband retreated to his study once more, where he sipped a sherry, and dwelled on the prospect of the rest of his earthly days. This required another sherry. There came an insistent knocking on the closed door that startled him out of his reveries.

"Your Lordship, your first guest has arrived, and her Ladyship is unavailable. I'm uncertain what to do with the lady."

Leaving the empty sherry glass but enjoying a bit of afterglow along with a slight twinge in his stomach, the master of the house went to greet the lady who had arrived unfashionably on time.

She stood with her slightly hunched back turned to him, gazing into the fire that snapped and crackled in the hearth of the sitting room.

"Madame, I fear we were unprepared for your arrival," he was saying as she turned.

Her hideous features nearly unmanned him on the spot. He stepped back until his legs came up hard against the small sofa, causing him to plop down with all the couth of a country bumpkin. From this position, he closely scrutinized this unsettling site. She smiled at his disconcerted response, showing how the greenish teeth remaining still in her mouth, looked sharp as small daggers. Her swarthy complexion told of many days in the hot sun, with its leathery look and deeply set wrinkles. Her eyes were a bold black, studying her host like a feral dog would an injured rabbit. Her hands were as gnarled as an ancient pear tree limb, and the long fingers she intertwined as if in prayer, were tipped with ragged fingernails, yellowed and hardened with age.

"Do forgive me, Madame. I seem to have had a bit too much sherry without the buffer of food against its effects. Can I assume you are our neighbor from Farley Wood?" he asked struggling to stand.

"I am Madame LaCroix, good sir, and my tiny estate, Farley Wood, has sadly kept us from previous meetings. But be assured, I know all about you and your dear wife. In fact, I am pleased to do your 'Calling' this very evening." Her voice was like a carriage wheel painfully turning without benefit of oil, rough with grit and dust.

"My...Calling? I'm terribly sorry, Madame LaCroix, but I have no idea what you mean by that. Perhaps you have confused this evening's event with another. Tonight, we dine together in convivial companionship only. There is no need for further entertainment."

When she moved closer to him, her somber black gown made a kind of hissing sound as if something alive were hidden beneath its heavy skirts. He unconsciously leaned back further into the sofa. She stood looking down at him, stretching her blueish lips into that terrible smile.

"You must allow me to perform this service sir or suffer the rest of your days living with your shrewish young wife."

"Madame! You speak slander, I fear! Have you not come in answer to our invitation, or have you used this as an excuse to harass me and mine?"

"You are a good man, my Lord, but simple in the ways of the designing woman you wed in your loneliness. I am here to extend another chance for happiness to be yours. "

Listening to her malicious words, he wanted to refute her statement in the strongest terms possible, but as he opened his mouth, the old crone pursed her withered lips and blew a red mist into his startled face. He breathed deeply in his shock, and then gulped for air before falling back into a deep sleep.

The witch, for that indeed, was what she was, swept through the foyer in her funereal garb, past the startled face of the door maid, and up the circular marble stairs. Finding the suite of rooms, the Lady of the house occupied, was no challenge. She merely listened for the constant complaints, and hectoring voice and followed.

Throwing open the door, the witch stepped in, and pointing to the Lady's maid, told her to leave. The girl responded with great haste, running from the sight of her, but also grateful to be free of her abusing mistress. The old crone stepped over the scattered dresses, avoided the boxes of discarded shoes, and came closer and closer to the stunned Lady.

"Wha...Who...How...?" the Lady stuttered weakly.

The witch drew even closer to the gibbering woman, her voice no more than a frog's croak. "I will now grant you the freedom you want from your Lord husband, just not in the manner you expected with his death. Know that I've seen you, slowly killing him with small doses of rat poison, put into his sherry and his warm milk at bedtime. You even planned a larger dose for this evening's meal, putting it into the plain wine he prefers, to your own pampered tastes. Assuring you and your guests would never be in danger. You have drained him dry of his joy in a life lived simply. You are greedy for all he possesses, and give nothing to his pleasures, not even your cold bed. I shall now take it all back from you with your own death."

As she moved closer, the Lady screamed out, "You can't do me harm! All will hear my cries!" She immediately began caterwauling like a fox in the jaws of the hunter's pack of dogs, but no one came.

"They are all under my spell, and now, you shall pay."

A dark red mist settled around the old hag and the beautiful young woman. When it cleared only the young wife remained, but only in body. The witch had taken full possession of the lovely form, running her hands down the slim waist and smoothing the lace bodice with a lovely smile. Dressing carefully, she returned the staff to their own normal, if somewhat dazed states, and reentered the guest parlor where his Lordship sat upon the sofa. He was staring at her when she entered, and when she leaned over and kissed his cheek, he jumped to his feet as if stung by a wasp. She came close to his rather stout middle, getting on tip toes, she gave him a deep kiss, his sherry flavored breath filling her beautifully shaped nose. This time the elderly man staggered backwards, and but for her strong young arms, would have collapsed onto the floor.

"Madame, this is...this ...what has happened to you?"

"Tonight, we shall entertain our guests, and when we are done with the lot of them, you shall come to my bed chambers and I will warm your body."

Dinner guests began arriving before he could process all that had happened, especially the promise of the night to be spent in his beautiful wife's bed. He ate sparingly, but drank copiously, unnoticed by his suddenly adoring wife. He'd already finished an extraordinary bottle of French wine and the server, knowing his love of the plainer bottle of red, poured until it too was finished.

The witch, in full possession of the lovely body of the young wife, was distracted by the feel of such beauty being admired on all sides, when she finally realized what had happened. Before dessert was served, his Lordship was standing to give a toast to his beautiful wife at the end of the long table. With his last words "my treasure" he fell over, squarely landing on his gold dinner plate.

The witch wanted nothing to do with being a Lady. Soon after the Lord's funeral, she let it be known she would be traveling abroad, and using that excuse, disappeared into her natural habitat in Farley Woods.

She settled in to wait for another to stumble upon her door, just as the unfortunate Corella had done all those years ago. Not taking to the plain, homely face and figure of the frumpy Corella, the witch disposed of her, hoping for a more appealing body to continue her long existence. When the invitation came to attend the dinner at the home of the reputedly most beautiful woman in the region, well, it was irresistible. But even the old witch had to admit, life can take such unexpected turns.

The Christmas Charm

The small box was likely hidden under the larger gifts scattered around the festively decorated tree. It had been over fifty years, but finding it represented the most important part of Christmas for the old woman. She soon tired of searching, sitting down with a deep sigh among the pillows of the rocker, set before the fireplace. The only sound was the crackle and snap of the kindling and fragrant pinecones in the newly laid fire, its warmth carried the fresh forest scent around the cozy parlor. Pulling her afghan up to the soft wattle under her chin, Bonnie Lou stared into the dancing flames, letting her mind drift with the orange sparks, as it always did in these quiet moments, late on Christmas Eve, and she was back again in 1936.

She was sixteen and a newly minted debutante, having had her Coming Out Gala in the scorching heat of a Mississippi summer. She was most unhappy when the little colored maids seemed more interested in staying cool in front of the large ice sculpture her Daddy commissioned, than serving the lemon parfait that was quickly turning to sludge along with the melting ice figure. It was supposed to be a sure likeness of Bonnie Lou, but with the sloughing off of the ice, the face took on the fearsome aspect of a gargoyle. Bonnie Lou was even more miserable.

Her Daddy did try to make her happy in their somewhat isolated, sterile life. Her mother died after a difficult childbirth. Not her's, Bonnie Lou was always quick to point out, but that of her sister. The child was named Margret by their father, which soon deteriorated to Mags, as if he couldn't bring himself to pronounce the whole name of the baby who took his beautiful Charlotte from him.

Mags seemed a normal toddler at first, but the family physician noticed her limbs barely grew in her first few years, leading him to declare she suffered the rare condition of Dwarfism.

She was, however, very precocious from a very young age. Being unnaturally short of stature, proved no handicap to her vital intellect and curiosity. At the astonishing age of six, her vocabulary had deepened enough that she became a prodigious reader, often found curled into a deep leather chair in her father's library, lost in a book even the girl's tutor found too obscure or ponderous.

Her mental acuity clearly surpassed her sister's, though she was two years younger. Soon, her sharp mind began to capture even the wandering attentions of her father. This was not an acceptable change in the life of the pampered Bonnie Lou. Their father recognized a rivalry was budding between the two girls. Being deeply averse to any unpleasantness in his household, he decided to treat them both with the same calculated indifference. This behavior came fairly easily to him as it turned out and the girls were left to themselves and their petty quarrels, while he was left in relative peace.

On her thirteenth birthday, Mags was called into her father's den to receive his awkward wishes and a gift. He loomed over his short offspring, handing the stunted child a box that just fit into her small hand. Mags pulled off the lid to discover a lovely silver charm attached to a braided silver bracelet. The bracelet was beautiful, but it was the charm that captured her heart! A lovely silver bird, its wings in flight, hung from the delicate band. Her father helped fasten it to her thick wrist and sent her off with a smile and an awkward pat on her head. Having done his duty by the girl, he quickly forgot her and returned to shuffling his papers.

When Bonnie Lou saw the precious gift on her sister's stubby arm, she was immediately taken by a fit of jealousy.

"It's not fair! You're way too young to be sporting such fine jewelry, Mags. I didn't get any such gift when *I* turned thirteen!" ...and so on...until Mags decided on a solution.

"Here, sister," she said pulling the bird off the fine silver bracelet. "You take the bracelet to wear, and I'll keep the charm. I will get you your very own charm for Christmas and that's just around the corner!"

And so, what began in petty jealousy, ended in a loving tradition. Every year since her thirteenth birthday, Mags made good on her promise, and using money she scrounged over the months preceding, purchased Bonnie Lou another charm for the silver braided bracelet. This went on until Mags presented her with the silver bird. She was lying under a heavy comforter, shivering with fever when Bonnie Lou came to sit by her bed.

"I haven't had a chance...to get your charm this...Christmas, Bonnie Lou. But I think...it's time to give you...this one."

She took her hand out from beneath her covers and reached for her sister. Bonnie Lou opened her own hand to catch the small bird, feeling the cold silver and sharp wings as she closed her hand around it.

"You can't give me this Mags! Why, it's your very favorite thing in the whole world! Besides, I'm twenty-three now and getting married soon. I don't expect you to keep up our tradition forever, you silly thing!" She chuckled and Mags smiled weakly, never taking her eyes off her.

When she realized Mags was determined she keep the charm, Bonnie Lou became very still. Her eyes glittered with tears, soon making long rivulets down her cheeks, while she silently watched the light dying in her tiny sister's eyes. She knew this misshapen young woman had changed her life forever all those years ago. The tradition of adding to her charm bracelet was firmly grounded in love and generosity of spirit.

Bonnie Lou reached for the hand that slipped off the covers and hung limply over the side of the bed. It felt so small in her own. Mags had gone very still and Bonnie Lou heard a long hiss of breath escape her partially open mouth.

All these years later, every Christmas, Bonnie Lou would place the silver bird charm in its tiny box. She'd ask her children, grandchildren, and now great grandchildren, to hide it somewhere among the many gifts under the tree, so she could discover it on Christmas morning.

When anyone asked about the oddity of this annual hunt, she'd say, "Traditions grow out of a need to maintain the familiar, giving a sense of permanency in our lives. But this one is to remind myself that the size of any gift is measured by the space it fills in one's heart."

Bonnie Lou never stirred when the youngest of her great-grandchildren tumbled into the room. She sat with her eyes closed, and the youngster laughed as he placed his plump hand on her arm, holding out a small box in front of her softly smiling face.

And So, It Ends

About the Author
Francesca Quarto

Francesca is part of a large Italian family where she discovered early on that a love of reading was as much a part of her DNA as her mother's skill at baking. Growing up in a house filled with laughter, screaming, banging pots, fighting and loving family bonds, shaped her life and heart.

She has worked in local television, a small city zoo, founded a non-profit tutoring agency for an inner-city neighborhood which eventually served local school districts, worked for an International Evangelical Television and Radio Station and for a non-profit organization serving challenged adults.

Francesca Quarto resides in a small town outside of Indianapolis, Indiana with her husband Patrick. She still has a great love of the written word and while she enjoys her E-Reader immensely, she still treasures the excitement of turning the next page.